THE FLAUTIST

Bryan Lawson

A crime mystery in which time, place and the characters all play a part.

About THE FLAUTIST Bryan Lawson

The internationally famous flautist, Evinka Whyte is scheduled to play in the inaugural concert celebrating the opening of a new concert hall in the historic city of Chester. However, things do not go as planned as she fails to appear on the concert platform.

DCI Drake and DS Grace Hepple are called in to investigate. It soon becomes apparent that Evinka Whyte lived a secret private life full of mysteries and rather at odds with her public image. To complicate matters, it seems that even the new concert hall has its enemies. Evinka's personal assistant has suspiciously disappeared and is eventually tracked down in Prague. The investigation uncovers the extraordinary history of Evinka Whyte's family which begins back in the mists of time in the musical city of Prague. But Drake and Hepple discover that Evinka Whyte was also connected with a secretive organisation based in Zurich.

What is the connection between Evinka Whyte's family history in Prague and recent events in Chester?

THE FLAUTIST is the fourth of Bryan Lawson's series of Drake and Hepple mysteries.

Other books by Bryan Lawson
A DEGREE of DEATH, 2017
WITHOUT TRACE, 2018
FATAL PRACTICE, 2019

About BRYAN LAWSON

Bryan Lawson is an architect and psychologist and has studied the relationship of people to place and published over 300 books and articles. For many years he was Head of School and Dean of the Faculty of Architectural Studies at Sheffield University. His first book "How Designers Think" has been in continuous print since 1980 and sold over 100,000 copies.

This is his fourth crime mystery.

Details of all books by Bryan Lawson together with news of forthcoming publications and a blog can be found at: - www.bryanlawson.org

V1 2021

Wherever possible this novel uses real locations. To see images of many of these go to the website www.bryanlawson.org

Select "novels"
Scroll down to "The Flautist"
Select "see locations"

My thanks to Rosie and Teh Kem Jin for their invaluable assistance.

Prologue

Those sitting opposite him in the Committee Room of Chester Town Hall reported later that the colour had just drained out of George Marshall's face. They said whatever it was that he saw on his computer must have scared him out of his wits. Two members of the committee dashed from either end of the table and lifted his collapsed body clear of his chair and laid him on the floor. One, experienced in first aid, revived George and kept talking calmly, trying to stop him lapsing into another fainting fit before the ambulance arrived. The trouble was that, as he fell, he dragged the chair over with him and his head crashed into the floor, so concussion had to be a possibility.

It had been George Marshall's dream job. He loved classical music. He had always worked with musical instruments and managed a significant professional orchestra. Opera was a life-long obsession. So managing the new concert hall and symphony orchestra in Chester would be the pinnacle of his career so far. The endowment left in the will of an anonymous donor gave him a unique opportunity.

In this final planning meeting, the chairwoman asked George to begin his presentation by reminding them about the original conditions of the legacy. He opened his laptop and flipped back to them. The computer was an unnecessary prop since he knew the terms and conditions off by heart. Most significantly, they specified that the concert hall should be able to accommodate a full symphony orchestra and to act as a small opera house. It was to be built on a site in the central tourist area of the city and specifically not on an out of town, characterless, greenfield site.

After much deliberation, the city had stepped up to the mark and identified a site and a bunch of architects were invited to propose designs with specific instructions that they should exploit the riverside site. George's research had included visits to Sydney Opera House and The Royal Shakespeare Theatre in Stratford-upon-Avon. He could still hardly believe that one day he might run a facility that could get mentioned in such illustrious company. He would plan an international winter concert and opera season. He could put on a series of summer events that would attract the substantial tourist market. He imagined audiences sitting in a restaurant or on a terrace overlooking the River Dee with its charming boats sailing under the delightful suspension bridge. In short, he could not wait to get started on it all.

In truth, so far it had not quite been the job George had envisaged. The site was extremely controversial. Even though it was close to two major car parks, some concerns were raised about the traffic it would generate. A small and little-used part of Grosvenor Park would have to be annexed to make the site feasible. This had triggered a stream of objections and even a public campaign to stop the concert hall altogether. The selected design also involved demolishing a listed building, albeit one in severe decay. George understood the objections and had tried his best to accommodate them, replying to every letter and email. He had modified the architects' brief to minimise construction disruption and to create public domain in and around the building that would offset the small loss of parkland. George had also added a requirement to the brief to uncover the second half of the Roman amphitheatre buried under the listed building. He had spoken at public meetings and tried to reassure people that the worst scenarios conjured up by the campaigners were mostly scaremongering and had no substance. That was when the torrent of abuse started on social media.

He was ready to counter any arguments at this final meeting. The committee room in Chester Town Hall had not seen a more significant event in years. Now was the time when they would get the go-ahead or abandon the project altogether. His laptop started to ping insistently. He knew he would be better ignoring it but somehow his right-hand forefinger got the better of him. He began to scroll the screen and, coming up from the bottom, came the most horrific image. He hit the escape key so hard that his laptop screen collapsed forwards and he tilted backwards. He did not remember any more of the meeting or indeed the rest of that day.

1

The sky was as blue as blue can be, and the early morning sun was warming commuters scurrying along The Groves to their place of work. The special day had arrived at last. The previous two days of testing and tuning the auditorium had gone well. The opening gala performance was now only hours away. Jimmy Caxton, the newly appointed caretaker, was standing by the river Dee a couple of hundred yards or so upstream from the new concert hall. Life was good, he thought, and a song thrush sang its agreement in a nearby tree. George Marshall soon appeared from the small house he had rented.

'This couldn't be better,' said George looking skywards and then across the river. 'The Dee looks so serene. All we need now is the music.'

The two men ambled along the riverside inhaling the fresh morning air. An almost imperceptible breeze wafted floral aromas from the carefully tended gardens to their right. To their left, a boatman was preparing one of the launches that provide the tourists with trips upstream round the great Earl's Eye bend and along the straight rowing course right to the edge of the city. The usual suspects were out in force. Swans giving their best impression of serenity, glided alongside George and Jimmy, hopeful of some tidbits. Out in the centre of the river, some gulls were in a more agitated mood, apparently arguing about matters of avian importance. Chester was putting on its best show as if it knew that this was an historic day. As they neared the Queen's Suspension Bridge, the two men paused to savour the view of their pride and joy. The new concert hall sat on higher ground looking down over the river as if it knew that it belonged. The architects had done an excellent job. The gala opening concert would confirm the hall's arrival on the Chester scene.

'Thank goodness the television people completed their setup last night,' said George. 'Thanks for working late on that, Jimmy. It leaves the hall free for the orchestra to rehearse with the soloist this afternoon. I don't really need to be here this early, but somehow I just had to come and make sure it's all ready.'

As they climbed the series of terraces up to the concert hall, Jimmy struggled with his new bunch of keys that clanged and clattered on a giant ring. The two men debated which key would open the stage door. They were so preoccupied that they failed to notice a small group gathering behind them. The key they needed was hiding and inevitably, it managed to be the last one on the ring that Jimmy tried. The door opened, making barely a sound. In an instant, the two men were swept aside as the small crowd barged in. Then more appeared, both male and female. Two of the men were wearing theatrical masks as if they had just left some Venetian ball. As Jimmy and George picked themselves up, an insistent rhythm of chanting began. Incongruously, it was about as unmusical as you could get and still call it chanting. By now, the main backstage corridor that ran right across the building behind the stage was full of this unruly choir. Being of a certain age, George thought they looked like sixties hippies. But they lacked the easy-going charm of the semi-drugged, flower power brigade. There was something more sinister and threatening about this crowd. Jimmy instinctively pressed the large round green button next to the stage door. The alarm leapt enthusiastically into action as if it had been waiting for this very moment. George covered both ears with his hands. A particularly scruffy man with a mask walked up to George and stood right in front of his face.

'Pull down the concert hall,' he shouted.

'Why ever would we do that?' demanded George quietly.

'It's a symbol of imperialist art created to repress working people,' came the sneering retort. Unable to compete with the strident alarm, George sought refuge in the main orchestra changing room. More people were sitting on the floor in there.

With a feeling of rising panic, he opened the conductor's room, to find a solitary and rather threatening occupant. Another couple of mask wearers occupied the soloist's room. George worked his way along the main backstage corridor, barging through increasing numbers of boisterous protestors. He pushed his way through the door into the front of house. By contrast, the foyer was spick and span standing ready and waiting to receive the evening's audience. Suddenly, a blue light flashing in the mirrors behind the ticket office temporarily blinded him. Then he heard the sirens.

'The alarm rings in the police station in town,' gasped Jimmy, dashing to open the front doors. A line of police officers emerged, all pulling on caps and helmets, as they emerged from three vans. They marched through the foyer to the backstage door. Rather ominously the first three or four were wearing flack jackets over their uniforms.

'I gather you've got a protest,' wheezed Sergeant Denson bringing up the rear with a red face. 'We 'alf expected this given all the protests on social media but we thought it was more likely to be this evening at the concert. We'll take 'em all through the back door where we have vans waiting to receive 'em. It may take a while I'm afraid. They're probably going to make us carry 'em out.'

The members of the audience arriving for the evening performance saw only an orderly and ready concert hall. Despite this morning's nonsense, the gala opening concert was already a huge success. Dr Laura Weeks, from the Deva University music department, had done all the introductions and announcements, Maestro Stransky had conducted in a suitably dynamic manner and the orchestra was absolutely on form. The first half performances were greeted with such persistent applause that several encores had been necessary. The full half an hour for the interval had been George Marshall's idea. Judging by the crowds outside on the terraces with their drinks and snacks, this had proved popular.

Even the Chester weather, not always as reliable as its citizens wished, had caught the mood and put on a perfectly balmy summer evening. The sound of the bell announcing the imminent continuation of the concert drifted right down to the riverside. The audience hastily finished their drinks and began to reassemble. The foyer gradually filled up as people arrived from the riverfront or from the site of the Roman Amphitheatre. A few more drifted in from Grosvenor Park.

The programme after the interval was going to be special and everyone was talking about it. George Marshall had pulled off a real coup by persuading one of Chester's most famous celebrities to appear. Evinka Whyte was never going to be a regular here due to her international reputation and consequent global bookings. However, the attraction of opening the hall and the sales of broadcasting rights had apparently proved just enough temptation and she had suddenly found that her diary was clear. She had reduced her fee and promised to play one of the Mozart flute concertos as well as his concerto for flute and harp. She anticipated that these would be followed by encores and prepared a couple of dazzling solos. She had even agreed to sit in the foyer after the performance and sign copies of her best selling compact discs and biography. The steering committee could not believe their luck and unanimously passed a motion congratulating George Marshall. All the newspapers and magazines had sent critics. A television company was recording the concert for later transmission and several European countries had bought the rights. They would make a huge splash nationwide and even internationally. Everyone had worried that more protestors would spoil the evening, but the police had held them well back from the building.

The house lights dimmed for the second half, leaving the orchestra as the focus of attention. Dr Laura Weeks climbed the five steps to the far right of the platform and stood motionless until the chatterers gradually caught the mood and fell quiet. She spoke in a loud clear voice.

'Mozart composed three concertos for the flute. The third has a harp accompaniment and we shall hear it later. The first in G major

K313 was written in 1778 while Mozart was in Mannheim. Here to perform it is Maestro Stransky with our new orchestra and special soloist. Despite her international life, she still lives here in Chester and therefore qualifies as one of our most famous Cestrians, Evinka Whyte.' Laura returned down the steps to regain her seat at the end of the first row.

All was set for the star to appear. The door from the back of house area onto the stage slowly opened. It was only visible to the musicians in the back row of the orchestra. The third French horn looked over to his right and saw Maestro Itzhak Stransky standing in the open doorway. A stagehand behind him started to clap. The French horn took his cue and, soon, the applause began to ripple around the whole orchestra with the audience enthusiastically clapping their tribute to the conductor and soloist. Nothing happened. The French horns all looked over to see that, far from making his entrance, Maestro Stransky had disappeared. The horns stopped clapping. The rest of the orchestra gradually followed suit. The audience was more persistent but, eventually, they too fell silent. Still, there was no sign of Maestro Stransky and Evinka Whyte. Members of the orchestra began to ask each other what was happening. Chattering spread around the audience. The two bassoonists exchanged their plans for the late evening meal after the concert and a couple of second violins discussed itineraries for summer holidays abroad.

At last, a figure appeared through the open door and the audience began to applaud again. But the members of the orchestra sat still and now silent. They recognised one of their ushers. He walked briskly onto the platform, weaving his way through the heart of the orchestra. He bent over to speak in the ear of the principal flute player. The applause died down for the second time. The flute player got up and, carrying his instrument, followed the usher across to the door. It opened as if by magic to let them through and shut behind them.

Murmuring had begun again at this mysterious event and this changed to hesitant applause when the usher reappeared with a music stand that he positioned next to the conductor's rostrum. He performed an elaborate ironic bow to the applause and disappeared.

George Marshall took to the platform wearing a grim expression. His slow and deliberate tread took him to centre stage where he stood next to the music stand.

'Lord Mayor, ladies and gentlemen. I am desperately sorry to have to inform you that Evinka Whyte is indisposed...' His announcement was interrupted by a communal groan. 'But the show must go on. Our principal flautist, Anders Hagen, has, of course, rehearsed the programme with the orchestra and he has kindly agreed to perform the same concertos for you.' As George left the platform, the conductor and soloist emerged triggering applause that was polite rather than enthusiastic. There was little doubt that the audience was disappointed.

George Marshall, Jimmy Caxton and the orchestra ushers gathered in the main backstage corridor outside Evinka Whyte's dressing room. The sounds of Mozart's first flute concerto drifted in from the auditorium but not one member of this small group appeared to be listening. Eventually, the dressing room door opened slowly to reveal a paramedic.

'Who is in charge here?' demanded the medic rather abruptly.

George nodded and half raised his right arm.

'I'm afraid that there is nothing that we can do for her,' said the paramedic. 'I'm no pathologist but I would say she has not been dead all that long, perhaps two hours, maybe less. Normally, we would have taken her to the hospital but it seems to us that this death may need investigation. I've just called the police. Of course, we will stay here until they arrive.'

2

The small group stood in the corridor with little appetite for conversation. In the background, Mozart's G Major flute concerto was reaching its conclusion. It was followed by rapturous applause. In normal times it would have been a cause for celebration that Anders Hagen had done so well but these were not normal times. One of the ushers rushed down the corridor to open the stage door. It was as if someone turned up the volume on a giant Hi-Fi system. Soloist and conductor appeared in the corridor briefly but the applause demanded that they return. They played this game with the audience one more time returning to wipe the sweat from their brows with cold towels supplied by the usher. Gradually the applause died down and then there was a silence as the orchestra sat down. After Dr Laura Weeks had made her introduction, Maestro Stransky returned to the platform to conduct the Intermezzo from Cavalleria Rusticana by Mascagni. He left Anders Hagen to receive the well-deserved plaudits from the small group. They were soon joined backstage by a harpist. They chatted nervously until there was more applause and Maestro Stransky returned to collect them to perform the final work, Mozart's Flute and Harp Concerto.

'Mr Marshall?' enquired a gentle female voice just rising above a quiet passage in the music.

'Yes,' replied George, turning to see a slight but striking woman dressed in a smart black suit over a pure white blouse.

'I'm Detective Sergeant Grace Hepple and here is my ID,' she said, smiling and holding out her card for inspection. The others thought George seemed to freeze. 'Could you please show me to the dressing room?' Now her tone was just a touch more insistent.

'Yes. Of course. I'm sorry. It's right here,' said a flustered George, opening the door for her.

'Thank you. My colleague will be along in perhaps ten minutes.' With that, the young policewoman disappeared and the small knot of concert hall staff resumed their dismal wait.

'Drake,' said a voice coughing out of control. A large man, slightly stooped as if embarrassed by his excessive height, was spluttering his way along the corridor. 'I was supposed to be at this concert, but I'm coughing so badly that I thought it would be too disruptive.' George held the door open for him silently. Drake stopped momentarily, his head cocked slightly to one side. 'Ah Mozart,' he said. 'Would that we could have this playing at every crime scene. I've always wanted to hear a live rendition of this seldom-performed piece and here I am at last but a rather inconvenient murder is taking me away.'

DCI Drake stumbled across the room still coughing. He crossed between the two paramedics and Grace Hepple to examine the body. It was slumped in a chair facing the mirror. Drake stared at the reflection of the long golden gown flowing over the arms of the chair on its way down to the floor. He moved forward to look back at the head obscured from the side by glossy black locks of hair falling over the shoulders. He raised his eyes to the mirror where he could see the reflection of Evinka Whyte's head collapsed on her left shoulder. DCI Drake had looked at many dead faces in his career. Some were contorted in expressions of terrible agony. Some looked startled or enraged, others were the image of repose, expressing the calm sleep that must have preceded their death.

This one was somehow different. It was strange to see this familiar face in such circumstances. Drake had always enjoyed the flute. It seemed to him to be at once lyrical and yet athletic. He had collected Evinka Whyte's discs. He had watched her perform and give interviews on television. He had even attended a couple of her concerts. That she could express emotion was not in doubt. The sparkling blue eyes and high cheekbones gave her a liveliness and spirit that, together with her outstanding musical talent, had been her immense good fortune in life. That luxurious head of flowing shiny black hair would bounce as she played or talked. The mouth, lips delicately pursed in playing, was now formed into a semi-snarl and her face appeared to stare quizzically into empty space. She seemed to be demanding the response to a question. She would never get an answer. That had become Drake's task.

The door opened to reveal a rather portly man carrying a large leather bag. The sounds of Mozart were heard once more to Drake's delight. 'Professor Cooper, pathologist,' said the newcomer in a jovial tone. Drake turned and held out a hand of greeting. The two men slapped each other on the back. It was Drake who spoke first.

'Do you know, Prof, some historians claim that Mozart detested the flute but just listen to that. How could such heavenly music be the product of hatred?'

'I wasn't expecting to see you on this case, Drake,' said a cheerful Professor Cooper, 'What delights have you got for me today?'

'Well, I was expecting to see you,' laughed Drake. 'Pathologists don't usually change jobs all that often.' Several of the pathologists that Drake knew had a similar overtly cheerful manner. Drake assumed that it was a way of distancing themselves from the awful sights they must investigate. He liked Cooper even though his jolliness often felt at odds with the situation in which they usually met.

'True enough. We dig our rut and practice in it for the rest of our careers.'

'Well, you might see even more of me now,' said Drake. 'I've taken over from Inspector Henshaw for a couple of years at least.

He's gone off to Hong Kong on a mission to sort them all out over there, though goodness knows what he can teach them that they don't already know. I rather took to Chester when we were dealing with that Singapore case, so I quite fancied coming here and having a break from London. I've brought Sergeant Grace Hepple with me too.'

Grace looked up from her notebook, nodded and smiled her greeting before continuing to jot. Her silence had as much to do with Drake inadvertently reminding her of the decision not to accept Martin Henshaw's invitation to accompany him to Hong Kong. Now she knew that she missed him. Most days she put this out of her mind but, if she was brutally honest with herself, just occasionally she wondered if she had done the right thing. Inconveniently, this was one of those times. She tried to concentrate on the case.

'I guess we'd better get to work then,' said Professor Cooper. 'What has happened here?'

'A sudden unexplained death,' said Grace, coming back to the present. Professor Cooper walked around the chair to look at the body.

'I recognize that face,' he said. 'Can't think for the life of me where from. Is she local?'

'In a way,' said Grace. 'I believe she has a house here but her life is pretty international and I don't know how often she comes back to Chester.'

'Who did you say she was?'

'I didn't,' said Grace. 'Of course, this is…was Evinka Whyte the world-famous…'

'…flautist,' interjected Professor Cooper. 'I remember now. I read in the newspaper about her coming to play at the opening of this hall.'

'Well she never made it,' grunted Drake. 'The stage manager came to take her to the stage after the interval and found her like this. He called the ambulance.'

'hmm yes I see,' muttered the pathologist turning on his voice recorder and talking into it like an old friend. 'Middle-aged female, probably late forties…'

'Miles out,' growled Drake, 'I'm sure a recent article put her in her sixties.'

'…Really?...face showing signs of extensive make-up so maybe that is fooling me but she certainly looks younger than sixty. Wearing a formal long, sleeveless dress, apparently ready for public performance. No immediate signs of injury or trauma. No obvious cause of death. No immediate evidence of her being attacked. Sitting in the seat in front of mirror some distance from phone suggesting she had not attempted to call for help…'

'Her mobile phone is here, sir,' said Grace to Drake. 'It appears to be turned off.'

Professor Cooper pulled out his illuminated magnifying glass and began examining Evinka Whyte's face. He hummed to himself a couple of times before changing to examine the left hand, which was lying on her lap. The right hand, resting on the arm of the chair, came under inspection before the pathologist moved steadily up her left arm pausing just below the shoulder. He put his face right up to the magnifying glass and moved it around in small circles.

'Pinhole with possible speck of bleeding on left upper arm. Possible recent injection.'

Drake looked over immediately.

'What does that mean Prof?'

'Can't say at the moment. Does anyone know if she was diabetic or took drugs?' He addressed the question to thin air. There was no response so he continued his preliminary examination.

Drake prowled around the room. Lacking the wear and tear of use, it had a minimalistic quality. The walls were all bare save for a door in the centre of each flanking wall. Drake turned the brass knob of one and it opened easily but only to reveal another door a few centimetres away. He tried the handle but this one would not open.

'What is this door for here?' demanded Drake without looking round. 'Any ideas on that Grace?'

'No, sir. No idea at all. I thought the next room was for the conductor but the door is some way down the corridor.'

'Can we see the manager?' asked Drake. 'What's his name?'

'A mister George Marshall,' replied Grace checking her notebook.

'OK let's have a quick word with him in another room.'

Grace led the way out into the corridor but there was no sign of George Marshall.

'Does anyone know where Mr Marshall has gone?' she asked.

The caretaker, Jimmy Caxton, pointed silently to the next door along the corridor towards the stage door end. Grace opened the door to reveal a man sitting alone and from his expression, in something of a state.

'This is Mr George Marshall,' said Grace. George rose as if to greet his visitors but immediately stumbled back into his chair.

'Sorry I don't feel awfully well...' Grace went over to the washbasin and drew a glass of water from the cold tap.

'I'm sorry Mr Marshall,' said Drake. 'I do understand the shock. We'll let you go in just a moment. First, can you tell me about the additional door in the soloist's room used by Evinka Whyte this evening?'

'Ah, that was my idea,' answered George Marshall stuttering. 'To be honest, that's not entirely true. I got the idea in Germany. It is a practice room complete with piano. Some soloists like to play a little while they wait to perform. We have two of these rooms. They interconnect for flexibility.'

'So could someone have entered Evinka Whyte's room through that door?'

'Unlikely. I think it was locked.'

'I certainly couldn't open the second door,' said Drake.

'I wish I had checked on Evinka now,' said George Marshall. 'I thought it best to leave her alone. I knew her personal assistant was with her and would call me if they needed anything and she had

Maestro Stransky in an interconnecting room if she needed to discuss the concert.'

'Where were you between rehearsals and the second half of the concert?' enquired Drake.

'Where wasn't I?' replied George Marshall. 'It being our first concert, I wanted to know how things were going. I couldn't sit still. I kept checking around everywhere. I even went outside in the interval to see how the terraces were being used.'

'You didn't see anyone else going into Evinka's room?' asked Drake.

'No, but I wasn't keeping a watch on it. In theory, any one of dozens of people could have visited her.'

'Mr Marshall, we will need to have a much longer conversation with you but it is already late in the evening. I suggest you go home and please come back tomorrow morning. Do you have far to go? I can get a constable to drive you.'

'No thank you, I can walk, it's barely five minutes along the river.'

'OK then,' said Drake. 'Please come back in the morning to help us understand more about the context here. You are free to go home now. Grace, let's go and see what Prof Cooper's up to.'

'Hello, Prof. How are you getting on?'

'Well that all depends on what you consider progress,' said the pathologist. 'As DS Hepple said, this seems to be an unexplained death. Of course, I need to conduct a proper post mortem but right now I would have to confess that I have no idea how she died. I can say that it was probably at least an hour ago but maybe no more than say five hours. That is purely based on the temperature of the body and that greatly oversimplifies the matter. From what I can see at the moment there is no sign of any injury and the dress appears entirely unscathed and indeed rather beautiful. There is no indication of strangulation or suffocation, either of which would almost certainly have caused major disturbance and probably left signs on the body. The only possibility I can entertain at this stage is that there may have been a recent injection in the upper left arm. I'm not certain about that but looking purely with the magnifying glass, there may be evidence of previous sites. She may be a drug addict but again there is no real evidence of this. However, the location of the possible site of injection is not a natural one when performed on oneself. Of course, you can do it there but it is difficult and unlikely. I will certainly request toxicology tests. You can have the room for the scene-of-crime team now.'

3

'Grace, would you get Tom Denson and his lads to tape off the soloist's room,' Drake asked as they left Professor Cooper packing up his kit. They turned down the corridor towards the stage door. 'I can't see the scene-of-crime boys getting very far this evening. We will need an overnight presence here, so that needs to be organized with the caretaker.'

There was a commotion ahead of them that quickly turned into angry shouting. As they reached the end of the corridor, Jimmy Caxton appeared trying to prevent a short and rather stocky woman from coming towards them. She seemed quite threatening.

'What's the problem?' asked Grace.

'I've been waiting out in the empty auditorium for ages,' replied the woman. 'I demand to be allowed to see my sister.'

'Sorry,' said Grace in her most reassuring tone, 'but can you tell me who you are?'

'I'm Renata Kubicek. Evinka Whyte is my sister. They said she was unwell. I want to see what is wrong with her that she couldn't play but this man is preventing me from getting through.'

'Of course, follow me,' said Grace opening the door to the room George Marshall had been using.

'Perhaps you would like to sit down in here for a moment.'

'Thank you. I was listening to the concert. I thought Evinka's stand-in was tremendous and gave a good account. I don't think the audience was too disappointed in the end. Evinka needs to look out!'

Drake had followed Grace and Renata in. He was silently studying this rather bumptious woman with short black hair and a round face. She seemed excitable and clearly used to getting what she wanted. Grace moved the chair slightly round from its position facing the mirror.

'I'm Detective Sergeant Grace Hepple and this is Chief Inspector Drake.'

'You are police? Why is this?' demanded Renata Kubicek.

'I'm afraid we have to tell you bad news,' said Grace. She watched Renata Kubicek as she half rose from her chair.

'Where is she? What has happened?'

'It would be better if you sat down,' said Grace. 'I'm afraid we have rather bad news for you.' Grace paused to make sure Renata was ready. 'I'm sorry to have to tell you that your sister has passed away.'

Renata looked stunned. 'What? How can that be?'

Drake took over. 'When the orchestra's usher went to call her for the second half of the concert, he found her unresponsive in her chair,' said Drake quietly. 'They called 999 straight away and some paramedics were here in a few minutes. Unfortunately, there was nothing they could do.' Renata Kubicek sat silently for, what seemed like several minutes but was almost certainly no more than a few seconds while Drake and Grace waited for her to absorb the situation. She began to talk again. She looked into mid-air and seemed to be talking to herself rather than anybody else.

'I flew in late yesterday from Prague. I had breakfast with Evinka this morning. I came over and listened to the rehearsal. She looked as well as I have seen her for a long time. I need to see her. Where is she?' Renata tried to stand up again, so Grace held her gently by the shoulders and helped her back into her chair. Drake muttered his best attempt at some calming words.

'When you feel able to, we would like to talk to you,' he said. 'There is no urgency. George Marshall has identified her, so the task does not need to fall to you.'

'But why are you involved?' asked Renata. 'I can't believe this. How did she die?'

'I'm afraid that at the moment we don't know how she died. Because it was sudden and unexplained, we get called in to see if there is anything that needs our attention. You said she was better than you have seen her. Has she been unwell then?'

'No. Oh, dear. I didn't mean that. I can't think straight. You are confusing me.'

'I understand,' said Drake. 'When you feel able to go, Sergeant Grace Hepple here will arrange for a woman constable to drive you home. Where do you live?'

'Mostly in Prague,' replied Renata. 'The family still has a house there. I was going to call on a friend and she would have put me up but it is really late now. I think I will go to Evinka's house. I need to collect some belongings. I have often stayed with her and I have a key. It's not far away but I do feel a bit wobbly so thank you a lift would be appreciated.'

'Perhaps we can come over and see you at her house tomorrow afternoon?' asked Drake. Renata nodded her head in silent agreement.

'Who else do we need to see this evening, Grace?' asked Drake.

'Perhaps the conductor of the concert,' she replied. 'I understand that he has remained in his room.'

'Let's do that now, while Prof finishes his preliminary examination.'

Grace ushered Drake to the next room and tapped gently on the door.

'Come in, come in.'

'Ah Maestro,' said Drake holding out his right hand, 'it's a privilege to meet you.'

Itzhak Stransky looked older than the picture of him in the programme that Drake had picked up from the entrance lobby. As a veteran concertgoer, this did not surprise Drake. Most programme pictures flattered their subject and somehow rarely got updated. But the way he got out of his chair and stood rod straight suggested a younger, more athletic man than his face and greying hair indicated. Drake wondered if a lifetime of conducting was indeed good exercise for maintaining fitness. He thought of conductors like Bernard Haitink, working right up to ninety and Otto Klemperer in his late eighties.

'This is terrible, terrible,' said Stransky, speaking with a slight mid-European accent. 'They have told me that poor Evinka, she is dead. I cannot believe it. We were making music together so well this afternoon. How can she not be with us now?'

Drake indicated that the Maestro should regain his seat and he took a stool from the other side of the room. Grace leant back against the door.

'Did you notice anything unusual during rehearsal?'

'No, not really. I know her playing well. I would have noticed anything unusual. I'm sure that I would. Perhaps she lacked a little of her usual attack but I thought maybe she was saving herself for the performance. To play two concertos and a series of difficult solo encores is demanding for anyone and she is not as young as she was.' He shook his head and pulled out a red handkerchief that was stuffed in the breast pocket of his jacket hanging over the back of the seat.   He dabbed his forehead.

'When did you learn that Evinka had died?' asked Drake.

'After the concert. At the interval, I was told only that she was unwell. The principal flautist from the orchestra took her place. He played wonderfully well. His phrasing was so good that I doubt, if the audience were blindfolded, they would have known. Of course, I have worked with this wonderful new orchestra for three days now. During the first two days, we had to test the acoustics so the architect could supervise adjustment of all the wall panels. This is a clever idea I have only seen something similar once before. By sliding these panels to and fro they can change the reverberation time and other aspects of the acoustics. So for these two days, the principal flautist took Evinka Whyte's place. It was obvious then that he is an extremely able player. This afternoon was the first time I could rehearse with Evinka. Everything has been thoroughly prepared. I'm embarrassed that I have forgotten his name, the principal flautist.'

Drake looked at the programme. 'I think it must be Anders Hagen,' he said.

'Yes, of course, Anders Hagen. Well, he deserves a solo career. It was certainly a busier evening for him than he must have expected. Yes, he is a remarkable musician. I suppose there must be many orchestral players who don't get the break to become solo performers but if there is one glimmer of brightness in this whole affair, it is that he might now get noticed. I shall certainly speak for him whenever I am asked.'

'Strange how things happen,' muttered Drake. 'This might turn out to be his big chance.'

'Yes,' said Stransky. 'I started out as a violinist and had a similar lucky break. Then I began to conduct small orchestras while playing the main violin part. This was mainly baroque music, which originally would have been performed that way. Then someone from a major orchestra heard me and since then I have had an endless set of appointments to conduct really good orchestras. I know all about the sort of lucky breaks that an orchestral player needs.'

'So when was the last time you saw Evinka?' asked Drake.

'Afternoon rehearsal.'

'Did you rehearse all of both concertos?'

'Oh, no. We would rarely do that on the day with a professional orchestra and an experienced soloist. We went through a few sections that I wanted to make sure things were working. I wanted to be certain I knew how she would play them and the orchestra would know too. In particular, we worked on the flute and harp concerto. We decided to keep the harp at the rear of the main floor of the orchestra. It is a major thing to move it to the front. We needed to make sure that was working for both soloists and myself and the orchestra. We also listened to her cadenzas. This is where the soloist plays literally solo and effectively extemporizes. Mainly it was so I knew how and when to bring the orchestra back in.'

'So you didn't see Evinka Whyte between rehearsal and the concert?'

'No. I respect soloists' wishes in such cases. Usually, they want to be left alone.'

'Let me get this entirely clear,' said Drake. 'You arrived three days ago and are you leaving Chester tomorrow?'

'No, I had planned a short break. Chester is not a city I know, so I wanted to explore for a couple of days. The week after next, I have to return to give another concert here. I shall rest and study some scores.'

'Where are you staying?'

'On George Marshall's advice, I think it is called the Grosvenor Hotel.'

'Good choice,' muttered Drake. 'Were you expecting to see Evinka during that time?'

'She only arrived this morning but I am sure we would have had dinner together after the concert.'

'Do you know Evinka Whyte well?'

'I wouldn't say that but we have some things in common. We have played together in Prague several times. You know she comes from a Czech family and there is some remote connection between our families. We have plenty to talk about when we meet and we enjoy playing together.'

'Thank you, Maestro. We may need to speak with you again. I would be glad if you would let us know when you are leaving.' Drake handed over an address card.

'Yes, of course, anything I can do to help. It's a terrible business. I can't believe that I shall never see Evinka again. It's terrible, terrible. But tell me how she died. Was it some kind of accident? She seemed well enough earlier today.'

'I'm afraid we don't yet know how she died,' said Drake. 'I suppose you couldn't help us with that?'

'No. I'm shocked. I have no reason to believe that she was ill. Was it a heart attack or something like that?'

'The pathologist will examine her in detail,' said Drake. 'We hope to understand more then.'

Drake and Grace Hepple were making their way out into the car park through the auditorium. Drake stopped about halfway across and looked slowly around.

'I wonder what Cynthia would have made of this,' he said.

'Your wife could always sum up a piece of architecture in a few sentences,' replied Grace.

'Yes but she did have the advantage of a ridiculously long professional training,' grunted Drake. 'I think I am getting better at my architectural appreciation. I do think she might have liked it. Ah no! I have made a mistake already. Cynthia always said that it didn't matter whether she liked a building or not. What mattered was whether she could admire it. Today, she would have said that it was like music. You don't like every piece even though it might be excellent. So it is with architecture. I wish she could have been here.' He stumbled momentarily and held tightly onto a seat back. Grace remained quiet. She knew that he still missed his wife but had never seen him so openly emotional before. To her annoyance and regret, her mobile phone interrupted the poignant silence. Drake regained his balance and walked on past a few more rows of seats.

'Hello. DS Hepple...Yes. Oh, hi there. Yes, of course, I remember...good gracious...Oh no! And how are you?...OK, that's good. Yes, thank you for calling. I'll deal with it at this end.'

Grace looked lost in thought as she put her phone away. Drake waited at the back of the auditorium studying the proportions of the space.

'That was one of the paramedics who came to look at Evinka this evening,' said Grace catching him up. 'He was telling me that, as he drove back to their on-call parking site, his colleague was unusually quiet. Then suddenly, he groaned and collapsed in his seat. The driver stopped and tried to help him but he said it was beyond him. Apparently, his heartbeat was weak and erratic and his breathing shallow and leaving him gasping for breath. He seemed unable to communicate. So the driver put his blue light on and drove back to the Countess of Chester Hospital in emergency mode. They have just updated him. The news isn't good. His colleague is in a really bad way, so they intubated and put him on a ventilator. He's in the intensive care unit but the doctors are still trying to understand his situation. The driver thought we ought to know.'

'Right,' said Drake decisively. 'Let's get everyone out of that room until we know more about the situation. It must be locked and guarded overnight. Make sure the caretaker doesn't go anywhere near it until we get the scene-of-crime team properly kitted out tomorrow morning. You ought to let Professor Cooper know this too.'

4

Grace arrived early the next morning and entered the building with the caretaker, Jimmy Caxton. She was keen to make sure that he did not unlock the rooms that the scene-of-crime team was going to search. First on her list was the soloist's room where Evinka Whyte had been found dead. Grace unlocked the room, checked inside and put standard police blue and white tape across the door. She did the same for the conductor's room and, just to be sure, the second soloist's room. Next, she went and looked around the orchestra platform. Evinka had been there in the afternoon but then so had nearly a hundred other people. She stood wondering if there was any point in searching here. She wandered around almost aimlessly. In her earlier life as a ballet dancer, she had looked down into orchestra pits and marvelled at the sound coming out but she had never stood on an orchestra platform before. She felt an unexpected and uncanny thrill as she took to the conductor's rostrum.

'I hope you're not thinking of another change of career,' came a voice from the back of the hall. She could hardly fail to recognize the mock grumpiness that was Drake. The two of them laughed with Grace waving her arms about as if commanding eighty musicians.

'Now that I have found a house to stay in, I don't need to lose the most valued member of my team.'

'Oh that's good news,' said Grace. 'Where are you going to live?'

'I've had a spot of luck,' said Drake, 'A tiny little house right on the riverfront just down from here. It was advertised to let. I snapped it up.'

She left Drake in an uncharacteristically jovial mood prowling around the hall and returned to the main backstage corridor ready to receive the scene-of-crime team. She turned left and walked to the end and into the stage entrance lobby.

As the door to the lobby closed, she heard another door slam. She opened the lobby door and looked back along the corridor. All the doors appeared shut, and there was no one in sight. She was sure that Jimmy Caxton was the only other person in the building and she had left him tidying up in the main auditorium. She walked steadily along the corridor, passing each door and pushing it gently. There was no movement detectable. She reached the far end where the fire escape door was closed. Then she saw it. There was a rubber wedge on the floor of the kind used to hold doors open. She pushed on the fire escape door. It was closed. She opened it by pushing the bar down and put the wedge into position. Sure enough, the door closed almost all the way but without engaging the lock. She guessed the staff used it to keep the door open while unloading instruments and so on from vehicles outside.

But there was another possibility. Had someone planned to come when the building was closed and re-enter? She walked back along the corridor, quietly opening one door at a time. First, the second soloist's room. Empty. Then, and with even more care than before, she leant over the blue and white police tape across the soloist's door and pulled the handle down slowly. She looked in. Empty. Perhaps she was imagining things.

She came to the conductor's room. She opened the door, again carefully. The handle creaked, almost imperceptibly, as it moved down. She leant over the tape and looked into the room. There was a loud crash. The figure that barged past her was just a blur. It knocked her against the doorjamb. She fell to the floor across the doorway, breaking the tape. The door closer operated and pushed the edge of the door between Grace's left shoulder and her chin. Her head would not go back any further with her back pressed against the jamb of the doorway. She was momentarily stuck with a feeling of panic welling up inside her. She told herself to calm down and slow down. After a couple of determined efforts, she managed to wriggle free so the door could close behind her. Her brain was in a spin. She struggled to her feet and looked up and down the corridor. It was empty. She rushed down to the fire escape door. It was shut firmly with no sign of the rubber wedge on the floor. She opened it and looked out. There was nobody in sight. She could only conclude the intruder had escaped and taken the doorstop.

Grace took slightly stumbling steps back to the conductor's room. Now that she was walking rather than running, curiously she felt less steady. Grace stopped and took a deep breath. Back in the conductor's room, she noticed a cupboard open. On the shelf inside was a mask. It appeared to be made of reddish brown leather and ended just above the mouth. The face was wrinkled and contorted. She held it in front of her while she looked in the mirror. It appeared to give her a leery and mischievous, sort of grin. She heard the door open again behind her and wheeled round.

'What?' exclaimed George Marshall. 'What the hell is happening here?' Grace realized that she was still holding the mask in front of her face.

'Oh sorry,' she said, revealing herself. 'I just found this here.'

'I remember it,' said George. 'That was the mask worn by one of the protestors yesterday morning. There were two of them wearing masks.'

Drake arrived behind George in the open doorway. Grace told them what she had discovered.

'So at least one of the protestors seems to have planned to return and was interested in this room,' said Drake. 'Perhaps he came to recover the mask. I guess that the two mask wearers left their disguises behind when our uniformed colleagues were arresting protestors and, to avoid being arrested, left via the fire escape.'

'If so, why did he leave the mask behind again just now?' asked Grace.

'I suppose because you frightened him and he panicked. For some reason, he doesn't want to be associated with the mask.'

'I remember the other mask now,' said George Marshall. 'It was white overall and covering the whole face. It had a tear on the left cheek as if crying.'

Drake grunted and looked thoughtfully at the mask in Grace's hands.

'This is ringing a bell,' he said, 'but my brain isn't being any more helpful than that. By the way, Grace, You should put that in an evidence bag with a note that you handled it first.'

'Oh, No!' said Grace. 'How stupid of me to pick it up.'

'You were a bit startled,' said Drake in an unusually forgiving manner. Grace assumed that finding his house on the riverfront was still keeping him in a good mood. 'Now, perhaps someone will explain to me what all these protests were about.' Grace and Drake both looked at George Marshall.

'This is a long story,' said George. 'The city received a huge donation made anonymously in a will. It was to enable Chester to have a proper concert hall. Before this was here, they would have had the odd concert in the cathedral or much smaller venues. This new concert hall was to be able to accommodate a full symphony orchestra. We have been able to fulfil that condition. Music lovers would previously have had to travel to either Manchester to hear the Halle or to Liverpool to hear the Philharmonic. The donor had been a wealthy Cestrian who had been frustrated by that all his life. I think I know who the donor must have been but, of course, I couldn't possibly discuss that, but anyway, it makes little difference to the story. That is except for one thing. A condition in the will of the grant was that it was to build a symphony orchestra hall in the centre of Chester. The conditions specifically stated that it should not be on an out of town greenfield site. I was appointed, initially only to investigate the possibilities and make recommendations to a planning committee. The committee was itself keen to see the hall not only serving the residents but also contributing to tourism. In my interim report, I argued that evening concerts were likely to extend the length of stay of tourists and thus increase expenditure in the city.' George Marshall paused as if trying to remember events. He took a deep breath and continued.

'City centre sites are not in abundance here. We have so many listed buildings that we soon came down to looking for open spaces. As you can see, the site where we eventually built was one such. There had been a running argument for many years about the convent that occupied part of the site. It was a listed building though in poor condition and was not a particularly remarkable piece of architecture. Moreover, there had been no developers interested in finding new functions for the building. It also partially overlapped the Roman amphitheatre, which you see, is now being fully excavated.' George paused as if to see whether his audience was attending.

'It then became an argument between conservationists, those who wanted to keep the convent and those who wanted to see the amphitheatre fully excavated. On the same side as the convent supporters, were those who were outraged at losing part of the park. It was an argument that could not be resolved by some compromise. Only one side could win otherwise the impasse would continue so we would lose the concert hall. Supporters of music thus joined sides with the Roman remains advocates. The argument got more heated and, somehow, the two sides started to recruit supporters from outside of the city. Sadly along with these came some much more undesirable characters. These extremists became dominant and took over the whole campaign with city residents pushed out of the debate.' George groaned.

'This is when it got nasty. I was abused on social media and eventually, on the day of the final meeting, threatened with my daughter getting murdered in a particularly unpleasant manner. They sent me pictures of her shopping and the kids going to school. The message couldn't have been clearer. It is these people we suspect of mounting the demonstrations on the day of the opening gala concert. We had wind of it happening but, sadly, we hadn't thought of them invading through the rear doorways just as the caretaker was opening the building for the day.'

'I see,' said Drake. He turned to Grace. 'Why wasn't I informed about all this?'

'Nor was I,' said Grace. 'I understand it all began long before we both arrived in Chester and was being dealt with by the uniformed branch. In truth, I don't think anyone anticipated it growing out of control.'

'I didn't share the emails with officers I'm afraid. I was just too anxious,' interjected George Marshall, 'I can't remember the policemen's names and I got the impression they weren't taking it seriously enough, but that's probably partly my fault.'

Drake grunted. 'This is a lesson we must learn but that is for another time.'

'Uniformed officers did take videos of the occupation and again in the evening,' said Grace. 'Perhaps we could send them down to our people in the Met Special Operations.' Drake nodded his approval.

'The use of masks and the return to recover things suggests these people are pretty serious,' said Drake. 'They do not want to be recognized. On the one hand, that creates problems. On the other hand, it probably narrows down the list of possible culprits to some extent. We certainly need to take it extremely seriously now. A key question is whether this is connected to the murder of Evinka Whyte.'

A bell broke the conversation before Grace could think of anything to say.

'That sounds like the stage doorbell ringing,' said George Marshall opening the conductor's room door.

'Probably the scene-of-crime team have arrived and can't get in,' said Grace. Sure enough, Jimmy Caxton arrived a couple of minutes later with a group of police officers ready to investigate the crime scene.

'Mr Caxton,' said Drake, 'what we really need is a list of the people who might have visited Evinka Whyte's dressing room between the rehearsals and the concert itself.'

'Not possible,' said Jimmy. 'The whole orchestra, the conductor and the stage managers would all have been up and down this corridor. Any one of them could have been into her room. I wasn't around here checking, so I can't help. Then there are the demonstrators. I can't be sure the police got them all out. They could easily have been hiding somewhere.'

Drake grunted his most grumpy grunt. 'I see this is going to need a real effort to narrow our enquiries down. Grace you should go and warn the SOCO about the paramedic falling seriously ill. They may need to conduct a careful examination and wear protection.'

'One person who was definitely in her room was her assistant,' said Jimmy Caxton. 'They arrived together. Now let me see.' He consulted the large book that had been under his arm. 'Yes, here she is. Look, Miss Whyte signed them both in. Evinka Whyte and Jelena Novakova it says. I saw her, the assistant, what was her name again? Oh yes, Jelena Novakova. Well, she left and didn't sign out. She was in a real hurry she was. Yes, look I made a note. It must have been just as I was making myself a cuppa. In a real rush, she was. I haven't seen her since.'

'Can you give Sergeant Hepple a full description of this Jelena Novakova?' said Drake.

'Sorry no. Thinking back she stood behind Miss Whyte coming in and she rushed out. All I saw was her back. I haven't the foggiest idea what she looks like.'

5

Drake and Grace had left the scene-of-crime team to their work, and Grace was driving them to Evinka Whyte's house. They set off back onto the main road that was part of the one-way system and found themselves circling the city centre to get back onto the road through Boughton. First, they went right down past the castle and almost to the Grosvenor Bridge. Taking a right, they joined a street that took them around the city past the new bus station where Grace pointed out the grass-covered roof.

'Chester is having a bit of a go at sustainable construction,' chuckled Drake.

Grace was too busy looking for the next turning to respond except for a brief nod of her head. She took another right back into the one-way system and was soon following the signs out of town towards their destination. The traffic thinned out a little as they reached Boughton and turned right off the main road. Almost immediately, Drake could see an imposing red brick and white stucco structure. Drake thought it might be pretending to be a little older than it actually was. It sat foursquare, puffing itself up with delusions of grandeur but there was no arguing that this was a desirable place to live. On close examination, the building had to admit that it was not some grand country house but a terrace of much smaller ones. Grace parked up, and they stood in front of what Grace assured Drake, was Evinka Whyte's house. From the road there appeared to be two floors but as they got closer, Drake could see an extra one below ground level with a narrow cutout giving it limited daylight. Grace rang the bell or, at least she pressed the button. No sound was discernable from inside. A minute passed without a response.

'That's odd,' she said. 'Evinka's sister Renata said she would be in and available to show us around all morning.' Grace pressed the bell again and, this time, after a short pause, Renata Kubicek opened the front door.

'I'm so sorry,' she said. 'I assumed that Evinka's P.A. was in, and she would normally answer the door. She seems not to be here, and I was up in my bedroom.'

'You have a bedroom here?' asked Drake.

'Yes, at one time I stayed here when I visited friends or my father in Chester.'

'You imply that you don't normally stay here now, asked Drake.

'No. In recent times Evinka and I had a bit of a falling out so it is easier to stay elsewhere.'

'This falling out,' said Drake. 'What was it about?'

'Oh, just silly things about what to do when our father dies. He is rather old now. Perhaps you had better follow me.' Renata turned with Grace and Drake following her through a small lobby into the central hallway. There were doors ahead. There were flights of stairs at the back leading both up and down. The floor of almost white marble was uncarpeted, and pale grey fabric covered the walls. An elaborate plaster cornice ran around the ceiling, and the doors were painted white with deep moulded frames. Daylight shone down from above. Looking up, Drake could see an octagonal roof light with an elaborate crystal chandelier hanging from the centre. There was an air of peace and calm. This was a house belonging to someone who was comfortably off. Renata opened the door ahead to reveal a large carpeted sitting room. There were two sets of floor to ceiling windows that gave a panoramic view of a tiered garden leading down to the River Dee below. Beyond the generously curved river, meadows and green fields stretched as far as the eye could see.

'Perhaps you should see the practice room,' said Renata. She ushered Drake and Grace out and down by one floor to the room below. It was more business-like with only a couple of small rugs on the otherwise timber boarded floor. Towards the rear of this room was a white baby grand piano. Shelving containing music scores and compact disks surrounded the piano. One set of shelves housed an industrial-looking music system feeding large loudspeakers standing on either side of the room. In the window were two music stands facing back into the room. On the adjacent wall was a collection of musical instruments. Drake counted five conventional flutes as well as a couple of piccolos and, what he took to be a larger bass flute. There were also several, relatively basic, wooden flutes and some recorders of varying sizes. This flute practice area was partially separated from the piano by a large chimney breast. Set into this in place of a fire was a large and extremely secure looking safe.

Grace turned to their guide, Renata.

'I think that once our scene-of-crime team has finished their work in the concert hall, we may need to bring them here,' she said. 'There is always the possibility that we might find something that gives us an insight into Evinka's death.'

'My goodness,' said Renata. 'I hadn't thought of that. I can't imagine you would find anything but of course I shall make the house available. Anything we can do to bring some closure to this awful business.'

'It would be best if you were to leave the house and its contents exactly as they are,' said Grace. 'Is it possible for you to stay somewhere else?'

'I intend to go back to Prague tomorrow,' said Renata. 'I do some work as a curator for a couple of museums there.'

'I think we need a longer interview with yourself too,' said Grace. 'As we search, there are questions that you might be able to help us answer. If you could check into a hotel for a few days, we would be most grateful.'

'No problem,' said Renata. 'I have a friend who lives on the other side of town. I'll call her.'

'What about this housekeeper?' asked Drake. 'You mentioned her earlier.'

'She's not so much a housekeeper as a personal assistant,' replied Renata. 'She would normally travel with Evinka. I've no idea where she is except that now I remember Evinka saying something about her having a holiday and how inconvenient it was. But she surely must have been there for the concert. I have her mobile phone number. Would you like me to call her?'

'What did you say her name was?' Drake responded.

'I don't think I did,' said Renata, 'but she is called Jelena Novakova.'

'Oh yes, Jimmy Caxton, the caretaker mentioned her dashing out just after the concert started. She didn't appear after the concert did she, Grace?'

'I've no recollection of her at all appearing after the concert.' Grace checked her notebook and shook her head.

'It must be a possibility that Jelena Novakova was the last person to see Evinka Whyte alive,' said Drake. 'Please don't call her but give the number to Sergeant Hepple.' With that, Drake turned to open one of the tall windows behind the two music stands. He sensed the fresh air and gentle noises of the River Dee below. Some indeterminate floral aromas wafted up from the garden He could see how this house combined tranquil views with a high level of privacy. It was an ideal residence for a famous and busy musician. He turned back to look across the practice room.

Suddenly there was a new mystery. What had happened to Jelena Novakova? Grace rang her number but it went to answerphone. Wherever Jelena was, she clearly had no intention of answering her phone.

'We'd better put out a call to all forces with that description, Grace.'

Drake had been mostly silent during their lunch at a nearby pub, so it was clear to Grace that he was deep in thought. She decided to keep quiet. She rang Jelena Novakova but her call was unanswered again. After a while, Drake hummed some tune to himself, turned to his copy of The Times lying on the table beside his plate and scanned the first page. He groaned at the headlines and turned it over, pulled out his pencil and studied the crossword. Grace had long ago realised that this activity often accompanied a new insight from Drake. She wondered how he did this. Most people would struggle with The Times crossword even when devoting their complete attention to it. Drake, however, seemed to use it as some sort of meditative stimulus. Grace waited for him to announce a new direction. This time he just grunted, looked at his watch and turned to her.

'How long would it take us to drive back to the concert hall?' he asked.

'Oh no more than ten minutes if the traffic is light,' she replied. Drake looked back at his crossword, filled in the answer to another clue and stood up.

'Let's go then,' he said. 'We have been kept out of the scene-of-crime. I want to see how things are going with the SOCO team. I also want to see the building properly from the outside. We need to do a walk around to make sure we understand all the ways in and out.'

'Can I ask you a personal question, sir?' asked Grace as she gathered her belongings and followed him out of the pub.

'Oh dear,' grunted Drake. 'Whatever is this?'

'It's just that I have noticed you seem to think about things to do with the case while you do the crossword.'

'Do I?'

'Yes, I've noticed it quite often.'

'Well, right now I'm at the beginning. I scan through and there are always just a few clues that I can answer straight away. They don't need mental effort. After you've done these things for as long as I have, you see through some fairly standard tricks that the setters get up to. I suppose I just recognise them. It's a bit like that at a scene-of-crime come to think about it,' he grunted. 'Perhaps I have been at this game too long.'

'What,' said an astonished Grace opening the driver's door. 'You're surely not thinking of giving up your crosswords.'

'Good gracious no,' replied Drake over the top of the car. 'I meant policing. Maybe I'm missing things because I jump to conclusions. Perhaps it's time to retire.'

'And exactly where would that leave me?' demanded Grace laughing. Drake grunted again getting into the car. They drove on with Grace silently wondering if Drake was serious about retiring. Drake was suddenly pondering on it too. Had he meant to say that? Of course not but...his brain was ahead of him. Chester was growing on him. He now knew that he liked the same cities that Cynthia had often waxed lyrical about. Free of family ties and responsibilities for the first time in decades, he could travel. Perhaps he could even have a go at compiling crosswords. Perhaps he could take a degree in architecture. Not at his age! Why not? These ideas were all well and good but he still thrived on the business of unpicking a case. Surely he could not give that up?

'Now let's look at this building afresh,' said Drake as they pulled into the small service yard at the concert hall. He set off down Souter Lane towards the main road. 'This is the approach most people will use. Look from here you can see quite clearly the game the architect is playing.'

'I'm afraid I can't,' said Grace.

'Oh yes, it's a fairly well established architectural idea. Cynthia taught me that much. She always maintained that in a given situation, there would be an infinite number of solutions but a relatively small number of basic strategies.'

'I see,' said Grace. 'Actually no I don't see.'

'It's simple,' said Drake. Can you see where the entrance is?'

'Yes, of course. There are many entrances. You can see the revolving doors in the glazed wall.'

'Can you see the main foyer and the crush bars?'

'Yes. It's all glass, apart from the doors.'

'Exactly. Can you see the auditorium?'

'Well, I can see where it is but not into it.'

'Well, there you are then,' exclaimed Drake with the air of someone winning a long argument. 'The architect has made the public areas open to view. We can all see them. The solid stone behind encloses the auditorium. Only people with tickets can go in there. It's all quite simple really. Analysing it is a bit like looking at a crime scene. You have not only to see but also to understand and make sense of it.'

'Gosh,' exclaimed Grace. 'I didn't realise being an architect was so easy!'

'It's not easy,' grunted Drake, 'but as with many things, the experts can make it look simple. I've been cheating a bit,' he laughed. 'I've seen a concert hall that uses the same strategy in Aarhus in Denmark, so I recognise it. That one is rectangular. This one is curved probably in response to the curves of the Roman amphitheatre. Look again and you can see the architect has used Cheshire red sandstone for the solid walls to fit in with the local buildings.'

Drake stood looking around and then slowly walked towards the building. 'As you correctly said, there are many entrances. That's a sensible idea given that people can approach from here, from the park or the river. These multiple doors will also let the audience out at the end without causing a blockage. Let's go and find the stage door. That won't be so obvious of course.' Drake set off around the building until they reached the stage entrance where Jimmy Caxton had his office. He immediately let them in.

'Mr Marshall was asking if you were here, sir,' he said. Drake nodded and pointed again to Grace. 'Look down this long corridor. It goes all the way across behind the auditorium with a fire exit that you found so spectacularly yesterday. There are ways out of this building in every direction. It's logical architecturally but it will make it a nightmare for us trying to trace people escaping. Now come down this corridor with me and let's sort out all these doors…OK here we are at the soloist's room where Evinka Whyte was found dead. The next door isn't labelled and is locked. The following door is the conductor's room where we briefly interviewed Maestro Stransky…Ah good it is unlocked…I thought so. Look inside,' said Drake in some satisfaction.

'What am I supposed to be looking at?' asked Grace.

'Look at the door in the middle of the flanking wall. It's just like the one in the soloist's room.' Drake strode up to it and turned the handle. It opened to reveal another door immediately behind it. Drake turned the handle and it opened to reveal the practice room complete with a baby grand piano. 'Come,' said Drake excitedly. He crossed the room to the door on the far side. It opened, again revealing another door, which also opened. 'See,' said Drake. 'We are in the soloist's room. Maestro Stransky could have visited Evinka Whyte without going out into the corridor. No one would know whether they met after rehearsals or not.'

'But that second door was locked when you tried it in the soloist's room,' said Grace.

'Yes, but that was from the other side,' said Drake. 'It probably locks only from the practice room side.'

'That puts another complexion on things,' said Grace.

'Certainly does,' replied Drake. 'We need to speak with the Maestro again. Anyway, let's go and see the SOCO.'

6

The SOCO team were packing up all their kit when Drake and Grace arrived.

'Good timing,' said Sergeant Phil Kline. 'We were just about to leave.'

'Found anything interesting?' asked Drake.

'We did a radiation test wearing full HAZMAT suits before we started,' said Phil. 'No sign of any issues at all. We took our kit off but as usual, kept gloves on as we did the rest. We've not seen anything that could have the potential to make anyone sick, so we can't help you on that score. There is nothing on the floor. We've printed the obvious places like door handles and taps. We'll let you know about that later. I assume you will print any suspects for us.' Grace nodded. Phil continued. 'There are two bags. The first is a knapsack kind of affair in black reinforced fabric. It has lots of pockets and several are lined with foam cutouts. Inside one pocket there is a disassembled flute. It looks identical to the assembled one sitting on a stand on the counter. Maker's name is Nagahara. The one assembled has Evinka Whyte engraved onto it. There's no engraving on the other one in the bag. Another pocket has several pieces of music. Two of them match the pieces played at the concert. The third seems to have lots of smaller pieces and is called...' He stopped and looked at his camera. 'Orchester Probespiel Flöte,' he said reading slowly. 'I've no idea what that means. Other pockets have what look as if they are tools for cleaning the instruments. The other bag on the floor is a leather shoulder affair. It has all the usual contents, handkerchiefs, makeup bag with lipstick, eye shadow, powder etc. There's an unusually large comb. There's a wallet with credit and debit cards and driving license, all in her name, and some currency, both sterling and euros. Then there's her iPhone. As usual with those darned things, we can't turn it on and if you try to break into them, they delete their data. The only things we can't identify were lying on the counter along with a refillable water bottle and an empty mug. The bottle wasn't full so she may have drunk from it. The mug was almost empty and it looked as if it had coffee in it. We've taken samples for toxicology tests just in case. Have a look at these odd objects.'

Drake put on his rubber gloves and peered at the first item. It was in black plastic and seemed to have four small pistons in a close line with springs on them. 'I've no idea what that is,' he said. The second item was a small blue cardboard box about 6 centimetres square. It was almost as high with a lid that slid right down over the base, which Drake slowly lifted. Inside were four items more or less filling the box and wrapped in white tissue paper. They looked identical. Drake unwrapped one. It was a small block of wood, pale in colour and with a mottled grain. It was probably just less than 6 centimetres square by 5 millimetres thick at one end and 2 millimetres at the other. The two main faces were not quite parallel, making it like a wedge with the tip cut off.

'Anyone any ideas about these?' asked Drake. Everyone peered at them and shook their heads.

'Perhaps they're wedges to hold doors open,' laughed Grace.

'They'd have to be bloomin' small doors,' grunted Drake.

'What's that inside the lid,' asked Grace pointing. Drake picked the lid up and turned it over. He turned it back and shook out a piece of white card with some printing, which he read out. "Acer Campestris, Lombardia."

'Acer means maple doesn't it?' said Grace.

'Yes,' said Drake, 'and Campestris, now let me think. The answer is somewhere in the depths of my schoolboy classics memories. Yes, I think the Campestris were minor female deities. If I'm not mistaken, I think they looked after the fields and meadows in classical Rome.'

Everyone looked even more puzzled.

'Doesn't get us much further, does it?' said Phil Kline

'Presumably, it is the kind of wood. They look like samples of some kind. Flooring possibly,' said Grace. Drake grunted in a way that indicated he was not impressed with the idea. A tap on the door broke the puzzled silence. Phil Kline opened it and in walked George Marshall.

'Sorry to trouble you but Jimmy Caxton is wondering how much longer you will need this room for?'

'I hope we can release it to you tomorrow,' said Drake. 'While you're here, can you help us with a few things? First of all, can you tell us what Orchester Probespiel Flöte means? Evinka Whyte had a book of short pieces of music with this title. I wondered if they were for encores.'

'Oh no. She wouldn't read music for encores. It's in German. These are pieces commonly used to audition flute players for an orchestra. I would think she used them for warm-up.'

'Ah that makes sense,' said Drake. 'Now can you help to identify the purpose of these two items?' Drake pushed the small collection of pistons towards the front of the counter. George Marshall walked forward to look at it.

'That's easy,' he said. 'It's a finger exerciser. Wind instrument players use them to strengthen their weaker fingers and get as near as possible to identical downward speed and pressure from each finger.'

Drake grunted again. 'Surely Evinka Whyte wouldn't need such a basic thing after so many years of practice?'

'You wouldn't think so,' replied George, 'but sometimes with ageing, the muscles drift out of sync. I think she was a perfectionist.'

'What about these little blocks of wood?' asked Drake. "There are four of them in this little box.'

'Sorry no idea,' said George, 'I've not seen anything like that before.' The little blocks of Acer Campestris sat on the counter remaining coy about their function.

Later that afternoon, the members of the orchestra shuffled their way through the fly-door and out into the auditorium. Each appeared lost in their thoughts with their collective footsteps making the only detectable sound. None of them seemed to want to sit in the front two rows, and none wanted to be alone at the rear of the auditorium. Between these empty extremes, they spread themselves around taking seats while leaving gaps. About ten rows were so occupied. The two stage managers and their senior manager followed them in and deferentially sat a row behind. Jimmy Caxton, the concert hall caretaker, sat alongside them on the end of the row in case he was needed. After a slight pause, the concert and orchestra managers came in chatting to each other in a whisper. The remaining administrative staff came in from the other side and sat halfway back down the stalls.

No one felt much like idle chatter, but gradually a few of the players began to compare thoughts on the situation with their neighbours. A quiet hum developed. To relieve the tension, one of the trumpets tried his hand at a running joke.

'If our beloved oboist can't sound a better "A" for us to tune to, we'll all be sitting down here every week.' The oboist responded by humming a perfect "A", provoking a bout of ironic laughter. It soon died away as George Marshall appeared on the platform with Drake and Grace Hepple a couple of steps behind. George Marshall stepped forward to the edge of the platform.

'Good afternoon, everyone. This is a terrible way to begin the life of this hall and you, our resident orchestra. First, I want to say how wonderfully well you all played in the opening concert. That was especially the case in the second half when you surely must have been somewhat distracted. I'm sure by now you are all aware that our celebrated soloist Evinka Whyte was sadly found dead in her dressing room just before she was about to perform last night. It is my duty now to introduce to you Detective Chief Inspector Drake and Detective Sergeant Hepple, who will say a few words.' George beckoned Drake forward and shuffled his way off the front of the platform to sit in the middle of the front row of still empty seats.

'Thank you, George,' said Drake. 'We are grateful to you all for coming this afternoon. This is indeed a dreadful day for you all, and I shall not keep you long. Our local pathologist is conducting an autopsy as we speak. He made a preliminary examination yesterday evening. At this stage, I'm not able to give you further information about Evinka Whyte's death except to say that we are treating it as needing some investigation. It is vitally important for our investigation that we ascertain, as far as possible, what Evinka Whyte may have done and what may have happened to her between the time she rehearsed with you here and the second half of the concert. If any of you have any information that might help us, however trivial or irrelevant you may think it is, then it is vital you come forward. We are happy to hear you speak now or possibly more suitably to visit us to discuss what you may know. The Director, Mr Marshall, has kindly allowed us to use his office upstairs for the rest of the afternoon. I'm sure you all know where it is. Are there any questions that anybody would like to ask?' Drake stood and said a few brief words to Grace Hepple and looked back into the auditorium. One hand had gone up. It belonged to one of the second violins. Drake pointed to her. 'Please go ahead,' he said.

'I'm new to Chester,' she said. 'I think quite a few of us are. After our rehearsal, I felt like exploring a little. Maestro Stransky had rehearsed the first half pieces with us after Miss Whyte finished, so it was a little while after she left us. I walked down to the river and along a little way. I saw her sitting on a bench, looking across the water. I think she might have been watching the boats or the swans on the river. I didn't think she would want to be interrupted and anyway wouldn't recognize me, so I just walked on. When I returned a few minutes later, she wasn't there. I'm afraid that's all I know.'

'Thank you,' said Drake. 'That is helpful. How long do you think this would have been after the rehearsal finished?'

'Oh, gosh. Maybe ten or fifteen minutes. No more.'

Grace Hepple made a note and Drake looked around for any more hands. There were none.

'Thank you,' he said. 'Sergeant Hepple and I will be upstairs in about five minutes. We would be happy to see anyone who can help.'

Grace and Drake were sitting waiting for members of the orchestra and staff of the concert hall to arrive when Drake's phone announced itself with the now familiar sound of Bizet's Carmen. The usual panic on Drake's part eventually found the offending sound.

'Drake here,' all went silent as Drake gave his phone an accusatorial look. It responded and Grace could hear a woman's voice. 'Oh hello Lucy,' said Drake, brightening up at the sound of his daughter's voice. 'Yes of course...look are you OK? What's the matter?...tomorrow...yes OK, There's a spare key with the lady next door to the left, see you then.' He put the phone back in his pocket with a frown on his face.

'Is there something wrong?' asked Grace.

'I don't know really,' said Drake. 'It was Lucy, she says that she's not dancing at the moment and could she come and see me for a few days.'

'Oh that's nice,' said Grace. Drake frowned again.

'I hope so,' said Drake. The two sat in silence with Drake looking blankly into space when they heard a tentative noise, almost a hesitant scratching. Drake nodded and Grace went to open the door. A young dark-haired and quite delicate, slight looking woman stood outside. She glanced nervously along the corridor and, presumably reassured, darted into the room. Drake beckoned her to a strategically placed empty chair and Grace pulled it back from the table for their visitor to sit down.

'Good afternoon and thank you for coming,' said Drake softly. 'Perhaps you would like to introduce yourself. I think you know that I am Detective Chief Inspector Drake and this is 'Detective

Sergeant Hepple.' The woman looked nervously, turning to nod an acknowledgement to Grace Hepple.

'Hello. Please call me Grace. My colleague never uses his first name.' Grace was smiling. Drake grunted again.

'My name is Penny Morris. I'm one of the first violins. I was ever so excited to get the job but all this has spoilt what was going to be a lovely occasion to remember.'

'Yes. Well done, congratulations,' said Grace. A flicker of a smile crossed Drake face as he nodded agreement.

'You have something to tell us perhaps,' he said.

'Yes. Oh dear, I hope it's not important but I saw them together. It was after the rehearsals. I went to walk down by the river. They seemed to be having quite a heated argument. She was almost shouting but lowered her voice as I walked down the footpath so I didn't actually hear what they were saying. They were walking up the path from the river to the stage door and stopped as I drew level with them. He was waving his arms. She had her hands on her hips. It looked like a real argument.'

'Who was that?' prompted Grace as Penny fell silent.

'Oh sorry. Of course, how silly of me. It was Evinka Whyte and Maestro Stransky.'

7

Drake was early in the next morning but he still arrived later than Grace. She had anticipated his wish to have all his work boards assembled in the case room. They had been left in Chester from the previous case. He liked her enthusiasm and dedication. She would go far in time.

'Ah good, Grace,' he said. 'You've had my work boards put up. That's marvellous. We can begin to sort information out now. I've got a suspicion that this case is going to be complicated.'

'I just phoned to get a report from the hospital,' said Grace. 'The paramedic is still in the ICU and they are not expecting any change in the immediate future.'

'We need to see the maestro again before he leaves Chester,' said Drake. 'I'd quite like to interview him at the concert hall. Something is bugging me about the rooms there. I want to have another look before we see him. Can you arrange for him to come there first thing in the morning?' Grace nodded.

'Look at this,' said Grace as Drake hung up his jacket.

'What is it?' asked Drake.

'It's the second page of the concert programme. There's a sort of brief biography of Evinka Whyte. I hadn't realized she was Czech.'

'I think I had read that somewhere,' said Drake.

'Even more astonishing,' added Grace, 'Her great grandfather was the famous composer Josef Kubicek. We danced a ballet by him when I was at the company years ago. It's gorgeous music.'

'What else does the programme say? Why don't you read it to me while I get a cup of coffee?'

Evinka Whyte – flute

Evinka was born in Prague into a musical family. Her great grandfather was Josef Kubicek, the famous Czech composer. She escaped from communist Czechoslovakia with her father in 1967. The people who helped them escape were part of a Chester based group saving musicians from persecution in the Soviet Bloc. Their immediate guide brought them from Germany to Chester and the family has lived in the city ever since. Her father was soon to marry one of the helpers, Clara Whyte. He and Evinka took the name Whyte to help cover their tracks.

Evinka started playing the piano and violin at the age of five but her new stepmother had played the flute in her younger days and the instrument was still in the house. Evinka was soon playing and astonishing small informal audiences of Chester society with her untutored prowess. She was to go to study at what has now become the Royal Northern School of Music in Manchester. She was soon playing in amateur orchestras and won the Young Musician of the Year competition, which led to her first album.

Evinka has straddled both the classical and popular worlds and has recorded many albums in both genres. She has always found time to teach and currently holds the post of Distinguished Visiting Professor here in Chester at Deva University.

'Well that is interesting,' said Drake over the noise of the coffee machine burbling enthusiastically. 'I think we need a long talk with Renata at the house so we get the whole family history. I have a feeling that it might be important. It's something the maestro said the other day. See if we can go straight up to see Renata this morning. Oh, and by the way, will you get a locksmith to see if we can open the safe in Evinka Whyte's music room.' Grace nodded and picked up her phone.

Drake and Grace were sitting in the music practice room at Evinka Whyte's house waiting for her sister to bring in some more coffees.

'By the way,' said Grace. 'I just rang the hotel but they said Itzhak Stransky had checked out. The only forwarding address they have for him is in Prague.'

'Drat,' said Drake. 'This case seems to be full of people who have disappeared. Luckily I think George Marshall said he was doing another concert here the week after next.' Drake got up and prowled around. The whole of the room was covered in shelving except for two pieces of a pure white wall. This was blank save for two posters about Evinka's concerts. One was in Venice and the other at the Berlin Philharmonie. He examined all the shelves and noted that they contained every piece of classical music for the flute that he ever heard of and plenty that he hadn't. There were books on music from every possible angle. There were bibliographies of all the great composers, books on musical theory and composition and books on wind instruments of all kinds. One shelf, just above the floor, contained a series of wooden frames. Drake pulled one out to discover it was a poster for another of Evinka's concerts, this time in Prague. The concert in Prague was in the opera house that Drake had once visited. He recalled that it was the theatre in which Mozart gave the premiere of Don Giovanni. He paused, looked at the distant landscape out of the window and reflected on being connected to such greatness in this room. Evinka had meticulously collected this library of her performances and yet they were not displayed but effectively filed, although ready to hang on a wall if and when desired. Drake pondered on what this might tell him about Evinka Whyte. He began to wish that he had met her before this awful event. He felt pangs of envy. He thought how wonderful it must be to play a musical instrument especially to do it so well. Perhaps when he retired he would learn to play the flute.

'That safe,' said Drake as Renata entered the room. 'It seems to occupy the whole of the fireplace. What did your sister need such a big affair for?'

'I think it was already in the house when she bought it,' replied Renata. 'But I do remember her saying how useful it would be. I've no idea why or what she kept in it. I guess the key must be somewhere around. I've never seen it open so I've no idea what might be in there I'm afraid.'

'Did the scene-of-crime boys find the key?' asked Drake, turning to Grace.

'No, they mentioned the safe and said they were unable to open it.'

'Renata Kubicek,' is your name. Is that correct?' asked Drake. Renata nodded. 'Technically my name should be Kubicekova because Czechs feminise the family name.

'Why do you use that name when Evinka used the name, Whyte?'

'There's a lot of family history behind that,' said Renata.

'Perhaps we had better hear it then, grunted Drake. Renata took a deep breath and began.

'All three of us were born in Prague.'

'Three of you,' Drake interrupted. 'There is another?'

'Yes, my brother, Dalibor. He's Evinka's twin. They were always close. Neither married and they still have houses in the same city. I'm the odd one out. They are a year older than me. Reading between the lines, I think I was an accident,' answered Renata, slightly impatiently. 'They must have been difficult times for our parents, especially father. At the time he was a young composer trying to find his voice. The authorities didn't like his work. They condemned it quite publicly as being too western and bourgeois. I think he began to fear that he might be made to disappear.'

'Really!' exclaimed Grace. 'How awful.'

'That sort of thing was not uncommon in those days. Czechoslovakia was in the grips of an authoritarian communist regime and very much under the thumb of the Russians. We don't know much about it. My father never talked about those days. Whenever we asked him, he used to say it was better for us not to know. Even after the Velvet Revolution in the nineties, he remained nervous. In recent years I have done quite a lot of research about it. I now think that my father was also tormented about whether his talent could live up to the name.'

'The name being Kubicek?' asked Drake.

'Yes, our great grandfather was internationally famous and successful and his name has gone down in history, probably for all time.'

'That's Josef Kubicek?' said Drake.

'Yes, his work is now much loved all over the world. During his life, he was greatly admired and his use of traditional Czech melodies endeared him to the whole nation. In his formative years, he was heavily influenced by Smetana. However, later he began to be inspired by what Dvorak had done when he went to America and developed a more international voice. This can be heard in his New World Symphony. Sorry, I'm an academic and I have been told more than once that I lecture people.'

'We are all ears,' said Drake.

'Well, to cut a long story shorter, our father, Karel Kubicek, must have been under terrible pressure. He wanted to be honest to his art but this brought him into conflict with dark forces in the communist regime. Eventually, he was forced to flee and in 1967 he took Evinka and Dalibor and disappeared. Our mother wouldn't tell me anything and I was really too young then to be able to remember now. I know now that my father, Evinka and Dalibor escaped on a well-travelled but dangerous route through what was then West Germany. A year later he organised for our mother, and me to get out via Austria. Again I can't remember much except that our mother disappeared on the journey. I was awfully frightened but there were some other children involved who kept me company. We believe now that mother was arrested but we've never got to the bottom of it. We never saw her again. Father met me off the train in Vienna and brought me here to Chester to join Evinka and Dalibor.'

Renata began to sob quietly. Grace got up and passed her a handkerchief. She sat and dabbed her eyes.

'I'm sorry,' she said. 'I should be able to deal with it better by now. I think my mother must have lost her life to free me from such tyranny.'

'Tell me,' said Drake. 'What name does your brother use?'

'He's Dalibor Kubicek.'

'So why did Evinka use the name Whyte?'

'A wonderful woman here in Chester called Clara Whyte organised a series of escapes including ours. Father fell in love with her and they married. Father changed his name to hers rather than the other way round. He remained nervous about the Czech authorities tracking us down. Of course, once the Velvet Revolution took place and, eventually, the Czech Republic was formed, we all felt easier. Mum, as we came to call Clara, sadly died of cancer and Dalibor and I changed our name back to Kubicek. I think Evinka was already making her name and worried about being compared to our great grandfather. Apparently, our grandfather, Václav, loved music and played the piano but had no real talent of his own and was also terrified of being compared with his father. My father told us that he never played in public. Sadly our father lost all contact with him after we came to Chester.'

'I take it your father has also died now,' said Drake.

'No. He is old. We are not sure exactly how old but probably ninety. He lives in a care home. We love him very much. He gave us the lives we now lead.'

'So you live in Prague?' asked Drake.

"Yes, most of the time. So I seldom see my father now. I'm an academic. Although I play the piano, I wasn't prepared to put in the practice so I was never going to be up to soloist standard. I am currently writing a biography of Josef Kubicek. It will be an important book.'

'Can we just go over the day of the concert with you?' asked Drake. Renata nodded.

'Yes, I had arrived quite late the previous evening and Evinka had gone to bed. The morning of the concert we ate breakfast together. Jelena prepared things for the concert.'

'Would that include a mug of coffee and a full water bottle?' asked Grace.

'The water bottle yes. Flautists may need to wet their mouth. I expect that Jelena made coffee at the hall.'

'Then,' prompted Grace.

'Then I went back to my room to do some important emails. Jelena and Evinka left for the hall. I left later and attended rehearsal. Then I had a walk by the river and went to the concert.'

'Did you see your sister again before she was due to play?'

'No.'

'You said neither Evinka nor Dalibor ever married,' said Drake. 'What about you?'

'I was in a marriage but it ended. Now I value my freedom too much for a long term relationship.'

'So why do you come to Chester?'

'I also had a post as visiting professor here at Deva University but I have just lost that.'

'Where does Dalibor live? Is he a musician too?' asked Grace.

'He lives here in Chester, in Curzon Park. No, Dalibor learned the piano as a child but he has little interest in music. He's an accountant and, of course, very well off compared with me as a miserably paid academic. He did all Evinka's accounts for her. She was hopeless at that sort of thing.'

'Perhaps we ought to speak with Dalibor,' said Drake to Grace. 'Renata, would you please give the contact details of Dalibor to Sergeant Hepple when we finish. You said a minute ago that you just lost your post at the university here,' said Drake. 'Why was that?'

'It's a long story. I'm not really happy to talk about it now.'

'I think we read in the concert programme that Evinka is a visiting Professor there too.'

Renata sat silently looking at the floor.

'Couldn't she have put in a word for you at the university?' probed Drake.

'Exactly,' said Renata fiercely. 'This is not the time to talk about it.'

8

Drake reached the end of the Groves where the road turned away from the river and climbed up the hill into the town. Sure enough, there was the sign for The Boathouse. He headed straight on under a roof spanning across an opening between two buildings. Once in the little courtyard, he turned right through the main building to a patio against which an old barge was moored on the River Dee. It was decked out with small tables and at one George Marshall was sitting waving his arm.

'A pint of bitter, George?' asked Drake.

'That's very kind. Yes please, JW Lees is on tap here.' Drake went back inside to order at the bar in what seemed a welcoming, traditional sort of English pub.

'I must thank you twice, George,' said Drake, arriving with two full pint glasses of the best local beer.

'Why is that?'

'Once for finding me this little house right here overlooking the river and once for bringing me a few steps further down The Groves to The Boathouse. It is an excellent little pub that will surely become my local. This place is just made for early spring evenings like today. It's a good place to sit and think, or just to sit. Oh dear, didn't Winnie the Pooh say that?'

George Marshall laughed. 'Then this is not likely to be the last time we meet here!'

'I'm very envious of you, George. Your job with so much music around must be a complete joy. I have always loved classical music but sadly never learned an instrument and I fear it may be too late to start.'

'Oh no,' exclaimed George. 'It's never too late to learn to play a musical instrument.'

Drake smiled. He still harboured an inner wish to play. He could not imagine anything more exciting than to sit in the middle of a great orchestra. Maybe when he retired and when he had more time. 'Tell me, George, how does one get a job like yours?'

'Oh, it was advertised, so I applied.'

'Yes, of course, but what I meant was how do you become qualified to do such a job?'

'For a start, you have to be prepared to be paid a pittance. My job was originally advertised at nearly twice what they are actually paying me. When I took the job, it was only to get the hall built. There was supposed to be a pay review then but somehow that hasn't happened. To be more serious, I suppose that I'm quite the opposite of you. I've been a musician from an early age. Strange really, my parents had no interest in music. With my brother, only a year younger, it was all about animals. Now he's a vet at a zoo in New Zealand. It's nice really how close we are still. We are also both in disappointing jobs.'

'It happens,' said Drake. 'I have a son in financial futures in Singapore and a daughter who is a ballet dancer. I've no idea how that came about. To be honest, I still don't understand what financial futures are. Tom has tried several times to explain it to me. And, as for ballet, I've no idea how Lucy does all that stuff while making it look so easy. So obviously I wasn't an inspiration to either of them. Their mother was an architect so they didn't get their skills from her either. So if your parents weren't the inspiration, what turned you on to music?'

'It was my aunt. She had an old half-size violin that hadn't been used for years, and it was just gathering dust. She let me play with it. I suppose I must have been no more than eight or nine years old. Of course, it was out of tune and in a terrible mess with broken strings and a bridge that was hardly holding the strings up. I think it had lost one of its tuning screws and only had three strings. I took it to the local music shop and asked them to tell me how to repair it. I think the guy there was amused by this little kid asking for help, so he took me under his wing. He let me into his workshop and gradually showed me what to do and, over many weeks of Saturday mornings, I managed to restore the little violin to working order. I started to play it with that wonderful innocence that small children have. Somehow I worked out what to do and managed to play a few simple tunes. My aunt paid for me to have some lessons and as I grew more capable, I had weekend work in the little music shop.'

'What a charming story,' said Drake. 'Do you mind if we walk back along the river? I want to get an image of the concert hall from the riverbank on my phone. Pictures often help me to think.' George nodded and the two men began to amble along the Groves past their houses towards the concert hall.

'So, what happened next in your life story, George?'

'Well I was never academic but I was lucky to have a natural talent and, over time, I played all the stringed instruments in the shop and got a Saturday job there. I left school as early as I could and got an apprenticeship at a major instrument maker's. Then I just happened to repair some instruments that belonged to members of a local amateur orchestra. One thing led to another and they asked me to look after their instruments and manage their concerts. Of course, I needed to earn a living and a job came up with a professional orchestra helping the concert manager and doing maintenance on their instruments. Eventually and quite suddenly, the concert manager died, so I took over in an emergency. In the end, they decided I could do the job and I've never looked back until more recently.'

'Wonderful,' said Drake. 'So I suppose you must know the repertoire inside out to plan concerts?'

'Yes, but my love of music meant I was well on the way, so then I just learned on the job. It has been a labour of love. I think I also know how to maintain and repair most of the major instruments of the orchestra so I understand musicians' problems. Of course, you should realise that planning concerts is a lengthy process. Good classical musicians get booked up probably two years ahead. I went to see Evinka a couple of years before we were due to open. I then had to rearrange because the building was late. Luckily she could fit us in not too long after we took possession of the hall. This job was to be my dreams come true but in recent times it has become more of a nightmare. Frankly, all the controversy about the concert hall continues to make my life pretty awful. The concert hall steering committee has not supported me at all. They have a lovely time playing at being important citizens of Chester. I am left all on my own to deal with all these protestors and their endless arguments. My life has turned out not to be making music. It's about dealing with awful people and getting no thanks. If these extremists are responsible for killing Evinka, then I hope you catch them and put them away for a long time.'

'I'm sorry about that,' said Drake. 'I suppose it has become my job to try to sort at least some of that out.'

George Marshall let out a hollow laugh.

'Well, there you are,' he said. 'I wouldn't have the vaguest notion about how you even begin to do that.'

'Sometimes, I wonder if I do!' grunted Drake. He stopped and looked downstream under the Queen's Suspension bridge soaring above them. 'I've always liked cities that have water in them. Sometimes on a big scale like Hong Kong or Sydney but there is something also so welcoming about the smaller scale. I fell in love with Chester the first time I worked on a case here. It's hard to believe on a lovely day like this but that case was a murder in the centre of that bridge,'

'Good gracious,' said George Marshall. 'You're right about this site. The moment I saw it I knew it was the right place to build a concert hall. Of course, Sydney was an inspiration but also Stratford with its wonderful theatre overlooking the river.'

'You have certainly been fortunate. It surely could become a real favourite,' said Drake. 'But first I must clear up the mystery of how Evinka Whyte died. Have you got any theories?'

'I cannot imagine anyone wanting to see her dead,' replied George. 'It is tempting to think the demonstrators were involved. There are some evil people among them. When the plans for the concert hall were being finalised I was sent some dreadful messages. One in particular showed my daughter being tortured. They must have got her picture from somewhere and spent hours on Photoshop. I saw it suddenly at a stressful time and I passed out and fell to the floor.'

'Have you still got all that material?' asked Drake.

'Most of it I deleted but I kept that image. I half thought somehow I might be able to use it to catch them but of course, I never did. I will send it to you.' Drake nodded his thanks.

'Yes, that might be useful,' he replied. 'Now I must take some pictures and do some thinking before tomorrow. Besides which, I'm expecting my daughter to have arrived.'

The two men parted and George Marshall set off back to his house. Within a few minutes, Drake had taken all the pictures he wanted of the concert hall. A blackbird was in full voice sending notes cascading down from a nearby tree. A gentle mist was beginning to spread across the river and climb up the banks on either side. The view upstream was charming and Drake clicked his shutter once more. The result on his little screen could have passed as a painting by Turner. Looking the other way, the suspension bridge seemed to be growing out of nothing on the far bank. Chester, and the Groves, in particular, had many ways of being charming.

Drake turned the key in the lock of his front door. It stuck once and then decided to co-operate. Drake pushed and the door flew open. 'Hello love,' he said as he shoved the door shut. 'It's lovely to see you. So why aren't you dancing then?' Drake advanced around the sofa towards his daughter. 'Oh, I see, stupid question.'

'Yes,' said Lucy. 'Ballet is hard enough anyway, but with a broken leg, it just isn't feasible.'

'How did you do that?' asked Drake.

'I landed badly, right on the edge of a trapdoor in the stage. You always need to avoid them as they don't have the give that there is in the rest of the stage boarding. It just went twang.' Drake pushed the crutch aside and sat on the sofa to hug his daughter. She started to sob uncontrollably.

'Whatever is wrong?' asked Drake.

'I don't know,' said Lucy. 'I've just lost my love for it. I don't know if I want to carry on dancing. I wasn't concentrating. That's why I broke my leg.'

'You know, that's odd,' said Drake. 'I said something similar to Grace yesterday. I didn't even know I was thinking of retiring. It just came out.' He pulled a face and they both collapsed laughing.

'Perhaps it's just the injury,' said Drake. 'When it heals, you'll probably recover your obsession.'

'That's a lovely thought, Dad. I wish I knew that. Somehow things have started to feel different. But if I give up dancing, whatever would I do then? That's made me realise I need to plan a future. Even if I get my mojo back, this is not going to be a long career. I've spoken to Tom about it. He says his tutor at college always used to say that a career isn't something you can plan. It happens to you. I think that's probably true. Look at Tom. If he hadn't met that chap from Singapore in a pub one night, he almost certainly wouldn't be over there.'

'I think I agree with Tom's tutor,' said Drake. 'It's amazing how accidents have a big impact. Your mother often used to say the same thing and look how well she ended up. If she hadn't got that awful cancer, she would still be at the top of her game.' Drake's voice cracked and he dabbed his eyes with a handkerchief. 'I still can't believe she's gone, Lucy. Life can be terribly cruel. Carpe Diem.'

'Dad, you've done it again. You're talking Latin.'

'Oh sorry, that's a bad habit,' said Drake. 'It means seize the day or live for now because we don't know what is around the corner.'

'Actually, I'm too confused to talk about it,' said Lucy. 'I think I'll have an early night. I might make more sense tomorrow.'

9

Midway through the following morning, everyone in the case room had settled down with the beverage of their choice when the phone rang. Grace picked it up. 'Oh right, Tom…thanks. I'll come down now.' Drake's rocking chair creaked as he looked over from his Times crossword. Grace nodded as she put the phone down.

'We've got an unexpected visitor,' she said.

'Name of…?' asked Drake.

'It's George Marshall. Tom Denson says that he's very insistent that he should see you.'

'OK bring him up,' said Drake returning to his crossword.

'Ah, Chief Inspector,' said George Marshall, as he was shown in by Grace.

'Please sit down and tell us how we can help.' said Drake, struggling to his feet and only succeeding at the second attempt. 'Why do they make these chairs so darned low? I'm sure they always used to be higher.' George Marshall laughed.

'I don't think they design for people your height,' he said.

'It's all a conspiracy against tall people,' grunted Drake. 'I never asked to be this tall.'

'Well,' said George. 'Surely it must be an advantage in your business. You see over a crowd and can terrify a suspect just by standing up, though I think you might need to do it a bit more quickly!'

'Why have you come?' asked Drake. 'Sergeant Denson tells us that you particularly wanted to see me.'

'Yes,' said George and then stopped suddenly. 'I was wondering how you are getting on with the case.'

'Steadily,' said Drake. 'Steadily.'

'Do you have any suspects yet?' asked George.

'We are keeping an open mind,' said Drake. 'We don't normally go public on someone being a suspect. You might sometimes hear the police say they want to find a particular person but even then that doesn't necessarily mean that they're a suspect. They might be thought to be a key witness.'

'I see,' said George slowly. 'I had hoped that we would be able to clear this awful business up by now. It's not the sort of publicity we need as we try to get the concert hall into the public's consciousness. We are starting to hold free concerts for the public soon and I hope this isn't still hanging over us.'

'I appreciate that,' said Drake, 'but I'm afraid murder investigations don't follow a timetable. We're not even sure that it is a murder. The pathologist has still not resolved all his investigations.'

'I see,' said George. 'That is rather disappointing. I suppose I had better let you get on with it then.' He rose slowly from his chair and then suddenly sat down again. 'Actually, there is something that I am wondering if I should tell you. It's been bothering me since I saw you at The Boathouse.'

'Would you like a cup of coffee,' asked Grace. George nodded his head.

'Yes, that would be nice.'

'I imagine you could drink another one, sir,' said Grace. Drake smiled and nodded his head. Grace disappeared behind all the work boards and the two men soon heard a promising hiss.

'When are these concerts then?' asked Drake.

'Well, the first one is on the Rows and at the Cross. We are hoping the good weather continues. The second one will be in the concert hall foyer in a couple of weeks.' George pulled his phone out and looked at it. 'Oh gosh no. It's only just over a week now!' Grace arrived with three cups of steaming hot coffee. George began to sip his tentatively. Drake pushed his across the table next to his empty mug. He had never drunk tea or coffee hot and he was not going to change now. It would need to cool down to his preference of moderately lukewarm.

'So, what is it that you wanted to tell me?' he asked George.

'Well, I still don't really know if I should tell you or not. I have been turning it over in my mind. After you did that little talk to the orchestra, I nearly spoke then.' He stopped and looked at his phone and cleaned the screen with a handkerchief from his top jacket pocket.

'It's about Maestro Stransky.' He blurted the words out rapidly and then fell silent.

'Yes,' said Drake.

'The fact is that I made a mistake. It was with the very best intentions but I wasn't to know.'

'Know what?'

'It goes back a while when I was planning the gala opening concert. When I learned more about Evinka Whyte's history, then I thought it would be a nice idea to have a Czech conductor. I was wrong.'

'Why wrong?' prompted Drake.

'When I told Evinka, to start with she was quite angry. I hadn't realized that there is some long-standing feud between the Kubicek and Stransky families. I wasn't to know. Evinka wouldn't tell me what it was all about but I gathered that it goes back a few generations so it's deeply felt. She said there had been violence in the past. I said I would change and find another conductor but when I went back to Stransky he fell back on a cancellation clause in his contract. He said that he'd already turned down another much more lucrative booking and he would charge us his full fee. I didn't need that to come out with the concert hall steering committee. It would have made me look completely incompetent and they were supposed to be reviewing my salary about then. I went back to Evinka, and she seemed calmer about it and said it didn't matter. She was sure that they could both do a professional job.' George wiped his forehead with the handkerchief that was still in his right hand. 'I suppose I should have told you before. I can't for one minute believe he would have done anything but anyway I just thought I should let you know.'

'Thank you,' said Drake. 'You were quite right to tell us. Do I remember that you said Maestro Stransky is coming back next week for another concert?''

'Yes, correct,' said George.

'Perhaps it would be better not to mention any of this to him,' said Drake. 'Leave it to us.'

'I'll certainly be careful not to mention it,' said George. 'Thanks for being so understanding. I feel silly now for not telling you sooner. Thanks for the coffee, Grace. I must be going. There's a lot to do on these upcoming concerts. I'll make sure you get a flyer about them and a couple of tickets, Chief Inspector.'

Grace had organized for Evinka's twin, Dalibor to come to meet them at Evinka's house. Drake was still engrossed in his crossword when Dalibor suddenly appeared rather early. Drake looked up and struggled out of his chair to greet the visitor. Grace pulled out a chair for him.

'I guessed you might be in here. I'm Dalibor Kubicek. I don't often get into this music room.'

'I'm Chief Inspector Drake and this is my Detective Sergeant, Grace Hepple. I gather you have a key to this house?'

'Yes, Evinka and I have always had keys to each other's houses. She was anxious to have a key holder nominated for the monitored alarm system. She is away a lot and I come round from time to time just to make sure all is in order.' Drake resumed his chair and put his copy of The Times to one side for later.

'This is a dreadful affair,' said Dalibor. I don't know how this can happen, especially here in Chester. We lead a quiet and comfortable life here. Evinka has been on tour to many cities that would have been much more dangerous than Chester.'

'Do you think she was in some kind of danger?'

'She certainly thought she was. She had become progressively more anxious. In recent months she said she was expecting "them" to come and get her. I've no idea who "they" were or why they would want to do her harm. She wouldn't tell me. There are not many secrets between the two of us so it was a bit unusual. I didn't take it too seriously I'm afraid. Perhaps I should have done. I half thought she might be suffering from paranoia. Presumably, whoever "they" were finally caught up with her. It's still hard to believe.'

'Were you at the concert?' asked Drake.

'Yes. I don't always attend her concerts. Most of them are in faraway places and I'm too busy to travel. To be honest they are not my cup of tea. I know it's strange for a Kubicek to say it but I'm not into classical music much. I found the first half of the concert rather tedious. When they announced that she was ill, I called her phone but she didn't answer so I left. If I'd realized it was serious, then, of course, I would have gone to see her. I texted her but got no reply. During the night I woke up worrying about her. The next morning, there was a text from Renata telling me to call her. Have you any idea who did this dreadful thing?'

'We are at the early stage of our inquiries,' replied Drake. 'Can you elaborate more on her anxiety?'

'Not really. I'm sorry to say it but poor Evinka was not a happy soul in recent years. If we were sitting here in the living room, she would hear things and keep going to check the doors. I tried to suggest to her that maybe she needed some help but she didn't take kindly to the idea.'

'You and Evinka were twins?' said Drake.

'Yes, we have a close relationship. We tell each other most things so this jumpiness of hers was a puzzle. Normally I'd have expected her to tell me if there was anything wrong. It's an odd thing but somehow we both seem to know when the other is in some sort of trouble. They do say that twins have some sort of extra sense. It often feels that way but I can't explain it.'

'Our pathologist has told us that there was evidence that she might have been taking drugs of some sort,' said Drake.

'Do you know?' said Dalibor. 'I have wondered that myself. I asked her assistant Jelena but she dismissed the idea. Surely she hasn't done something stupid and taken an overdose has she?'

'We do not have any evidence at the moment that might suggest that,' replied Drake.

'Thank goodness for that,' sighed Dalibor.

'How do you earn your living then?' asked Drake. 'I gather it isn't through music.'

'No. I was forced to learn the piano as a child but I never did the practice so I was hopeless. My teacher used to report me to my father who was rather more understanding. I do think though that I am a disappointment to him. I'm an accountant and I have a law degree though I have never qualified as a lawyer. I do mostly work on corporate accounts and advise boards of directors about the health of their company.'

'I suppose that might get rather repetitive and boring,' said Drake.

'Oh no! It is always fascinating. Every company is different. It's amazing how blind the directors can be to their situation.'

'You help Evinka with her accounts then?'

'No, I don't help her. I actually do them. She was hopeless at it. To be honest with you, without my work on her behalf, she would have got into a real mess. She had no understanding at all about her outgoings and income. I suppose in a way, it would be nice to be that carefree about money but it is rather dangerous. To be fair, her accounts are often complicated by payments in foreign currencies. I would occasionally have to advise her to be more careful. She would always tell me not to bother because she knew she was all right. Of course, this house is worth a fair bit. I suppose that I had better begin to wind up her affairs.' He looked blankly into the distance out of the window so Drake kept quiet. Eventually, Dalibor shook his head and sat up from the slump he had collapsed into.

'Is there any other way I can help?' he asked.

'Can you tell us any more about the worries that Evinka developed recently?' asked Drake.

'I did look at her diary. I always get it synchronized onto my phone so I know where she is. It seemed to start after she played a concert in Zurich. I asked her about it. She just denied it.

Whenever I asked her about it, she just got worked up so I stopped inquiring. I did, however, notice that she was regularly paying money to someone in Zurich but I couldn't find any trace of it so I forgot about it. Now I am wondering if I should have followed it up.'

10

When Grace returned from seeing George Marshall to the door, Drake was back in his favourite chair working on his crossword again.

'What do you make of that, sir?' asked Grace.

'Could be something. Could be nothing,' said Drake. 'See if you can get hold of Maestro Stransky's schedule. I guess that he has a web site. We'll start there.'

'This story about the family feud between the Kubicek and Stransky families is a new angle,' said Grace. Do you think it really possible that Maestro Stransky murdered Evinka Whyte as the result of a family disagreement?' Drake got up again and started to walk around his work boards.

'Well, we won't know if we don't follow it up,' said Drake. 'Certainly, Stransky had an opportunity to be the murderer because of the interlinking rooms. He could have moved between the rooms without anyone else knowing. We also have the evidence from that violinist, what was her name?' Drake scanned the boards. 'Ah yes, Penny Morris. She claims to have seen Evinka and Stransky arguing outside after the rehearsal. So how should we tackle all this?'

'Perhaps we need some further knowledge about this feud,' said Grace. 'So far it is only hearsay from George Marshall.'

'Well,' said Drake slowly, 'the only people we know of still alive who might know more are Renata Kubicek and her father, Karel. Why don't you call Renata and see if we can talk to her again? She could also give us the contacts for her father and we need her to give a full description of Evinka's assistant Jelena Novakova.'

Drake started prowling around his work boards again as Grace looked up Renata's number in her notebook. She was soon busy on the phone.

'I've made contact with Renata,' said Grace. 'She is staying with a friend on the other side of town and could come over to see us either here or at the house.'

'OK, let us go to the house,' said Drake. 'I wouldn't mind poking around again. Tell her we'll be there in half an hour.'

Drake and Grace arrived back at Evinka Whyte's house. They went straight to the music room and Drake prowled around looking at instruments, books, sheets of music and Evinka's collection of concert posters. But the room and its contents remained stubbornly silent. He stood in front of the fireplace looking at the large safe.

'I meant to tell you, sir,' said Grace. Our best locksmith has failed to open the safe. The lock completely defeated him. He says that it's pretty ancient. It has the maker's name on it; some company in Manchester that disappeared in the last century. He says the only alternative is to start drilling it but unless you know where to drill you can do more harm than good. He says they are trying old records to see if they can find the maker's instructions. They usually record alternative ways in apparently. No luck on that so far and it is not possible to pull it out without demolishing a load of the wall. They could then get it back to their workshop but even then they would still have to find a way in.' Drake grunted his disappointed acknowledgement.

'If there's a safe, there's a key,' he said gruffly.

'But nobody has found it so far,' said Grace. Drake continued his walkabout until the door opened. It was Renata.

'Thank you for coming,' said Drake as Renata walked in. She sat on a piano stool and stared out of the window at the River Dee below.

'It feels strange to be coming here without Evinka,' she said.

'We have some information that perhaps you can help us with,' said Drake.

'I'll try. Anything to help solve this awful business.'

'We have some information that suggests that the Kubicek and Stransky families know each other and there is something of a difficult situation between them,' said Drake.

'We certainly know each other. There was a marriage between the families several generations ago. My grandfather, Vaclav, had a sister called Daniela who married into the Stransky family. They are another Prague musical phenomenon. I always understood that things got turbulent around that time. I'm not sure the marriage was a happy one. Her husband was a violinist like Daniela. I understand they rowed a fair bit. But there are many stories; it might be sensible to call them legends. Most have been told through the generations of our family and they have almost certainly grown with the telling. All of them begin with our great grandfather Josef. As you know, Josef Kubicek was an internationally famous composer and remains so. In Prague, which was part of Bohemia then, he was a celebrity. Most say he was wealthy beyond what history has told. These stories say he kept some great treasure but nobody knew what it was or where it was kept. These stories end rather abruptly by saying this treasure was lost. A favourite version has it taken by the Nazis during the Second World War. Some say it went to South America, Argentina is a popular destination. One story says that it was part of a huge collection of art and precious objects that the Nazis packed onto a train in 1945 and sent to what is now Wroclaw in Poland but at the time was called Breslau and in Germany. Some claim this train was hidden in an underground tunnel and has never been found. Many people have searched for this train but none have found it.' Renata paused, took out a handkerchief and blew her nose.

'Trains feature in other stories. One says that when our great grandfather Josef was in his prime, the Habsburg Emperor Franz Josef came to Prague in his imperial train. At that time Bohemia was part of the huge Austro-Hungarian Empire. They say he heard Josef Kubicek play one of his compositions and the next day a dazzling gift arrived for our great grandfather Josef. I'm sorry, there are too many Josefs in these tales. The imperial train was well stocked with precious works of art, some from antiquity. The story goes, that Emperor Franz Josef hated some of the art, so whatever it was that he sent to my grandfather was likely not to be a loss felt by the Emperor. If any of these stories are true, and that is far from likely, the assumption was that great grandfather Josef handed whatever his treasure was to his son Vaclav, my grandfather, who then lost it. Vaclav was notoriously non-musical and disinterested in art of all kinds. They say hunting was his passion. Some stories say that Vaclav was so uninterested in this mythical treasure that he let his sister have it. In this case, it would have passed onto her Stransky husband. The Stransky family still claims foul play. I've heard versions that say it wasn't lost but was handed down to Karel and then to the twins Evinka and Dalibor. Both denied any knowledge. Now Evinka is dead no doubt more stories will appear. I don't believe any of them.'

'What a fascinating tale,' said Drake. 'What do you think this precious object was?'

'One version claims it was an invaluable Fabergé egg. Some tell of a priceless musical instrument. Others say it was a painting but they disagree about the artist. Some even say it was pure gold but that seems the least likely.'

'Do you think there is any truth in these stories?' asked Drake.

'We, that is Evinka, Dalibor and I, have always doubted it. Maybe there was some argument and some object got lost but I doubt the tales are more than rumour and invention.'

'How could we delve further into this?' asked Drake.

'The obvious person to ask would be Karel Kubicek, my father. He was always secretive about anything to do with the past of our family. He wanted to make sure that none of his children could be tortured for information by the secret police. He never really recovered from the death of both his wives. As I told you before, they were our mother who disappeared in Prague and the wonderful Clara Whyte who helped to rescue us all from Czechoslovakia. She sadly died many years ago now. My father is now old and beginning to suffer from dementia. He lives in a home in Wilmslow not far from here. I doubt that you would get any real information from him now. Do give him my love if you see him. The matron at the home says he is happy and I would prefer you not to tell him that Evinka has died.'

Later that day, Drake was fiddling with his work boards when the phone rang. Grace answered and listened for some time before putting the phone down.

'That was Traffic,' she said. 'They had a hit and run case last night in Curzon Park. The pedestrian was killed outright. This morning they were going house to house when they discovered what looks like burglary and they need us to look at it.'

'OK,' said Drake. 'I want to get all this a bit more sorted out. Why don't you go and take that young Constable Redvers with you? He's desperate to get more investigative work.'

Grace was quite pleased to get out and have a job of her own. She knew the Evinka Whyte case was already looking as if it would be a major enquiry. She could handle both. She gathered up her belongings and set off.

Drake was pleased to be on his own. Sometimes thinking needed to be done in isolation. This felt like one of those times. He needed to get all the main characters in the Evinka Whyte case set out on his work boards. Their activities, locations and possible motivations could then be added. So far, he simply had no real ideas, though Maestro Stansky was not being straight and he was a possible line of enquiry. Evinka's PA, Jelena Novakova had been missing and she needed to be found fairly urgently.

Drake was prowling around his newly assembled work boards when the phone rang. Grace could answer it, he thought. The ringing persisted until he remembered that she was out. He strode across the room as fast as his uncooperative legs would carry him to take the call.

'Drake.'

'It's me, sir,' said Grace's voice.

'OK, how is it going?'

'It's suddenly got more complicated,' said Grace. 'The man killed in the hit and run was Evinka's twin brother Dalibor Kubicek. It's his home that appears to have been burgled. I think you'd better come over and have a look.'

'Drat,' said Drake. 'I was just getting into things here. Now two of our important lines of enquiry are missing, first the personal assistant, Jelena, and now the brother, Dalibor. I'll get someone to drive me over.'

'Don't worry,' said Grace. 'I've sent Constable Steve Redvers over to collect you. He should be there in a few minutes.'

Drake was just getting his coat and scene-of-crime kit when Constable Redvers arrived. He was visibly excited as they walked out to the car.

'I guess I'm on the Evinka Whyte case as well now,' he said grinning from ear to ear.

'I'm not getting in that tin can,' said Drake. 'How do you expect someone of my height to clamber in there?'

'Sorry, sir.'

'Go and get the Range Rover, and Redvers, how tall do you think I am?' demanded Drake.

'About six feet, sir.'

'Not even close,' growled Drake. 'Not good enough if you're going to work with me in CID, you'll have to learn to observe better than that. See if you can find out how tall I am and tell me tomorrow.'

'Yes, sir.'

As they drove in silence up to and around the one-way system, Drake was busy making notes. Constable Redvers was wondering how he had already found so much to write about when a slightly muffled mobile phone started a rather tinny rendition of Bizet's Carmen. Drake began hunting for the culprit. Coat pockets, jacket pockets, leather bag all came under scrutiny. Eventually, the ringing stopped.

'Drake,'

'Cooper here. Have you still not learned to put that darned phone where you can find it?'

'Hello Prof,' said Drake. 'It's got a life of its own. How's the Evinka Whyte post mortem going?'

'Slow. We're in the middle of some tricky toxicology tests. I'll get back to you on it as soon as I can.'

'So what are you calling about?'

'This hit and run case. There's something a bit odd about it. By the way, I've just seen the name. He was Czech as well by the sound of it. Was he a relative of Evinka Whyte or is it just a coincidence?'

'Yes, he was her twin brother. An accountant, not very musical apparently.'

'Well, I've just done a preliminary scan. It's a bit unusual. I've no idea what was the cause of death. There are several possibilities but I don't think that matters. The fact is that his body is in a real mess. It looks like a fractured skull with bleeding on the brain. That could have done for him to start with. Then there's damage to virtually every major organ including the heart. Both legs are broken and superficial abrasions on face, hands, arms and legs.'

'OK,' said Drake. 'I get the message but what's odd about it?'

'Well from my experience of car impacts, and I've seen a good few in my time, I would guess an impact speed of well over the local speed limit. It's only twenty on those roads and this looks more like fifty or more. If I hadn't been told where the incident occurred, I would have guessed something like a dual carriageway or even a motorway.'

11

Constable Redvers pulled the police Range Rover up immediately behind the blue scene-of-crime tent. Drake slid sideways across his seat as Constable Redvers arrived around the vehicle to open his door.

'Thank you,' said Drake. 'You see I can just go in and out sideways with these vehicles and when I'm sitting inside I don't have my knees up under my chin. Don't forget. I want to know how tall I am tomorrow morning.' He chuckled to himself and Constable Redvers felt a little relieved that perhaps Drake was not as serious as he sounded.

Grace appeared out of the house. Drake surveyed the premises. It was not a new house by any means and its sweeping pitched roofs suggested that it was trying to be "Arts and Crafts" but in reality, it was more recent. Drake walked along the drive as it curved round in front of the house. There was a large double garage to the side with plenty of space to park several cars and still be able to get each one in and out.

'This front door was unlocked and slightly ajar,' said Grace. 'It opened easily when the scene-of-crime people pushed it. She demonstrated that the large and surprisingly heavy door swung open complaining noisily.

'No one could come to visit without you hearing them,' grunted Drake as he moved into the spacious but rather dark hallway.

'Straight across the hallway, is his study,' said Grace. The scene that met Drake's gaze was one of mayhem. What Drake took to be a normally tidy room with books and documents on shelves and in drawers, was now a complete mess. Stepping over some of the papers and files on the floor, Drake instinctively scanned the books on the many shelves around the room. Drake thought you could tell a fair bit about people from the books they read. This collection chiefly concerned accountancy, economics and some works on politics with a shelf of philosophy. There were biographies of the all the recent major conservative prime ministers. Some, especially Churchill and Harold Macmillan, were even described by several different authors. There were also books going back as far as Baldwin and Balfour. This was not the library of someone superficial. Drake guessed that he could probably quote facts from these books with a fair degree of accuracy. Drake scanned around looking for books on art, literature or the theatre. It was a fruitless search.

Drake was beginning to think that the man who had so often sat in this room was rather one-sided. Given his family history, it was noticeable that there was not one book that even remotely related to music. Drake moved around the room looking at the upper shelves where all the books were housed. The lower shelves were mainly filled with folders. It was a highly organized room. It suddenly occurred to Drake that he had not seen a single book of fiction until he found one shelf entirely devoted to crime mysteries. Intrigued, he pulled a few off the shelves. There were all the classics and golden era of crime writing, books by Agatha Christie and Raymond Chandler as well as collections of the shorter stories featuring Sherlock Holmes. This was a man of considerable intellect who nonetheless did not feel the need for art or nature in his life. Drake wondered what he would have been like as a dinner guest. The lower shelves were mainly box files. They seemed to contain letters and financial accounts of clients and were filed under names and dates. This man would have been able to find anything he wanted quickly and reliably in this room. He would have been horrified to see it in its current state.

Drake examined a lockable filing cabinet. All the drawers were pulled out and what had presumably been their contents strewn across the floor. Other papers were covering the generous desk that sat in front of a floor to ceiling window. Out of this window, Drake observed there was a tidy, if a little unimaginatively landscaped, back garden. Drake pulled on his rubber gloves and idly shuffled the papers on the desk in front of him. They were a mixture of letters and longer pieces of prose interspersed with sheets of accounts.

'Oh dear,' said Drake. 'It's no use me looking at accounts. I'm not bad at maths but as soon as pound signs appear, I lose all sense of what it is about. Accountants don't even seem to use plus and minus signs like the rest of us. It's just so confusing. Grace, can you find any accounts that look like Evinka Whyte's in all this mess?'

'Already looked, sir,' said Grace, 'and some of them are headed with her name. I'll try my best to curate them. Perhaps we can get them sent to our friends in Fraud at the Met.'

'OK,' said Drake but let's only send them copies. We need to be able to investigate this room as a whole. What is the rest of the house like?'

'It's all very orderly,' said Grace. 'In the bedroom, there are clothes stored systematically in wardrobes and cupboards. The living room has a huge screen television and massive leather chairs that rock and swivel. There are valuables and even money sitting on shelves upstairs. The victim had money on him together with all his credit cards and keys. This was not a burglar who came for cash for drugs, or things to sell for money. Would you like to see the scene of the accident outside before they clear things away?'

'Of course,' said Drake as Grace showed him back through the hallway and down the drive. A uniformed constable was standing guard over the blue tent, which he opened for Drake and Grace to enter. The location of the body was marked out on the road in chalk. Its limbs looked as if they were flailing around and the head was awkwardly turned to the side. There was still evidence of blood on the road for several meters away from where the body had come to rest.

'Prof Cooper has called me,' said Drake, looking at the outline of the body. 'He says that almost every organ in the body is damaged including a fracture of the skull. He says the damage is consistent with a fairly high-speed impact.'

'We are only in front of the adjacent house,' said Grace. 'All these houses here have a fairly wide frontage.'

'I notice that there are no cars parked in the road,' said Drake. 'Any visitor to these houses would be able to park in a driveway. Does that seem odd to you?'

'Well it's unusual in most streets of housing these days,' said Grace.

'Ah yes, but I was thinking of something else,' said Drake. 'Our victim is hardly likely to have stepped out into the road from behind a parked vehicle. Anyone driving along here would surely have seen him easily. The street lighting looks quite adequate.'

'Neighbours put the incident at just before dusk anyway,' said Grace.

'Did any of them get a good look at the car?'

'No, apparently, a couple of them heard the screeching of tyres and the noise of a car accelerating. One heard the thump. He said at the time he thought it was a vehicle-to-vehicle crash.'

'The noise of tyres suggests an application of brakes so there was some attempt to stop,' Drake observed. Are there any security cameras around here?'

'Yes,' answered Grace, consulting her notes. 'Pretty much all the houses have them except for the victim's but they all seem to be trained on their properties. It seems unlikely that we are going to get anything from them.'

'So if the vehicle's driver had a good view and it was still daylight, why did their car hit Dalibor Kubicek?' Drake was pondering aloud rather than asking anyone in particular but Grace volunteered an idea.

'Perhaps the driver was drunk or drugged.'

'But the car disappeared without, as far as we know, hitting anything else,' said Drake.

'Perhaps,' added Grace. 'It was deliberate.'

'Hmmm,' grunted Drake. 'Perhaps. Perhaps. But how does this incident out here relate to the burglary, or is that just a coincidence?'

'Good question,' said Grace. 'I've been wondering the same thing.' With that, Drake started to amble off down the road as far as the nearest bend, which was about a hundred yards away.

'Excuse me Sarge?' said Constable Redvers to Grace. 'Do you happen to know how tall DCI Drake is?'

'He's six feet six inches but he stoops so he looks a little shorter,' said Grace. 'I see you had the wit to bring him in the Range Rover. Why do you ask about his height?'

'First of all, I have to admit he asked for the Range Rover and then he challenged me to find out how tall he is by tomorrow.'

Grace laughed. 'Oh that's good,' she said. 'So he will be pleased and will likely admire your ingenuity.' Drake was soon back at the scene, huffing and puffing at his exertion.

'So what do we think has happened here?' he asked.

'Well,' said Grace. 'I guess it's possible that Dalibor Kubicek threw everything around in his study in some fit of rage but that seems rather unlikely. I think there has been a burglary.'

'OK,' said Drake, 'but has there been a break-in?'

'There's no damage to any of the doors or windows that we have been able to see so far,' replied Grace.

'The front door was unlocked and open when the traffic people arrived?'

'Yes,' said Grace. 'I assume Dalibor has come outside and left it open.'

'Perhaps. Perhaps,' said Drake. 'But what if he wasn't security-minded. He went out leaving his door unlocked and returned just as whoever was inside came out.'

'Quite possible I suppose,' said Grace slowly.

'I agree it is a less likely interpretation than the obvious one,' said Drake.

'Which is, I suppose,' said Grace, 'that he opened his door to the intruders.'

'Then what?' demanded Drake who then tried to answer his own question. 'Perhaps he was taken captive somehow, the burglary was completed and he broke free and chased the person or persons doing this out of the house. They then jumped into their escape vehicle and ran him down.'

'But, Prof Cooper thinks the collision was at some speed,' said Grace, 'and that wouldn't be likely.'

'Ah but that's where you might be wrong,' grunted Drake. 'I've just walked down the road. Always look at the context. This is a cul-de-sac. Perhaps the escaper's car was facing the wrong way. They had originally driven in just as we did. So they drove to the end, just around that corner, where there is a turning circle, and then came back at speed. Dalibor stood in the road in a rather foolish and futile attempt to stop them and got run over, receiving countless injuries that proved fatal. Grace, you've got Renata's contact details haven't you?' Grace nodded and pulled out her notebook. 'Better let Traffic have them. She must be the next of kin. The poor woman has lost both her siblings in quick succession.'

Drake paused and walked around in small circles looking down at the ground in front of him.

'So the next question,' he said. 'What was the intruder after?'

'Well,' said Grace. 'The house has many valuable items and there is even cash lying around. This isn't an ordinary break-in. They appear to have been looking for documents in Dalibor's study. There's no evidence of searching anywhere else.'

'So what documents could Dalibor have had that were so valuable or so important that this whole business was necessary?' asked Drake. 'If we can find that out then I have a feeling the rest of this case will fall into place. But what could it be? The next question is the obvious one.'

Grace looked puzzled. Constable Redvers stood open-mouthed and enjoying every bit of this exchange between the experienced Drake and his relative novice Grace.

'The question is,' Drake repeated himself. 'Is this purely a coincidence or does it have some connection with Evinka Whyte's death? If so, do the documents being searched for somehow reveal the murderer's identity? Now if someone will drive me, I need to get back home to see my daughter.'

12

Drake made two cups of coffee and transferred one to a table beside the sofa where Lucy was stretched out. 'You look like a beached whale,' he laughed.

'Oh thanks, Dad,' she replied. 'Look I'm feeling a lot better this morning but I'm worried about you now. Whatever would you do if you retired?'

'I might have more time to study architecture and visit all Mum's buildings,' he said.

'Oh Dad, that's a lovely thought, but are you sure you wouldn't just get miserable.'

'You may be right,' grunted Drake. 'I'm probably more confused than you are. Sometimes I just wonder if my old brain is up to it any more. You should always quit before you become a burden.'

'Perhaps you should ask Grace if you are a burden,' said Lucy. 'I'm pretty sure I know what she'd say.'

'Really!' said Drake, 'and what would she say.'

'She says she needs you around a bit longer to learn from you.'

'Oh, she's well on the way that one,' said Drake. 'I'm probably holding her back.'

'I got to know her quite well on the Opera House case,' said Lucy 'and I don't think so. Besides, she texts me quite a lot now and she's all confused about Martin and whether she should have gone to Hong Kong with him.'

'Perhaps the three of us should get together and hire a psychiatrist between us,' growled Drake.

The journey was not long but, for Grace, it had been quite long enough. She made a mental note to sit Drake in the rear seat of the Range Rover in future. There he invariably detached himself from the journey and did his crossword and thought. Often he just thought. Grace had noticed how useful journeys were to Drake as long as he could stretch his legs, he would normally be happy and mainly silent. On this occasion, and for some reason that she couldn't understand, Grace had held the front passenger door open for him and he got in without argument. He spent the entire journey arguing with the satnav. He had a map. Grace realized that he liked maps and that he felt they were far more authoritative than computer screens. He complained about the satnav voice, female of course, and the layout of the screen. But most of all he complained about the route. In the end, Grace followed the satnav, which Drake reluctantly admitted had won the argument.

They pulled up outside the care home where Karel Whyte lived. Drake sat in the passenger seat looking at the building.

'It's trying to be familiar and friendly I suppose,' he said, 'but oh dear, it is without any sort of soul. Cynthia would have hated it. If ever I get old and cantankerous I should hate to live in a place like this.'

'Well I don't think we need to worry about that for a good few years,' said Grace. Drake looked at her quizzically. He wondered if Lucy had already talked to her. They made their way down the short path to the front door, which opened just as they reached it.

'Hello. You must be Inspector Drake and Sergeant Hepple. I'm Helen Thompson. You spoke to me on the phone, Grace. I'm more or less in charge here. Some of the residents call me "matron" and I don't really mind that and it's certainly not worth arguing about. I have just moved Karel Whyte into one of our small sitting rooms where you can talk to him in private. We don't know how old he is but we think he must be around ninety. Occasionally he goes to sleep in the middle of a conversation. He doesn't mean to be rude. Don't try to wake him since he usually surfaces again in only a few minutes. If you interrupt his little sleep he wakes up confused so that won't help anybody. I'm afraid that I told him that you are from the police. That bothered him quite a bit. He has a past that he finds difficult to deal with. He seems to be remembering further back as his dementia develops. But by contrast, you'll probably find that he has already forgotten that you are police officers. I did feel it ethically correct to tell him and you might think that too.'

She started to walk down the hallway while she finished talking and Drake and Grace soon found themselves in the room where Karel Whyte was sitting looking out of a floor to ceiling window at the garden beyond.

'These are the police officers that I told you about, Karel,' she said.

'Police officers are you?' said Karel in a firm quiet voice that never the less seemed strong for someone of his age. 'I hope you don't mind if I don't get up. It takes me a while these days.'

'I understand your problem,' said Drake. 'I already find the same thing.'

'Ah but you are so tall,' said Karel. 'People used to say I was tall once. I must have shrunk.' Drake nodded to Grace and she took over.

'We've been talking to your daughter, Karel,' said Grace.

'I've got twins you know,' said Karel. 'They still come to see me. I thought they were coming today.'

'Your daughter sends her love,' said Grace.

'I've lost my wife,' said Karel. 'No one seems to be able to find her. I think the police took her. Do you think I will ever see her again?' Before Grace could reply, Helen Thompson appeared.

'How are you Karel?' she asked.

'I'm talking to these two people. They seem very nice but I don't know who they are.'

'They are police officers, Karel. They've come to talk to you.'

'You are police? What sort of police are you?' demanded Karel.

'We're Cheshire Police,' said Grace.

'Cheshire, why Cheshire? What are Cheshire?'

'Because we are in Cheshire, Karel,' said Helen. 'You live in Cheshire. These are nice people who think you may be able to help them,' said Helen. 'What is it that you want to ask, Grace?'

'We would like to know if you remember the Stransky family?' said Grace.

'Of course, I remember them. They're scallywags. They told the police. I'm sure they did.'

'Why would they have done that?' asked Grace.

'They said we stole from them,' said Karel. 'We didn't. I'll get my twins to tell them.' He suddenly burst out laughing. 'They believe all sorts of nonsense.'

'Who do?' asked Helen.

'The Stransky family. They believe anything they want. You know they even tried to take my violin. Can you believe that? My very own violin! Where's my violin now? They haven't got it have they?'

'I'll bring your violin, Karel,' said Helen. 'Perhaps your new friends would like to hear you play.'

'Everybody used to want to hear me play. I'm not so good as I was. I don't practice enough. That's the problem. There isn't time any more.'

'Why would they want to take your violin? Karel?' asked Grace.

'It's a really good one. I've always had it. They think if they get my violin they will play like me. But they're wrong aren't they?'

'I don't suppose anyone can play like you do Karel,' said Grace. Karel Whyte laughed and slumped back in his chair, closing his eyes. Drake wondered if he had gone to sleep. Helen came back with a violin. Grace marvelled at the service. Helen was even putting rosin on the bow.

'Here you are, Karel,' she said, putting the violin on his lap. He reached out for the bow with his right hand and lifted the instrument with his left hand shaking slightly as he did so.

'What shall I play?' he demanded but got no answer.

'Play us your favourite tune then,' suggested Helen. Karel Whyte tucked the violin under his chin, brought the bow across with his right hand and closed his eyes. He began playing, swaying in his chair. His body turned and twisted slightly in time with his bowing action. Drake suddenly looked up from making some notes. He looked at Grace and they both stared wide-eyed at each other. Gone was the shaking hand they had seen a few minutes ago. Karel's left hand gripped the fingerboard and slid effortlessly between positions, his fingers leaping up and then coming firmly down in precisely the right place. His right hand had a firm and positive grip on the bow and he moved it faultlessly back and forwards from one string to another. Karel Whyte was playing the most hauntingly beautiful tune. Grace thought she had heard it before. Drake swayed his right arm in time with the bow and closed his eyes. The sound swept around the room. Some pigeons on the lawn outside shuffled their feathers as the small audience listened intently to the enveloping sound. Karel reached the end as the music swept right up to the high concluding note. He sat still with his bow arm collapsed on the chair, lifted his head and opened his eyes.

'That was beautiful,' said Drake as the audience of three clapped their hands in genuine admiration.

'What's that called Karel,' asked Helen. 'He plays that a lot,' she said to Grace and Drake but we never know what to call it.' Karel sat silent and motionless except for a slight shaking of his bowing hand.

'It was the Meditation from Massenet's opera Thais,' said Drake. 'I've never heard it played more beautifully.'

'Oh, I knew that I'd heard it,' said Grace. 'We used to do ballet warm up to it years ago.'

'I've tried to get him to play when we have a singsong,' said Helen. 'I even got him the music but of course, he cannot get near enough to read it when he is playing. Anyway, the others all love to hear him play. He must have been a professional musician in his earlier years to have those memories so well embedded now.'

'I think I might have forty winks now,' said Karel Whyte as he passed his violin back to Helen Thompson.

'Now you know what to ask for next time he plays,' smiled Grace.

'No it doesn't work like that,' said Helen. He doesn't remember that way. 'It's hard to explain until you've lived with people in the early stages of dementia. He can sometimes suddenly remember things from his early life and tell us a story quite clearly. But he has probably already forgotten who you are. Even after so many years, it still affects me. It is hard for relatives to live with. His two children do come now and then but I think they travel a lot and are away most of the time.'

'His daughter was a famous flautist,' said Drake.

'Good gracious, of course,' said Helen. 'We have never made the connection. I think I have some of her records somewhere. So that is where she got her talent from then, poor dear Karel.'

'Does his other daughter come too?' asked Grace.

'No, not often. We only see one daughter and her twin brother. They are lovely people but both very busy. He has another daughter as well?'

'Yes but she lives in Prague.'

'Oh, he talks about Prague sometimes,' said Helen. 'He talks about police and a train, but we don't usually make any real sense out of it. I can tell though that it troubles him. His eyes have a look of sheer terror in them at times.'

'Could we just talk outside for a minute?' asked Drake.

'Of course.' She took them out and across the hallway to her office and pulled two chairs away from the wall.

'You may have read in the newspapers about the death of Evinka Whyte recently.'

'Now you mention it, yes. My goodness, so his daughter is dead?'

'Exactly,' said Drake. 'We are investigating her death. It is probably murder. If ever he says anything that you think might help us, please give Sergeant Hepple a call.' With that, Drake and Grace thanked Helen for all her help and got up to go. As Drake reached the door, he turned back to Helen.

'Thank you,' he said. 'It has been an honour and a privilege to talk to Karel and listen to him play.'

'We are lucky to have him,' said Helen. 'I try to get him to play often but as you saw it tires him. You do realize that soon his early memories will probably gradually disappear and with that his ability to play.'

'His daughter asked us to be careful not to tell him Evinka was dead,' said Grace.

'Of course,' said Helen, 'there's no need to distress him, though he would almost certainly forget that quite quickly.'

'That is so sad,' said Grace and she wiped a small tear from her eye.

13

'I've got some things to show you,' said Grace, 'but it will take a while and it's a bit complicated.'

'OK,' replied Drake, looking up from his copy of The Times and climbing out of his chair to cross the case room. 'The crossword can wait but I'm desperate for a cup of coffee. I'll be with you in a minute.' He rounded his work boards to find Steve Redvers at the coffee machine.

'Don't worry, sir. You can have this cup. By the way, I believe you are six feet and six inches tall.'

'Nope,' said Drake, 'Six and a half inches but not bad, not bad.'

'It's the accounts of Evinka Whyte that were found in Dalibor Kubicek's study,' said Grace, dumping a pile of photocopied spreadsheets on the table in the centre of the room.

'I'm all ears,' said Drake, 'as long as you don't expect me to understand accounts.'

'I'm not sure that I'm much better,' said Grace laughing. 'I'll do my best to tell a story from the rather odd data,' Drake pulled up a chair, sat down beside her and pushed his coffee out of the way to cool. 'The first thing to establish is just how luxurious her lifestyle was. She travelled extensively, I presume to give concerts. I've found a few airline tickets and they are all business class or even first class. However, in the accounts, we get hotel bills. I've checked the hotels on the Internet. Look here are a few I've underlined in blue on the accounts. There's the Four Seasons Hotel George V in Paris. It's only just off the Champs-Elysées. It has palatial rooms with private terraces looking over the city, a spa and a Michelin three-star restaurant. I'd be happy to have a few days there. Or you can look at Berlin, She's been several times to play at the Philharmonie and she stays at the Hotel Adlon Kempinski.

This is on the Unter den Linden right next to the Brandenburg Gate and the restaurant has two stars. I've no idea how she managed with only two stars! So it goes on, The Waldorf Astoria in Amsterdam or the Danieli in Venice. These are all five-star hotels in prime locations.'

'Yes, I get the message,' said Drake. 'But why is this odd?'

'Well,' said Grace. 'It's the lifestyle of a high living famous performer, but the accounts tell a different story. Look, see how now and then the accounts go into the red, sometimes quite substantially and she starts paying overdraft rates.'

'So she was living near the edge of her income,' said Drake. 'I suppose she was entitled to do that.'

'Look, I've got this pile of accounts here for the last three years. Her income is certainly substantial. She gets mainly concert fees, in some cases with expenses and then she gets royalties from her recordings. There seem to be two major recording companies. One pays her a whole lot more than the other. I checked it out and I think the higher paying royalties are for her popular music recordings and the lower one for her classical recordings.'

'Well done, Grace,' said Drake. 'You might just be on to something.'

'Ah, but I've only just started,' replied Grace. 'What happens to get her accounts back into the black on two occasions is that eventually there is a sum paid in by Dalibor Kubicek. I've no idea what it is for or who it actually comes from. I assume that he wasn't wealthy enough to subsidise her himself. Both sums amount to thousands of pounds.'

'Now that is interesting,' said Drake. 'How do we explain that?'

'There's more,' said Grace, wondering why Drake was in such a good mood. She could count on the fingers of one hand the number of times he had been so complimentary. 'The accounts in the files go back many years. I went back ten to fifteen years ago and guess what?'

'No idea,' snapped Drake.

'Her royalty payments were substantially more.'

'I see,' said Drake. 'Now I think about it, that doesn't surprise me. She was hugely popular for many years but perhaps we hear about her less now. So her popularity has waned and with it her income.'

'But not her lifestyle,' said Grace with an air of someone successfully concluding an argument.

'Yes it looks that way,' said Drake. 'So she got the taste of the high life and couldn't or wouldn't give it up to live within her means.'

'Just what I thought,' said Grace, 'but look as hard as you can through those earlier years and you won't find these payments from Dalibor.'

'I see,' said Drake, 'so either he has begun to subsidise her or she has somehow found another source of income that, for some reason, gets paid through Dalibor. Perhaps that's a kind of tax avoidance. I wonder if this is significant in terms of our case.'

'There's another oddity in the records,' said Grace. 'From about five years ago you will frequently but irregularly find payments made to some company or organisation called NmN. It's a Swiss bank account so I doubt we can delve much further. However, about eighteen months ago, NmN started to make regular monthly payments to Evinka. Look here they are in Swiss francs and virtually the same amount each month. It's about a thousand pounds. I guess the variation is explained by changing exchange rates. For the last couple of months, these payments haven't been made.'

'So what sort of thing could this be?' asked Drake. 'Is it some investment that she was paying into that now pays her interest or something like that? Maybe she was such a good customer that they started to pay her to advertise.'

'Possible,' replied Grace, 'but in that case surely we would have heard about it. I've no idea what NmN means so they seem to be keeping quiet. What is even more interesting is the underlining on the accounts. I didn't do that. I assume it was Dalibor Kubicek. Then, he underlines the new incomes and only three months ago, he scribbled, "check with Evinka" on the spreadsheet.'

'So perhaps he was puzzled by it too,' said Drake, scratching his forehead from above in that way he has with his arm over his head. 'Now I think about it, Dalibor mentioned it and said that Evinka started to show signs of anxiety after playing in Zurich. I assume you've done an Internet search for NmN.'

'Yes, of course. I've tried every which way I can. Absolutely nothing comes up. I'm inclined to think the letters stand for something but I don't think we have any chance of working that out. I tried it with "music" in the search and with "flute"...nothing. All I've been able to find is that the letters stand for a chemical compound called...I'll have to check my notes here... Nicotinamide Mononucleotide, which is a bit of a mouthful. It seems to be used in medicine for several purposes. I don't see any of that being relevant. A small number of British companies seem to manufacture and sell it but they don't use the letters for their name. I've drawn a complete blank.'

'More mystery then,' grunted Drake.

'Well not entirely,' said Grace. 'The scene-of-crime boys brought an iPad back from Evinka's house. To start with, it wouldn't turn on but technician Dave performed his magic on it and we have it working. Dave went through all her contacts on it and printed them out for me. I found a contact for NmN. All it has is an address in Zurich, Switzerland of 5a Oberdorfstrasse. I looked at the map and it's very central, in what they call the old town part of the city. I put the address back into an Internet search and found nothing. My feeling is that our only hope is to get someone to go there and see what can be found.'

'OK,' said Drake, 'but we can't afford to spend too much time on it. Why don't you get the people in charge to contact the Zurich Police and see if they might help?'

The next morning, Drake arrived in the case room, as usual, sometime after Grace. No sooner had he sat back in his favourite chair than Grace brought him a cup of coffee. In recent weeks, he had heard Cynthia's voice more than once telling him to make his own coffee. He reckoned quietly to himself that if his wife wouldn't make his coffee, then he should not expect his sergeant to do so. Grace was already living up to the productivity that her early career had promised. He was sure she had a high-flying career ahead of her but he secretly hoped that he would not lose her just yet. He had been trying hard in recent months to take his turn at making the drinks as part of an admittedly often-abortive attempt at giving Grace more independence and responsibility.

'Why thanks, Grace,' he said cheerfully as she plonked the mug down on the little table by his chair and strode off purposefully to her desk.

'As it happens, sir,' said Grace. I have something to show you when your coffee cools to your satisfaction. Drake wondered if he heard a touch of cynicism in that usually lilting voice of hers.

'Don't let's wait then,' said Drake. 'We'll strike while it's still hot.' He amused himself with his little joke and put down his copy of The Times.

'I've got all the papers over here on this table,' said Grace, ignoring the joke. Drake struggled up, gathered his mug and joined her.

'It was something you said recently that prompted this,' said Grace.

'Oh really,' said Drake.

'You said that Evinka might not be as popular as she once was. You were right. I've drawn up a list of all her recordings. She was once producing one, or even two, popular music discs a year. It is now more than two years since she made the last one. Look here you can see the titles.' Grace pushed a couple of sheets across the table and Drake began to scan them. He recognised several discs that he had bought himself or even got as a present from his daughter. The last disc he recognised as in his possession was now nearly five years old on the list. He grunted and nodded.

'Then there are her classical concerts,' continued Grace. She has documented those for us with all the framed posters in her practice room. They are even in order so she made life easy for me. Six or seven years ago, she was performing somewhere in the world almost once a week. Now she is only doing one or two a month.' Drake nodded again.

'Yes, Grace,' said Drake. 'That helps confirm what we thought and what Dalibor's accounts show in terms of fees.'

'But there is something else,' said Grace. 'This all set me thinking. Surely she wasn't turning work down and hopefully she wasn't in failing health so I looked on the Internet for reviews of her concerts. Look at this one only a few weeks ago. It sums up what several recently have been saying.

A dazzling evening of the Brandenburg Concertos and Suites

The variety and richness of Bach's work was stunningly demonstrated in this wonderful concert. The players were at the top of their form. All except perhaps for Evinka Whyte. Her playing seemed almost disinterested. Perhaps she is bored with playing these standards of the repertoire. This was nowhere more clearly demonstrated than in the famous Badinerie in the final movement of the Second Suite. It just did not skip along as it should. Evinka Whyte's attack was sloppy and her timing uncharacteristically imprecise. Luckily the conductor kept pace with her.

Another critic from a few months ago described her playing as sloppy. There are several reviews saying something similar, all of them in the last year. There is an interesting one that makes the same point while praising her "lyrical interpretation of the slow movement was even more laden with emotion than usual." The critic wondered how this could be. "Such a contrast within one evening." Grace made a point of standing back from the table as she waited for Drake's response.

'Now that's really interesting, Grace,' said Drake in genuine admiration. 'That must have taken a great deal of research to put together.'

'Steve Redvers has been helping me,' replied Grace.

'Well done both of you. It presents us with a clear picture that her work has been changing. Perhaps there was some illness. If so, I wonder if our friendly pathologist has discovered anything yet. I'll give him a call.' With that Drake stumbled back to his chair and pulled out his phone. He sat listening to it for some time.

'No response,' he said. 'I'll leave him a message.'

14

Grace stepped down from the airport train and looked up at the platform clock. It read 11:35, the same time as given for the arrival of her train in the printed timetable sitting on the shelf by her seat. In a moment of absurd pride, she looked at the watch on her wrist. It was not so much the time she was checking as the design. Sure enough, the face of her wristwatch proudly and neatly matched that of the station clock. Then a moment of stabbing anxiety took over. She had always admired this design with its beautifully clear Bauhaus inspired simplicity. She must have mentioned this once in a conversation with Martin. When he had departed for Hong Kong, she found this wristwatch neatly wrapped and lying on the table beside her bed. The message on the accompanying card read "Remember me every time you look at it. There's always a job for you in Hong Kong, love Martin." She stood there in the middle of the station concourse wondering yet again if she should have gone with him to Hong Kong. Of course not, she told herself, she would not have had this opportunity to come to Zurich for Drake. She had a chance to put her stamp on the investigation. Of course, she was not actually on duty. Drake had asked for the co-operation of the Zurich Police but it had been denied. So he was missing one of his cherished foreign jaunts and she was here instead, on two days leave. It had been her idea, which he grudgingly agreed to. She needed to deliver. She slung her neat overnight knapsack over her right shoulder and set off.

Leaving the station building behind, Grace looked at her map and then at the confusing traffic junction right outside the front of the station. The map showed that if she crossed this she would be right next to a bridge over the River Limmat which should connect with Lake Zurich a mile or so upstream. Walking across this bridge and another traffic junction she found Niederdorfstrasse, which her map told her would turn into the street where NmN had their address. Sure enough, she was soon walking along the pedestrian street that was Oberdorfstrasse. It was a narrow jumble of old buildings with pastel-shaded frontages crammed together as far as she could see. It was bustling with people, most of who seemed to be tourists occasionally stopping and looking into shop windows. The buildings seemed to press in on the narrow street. You could buy wine, coffee, jewellery, books and clothes, mostly for women, as well as, of course, watches and clocks. She checked her notes. Yes, this must be it, number 5. But where was 5a?

There was a small lobby leading directly into a wine and coffee house to the left. Straight ahead was an unmarked staircase. She tentatively climbed some steps and eventually, a small sign came into view next to a doorway off a landing. This was 5a. There was no nameplate but this was definitely the address given for NmN. There was no doorbell, so she tapped on the door. She waited but got no answer. There was a letterbox that she pushed open but she was met by a musty smell and darkness. A creaking floorboard below caused her to look down the stairs. A large man was peering up at her over half spectacles. He was wearing a blue and white striped bibbed apron over a bright blue shirt. He stood in the entrance to the coffee shop and spoke in German.

'Sorry,' said Grace, 'but do you speak English?'

'Yes, of course, Madame,' he replied with a short laugh as he twirled the end of his walrus moustache. 'How can I help?'

'I'm looking for the people at 5a,' she replied.

'No Madame, I think you must be mistaken. 5a is empty and has been for many years.'

'Oh,' said Grace, descending to the lobby. 'I'm so sorry I must have the wrong address. Perhaps I could have a small beer. Could I sit at this table in the window?'

'Of course, Madame.'

Grace sat so she could watch for anyone going up the stairs or coming out. Several cups of coffee and pieces of delicious cake later, she had seen nothing and it was now towards the end of the afternoon. She paid her bill and left to explore a little of the old town before darkness fell. She walked towards the station and turned up a narrow alley that took her along another pedestrianized street that passed through several squares until much larger department stores began to appear. She promised herself a small indulgence and started nosing around in them but finding things rather expensive.

When she finally came out into the street, Grace realized that she had been longer inside than she thought. Darkness was falling. She checked her map and decided to walk past the little coffee shop again on her way to the hotel down on the lake. Not wanting to stop, she walked straight past, looking up the staircase as she did so. There seemed to be a flicker of light up there. She wondered how she could check without running across the moustachioed waiter.

As luck would have there was a bookshop more or less opposite. She went in hoping it had an upper floor. It did. There was even an escalator. She reached the top and doubled back towards the shop frontage. Floor to ceiling bookcases were everywhere and she began to get disorientated. Moving towards the tourist section she noticed a gap between Europe and the Far East. It was just wide enough to squeeze through. She was now right in front of tall windows with low sills. She checked behind her. She could only see three people. One seemed to be stacking the shelves or more probably taking some kind of stock check. She was entirely engrossed in her work. Two others were browsing with their backs to her. She pushed behind the shelves to her left and found herself looking down into the street. She was right opposite the little coffee shop. Her eyes scanned up from the entrance.

Yes, there was certainly a light coming from one of the upper floor windows. She saw a shadow move. Someone was there. Her heart pumping, she eased her way back out into the bookshop. Nobody was taking any interest in her but she couldn't remain there and stay completely out of sight. There was nothing else for it. She needed to check 5a out again. Out in the street, Grace waited for the two waiters to disappear back into what, she assumed, was the kitchen or cellar. She darted across the road and swept up the staircase as quietly as she could. She checked for her phone and took a picture. Just as she expected, there was light coming out from under the door.

She pushed open the letterbox. It responded with a gentle rattle. Her heart was in her mouth. Had anyone heard? She got down into a squat and peered through the open letterbox. The room was surprisingly well illuminated. There, right in front of her was a large table with a huge lamp over it. Someone was working there with his back to her. To his left, she could see a stack of what looked like the boxes eggs come in but these were more sharply rectangular. They seemed to be made out of compressed cardboard in a nondescript grey colour. The man working would periodically take one off the top of the pile. To his right was a whole row of small cylindrical bottles, perhaps no bigger than a bird's egg. They had black plastic or rubber caps and looked to be nearly full of a colourless clear liquid. It could be water but Grace suspected not. Yes, he was taking bottle after bottle and pushing them down into the tray where they located in a neat row. She started to count. One, two…he pushed seven bottles into the tray, turned it around and pushed another seven in. Then the tray seemed to have a lid arrangement, which he flapped over the caps of the little bottles. He pushed the completed tray away from him slightly and picked a piece of folded cardboard. It opened out into a sleeve that fitted around the closed cardboard box. He taped up the ends and picked up a sheet from the table. Now she could see it was full of sticky labels. He tore one off and stuck it onto the lid of the tray. He picked up a pen and ran his finger down another sheet of paper. Then he started to write on the label. She watched the whole process being repeated. Yes, it was two sets of seven small bottles packed into each tray and labelled.

She released the letterbox flap but it stubbornly stayed open. She prodded it and it crashed closed as she grabbed at it clumsily Her phone slipped from her grasp. There was a crash from inside 5a. The light went out. Her heart missed a beat as her phone started to bounce its way down the staircase. Luckily, no one downstairs seemed to have heard. She tiptoed after it and picked it up. Then she became aware of a pair of large black shoes. She grabbed the phone and her eyes slowly came up over the black trousers, across the blue striped apron and on up to meet the gaze of the moustachioed waiter staring in a much less friendly manner than he had earlier in the day. He was swivelling his half-glasses around impatiently in his left hand.

'Oh, hello again,' said Grace weakly. 'I dropped my phone.'

The waiter continued his silent stare as Grace rose to her full height. Her face was still only up to his chest.

'You've been upstairs again,' he said. Grace sucked her tongue, wrinkled her nose and silently nodded her head.

'I thought I could see a light,' she said.

'Nobody is there to put a light on,' said the large waiter.

'I'm sure it was on. I saw it,' said Grace.

'Perhaps my assistant went to get something,' said the waiter hurriedly. 'We store some things up there. Perhaps you had better tell me what you want up there now.'

Several alternatives rushed through Grace's mind jostling for attention. Should she come clean? Should she buy another coffee? Should she just rush out and off to her hotel?

'I'm trying to contact NmN she said quietly. We have this address from them in correspondence.'

'I've told you there's nobody in 5a,' said the moustache quivering in a manner that Grace began to think was quiet rage. 'Perhaps you should contact their website.'

'Yes,' said Grace. 'That's what I'll do then.'

15

Grace stepped out of the door and down the narrow street in the direction of her hotel. As she walked, she tried to work out what was happening here. There had certainly been someone in 5a and he was definitely packing trays of small cylindrical bottles of clear fluid and then labelling the tray. Why were they in sevens? Perhaps it was for the days of the week. Maybe this was medicine. Why was the waiter so adamant that 5a was empty and then later admitted they use it for storage? Grace paused and looked idly in the window of a jewellery shop. They had every possible size, colour and detail design of the Swiss Railway Clock. It was then that she became aware of a large man standing two shops back staring at her. Was he the other waiter from the little coffee shop? He was certainly wearing a bright blue shirt over black trousers. Perhaps it was their uniform. He looked as if he had less training in following than she had in shaking him off.

Grace set off again along Oberdorfstrasse. She ambled steadily looking in windows as she passed. She was trying to remember her training. Her mind was a complete blank. She had to admit to herself that she was a little anxious now. She was an unrecognized police presence in a foreign country with absolutely no backup. She stopped by a dazzling baroque church, all frills and turrets. She took out her phone and held it up as if taking a photograph but with the camera facing her turned on. She could see her follower. He stood head and shoulders above the surrounding crowd. He was big, not exactly fat, just big. There was little doubt that he was tracking her and not being too subtle about it. He stopped too and looked in a shop window. There was something about the motion that gave him away. He definitely stopped first and then turned to look in the window. This was not the movement of a person who had caught sight of something turned and then stopped.

She felt her heart thumping. Why was she so alarmed? She couldn't really understand herself but she was getting more worried. She remembered the murder of Evinka Whyte. It had been done so cleverly that even Professor Cooper was struggling to identify the cause of death. This person or persons were serious and capable. What was it about NmN that made them so elusive? She moved on again and turned into a shop doorway. The door was recessed by about two meters with splayed windows on either side. She waited there looking intently in the window. Several seconds passed. She wondered if he had already stopped. Should she go into the shop for safety? Then suddenly, there he was. She felt his significant presence as he pushed past her and rushed into the shop.

She left again and began to hurry down the narrow pedestrian street. She slowed as she reached a little crowd standing talking. She got beyond them and looked back. He was following her again. She stood checking her map and quickly decided to turn to her right down a side street that should take her towards the lake. She let out a sigh of relief as she saw the water ahead. There were fewer people here. That made it easier to see him but she became more alarmed by his size. By now in her mind, he was a thug capable of doing serious harm. Increasing her pace, she turned left along a major road. This was a busy place and she felt safer. She scuttled along looking for her hotel. Then suddenly, there was the sign "Hotel Eden Au Lac". She was in through the generous doorway in no time. She rushed up to the counter and checked in and had asked for a room overlooking the lake so the concierge was going through the administration and looking for a room at the front. She found one and told Grace it would have to be on the top floor. Grace scanned around while the concierge was setting up the electronic key. She felt safe now. She couldn't see him anywhere. When she looked back, the concierge was holding out her room key and looking a little puzzled. Should she go back to the doorway and look for her follower? Why? What could she gain from that? It seemed that she had uncovered more of a mystery than before she started on this trip.

Grace found her room and waved the little plastic card key at the lock. It clunked in a "here to please you" sort of way and she pushed the door open. She was on the sixth floor in an attic bedroom. She peered into the bathroom as she passed it. It all looked comfortable. She passed the bed on her right and reached the window. It had a low sill and a wonderful view of the lake. Then she saw him. She could not miss his large frame. Her pursuer was standing on the other side of the road looking up at the hotel. He seemed no longer even to be trying to mask his intentions. What were his intentions? Even across this considerable distance, their eyes met, if only for a brief second. Grace turned and dashed to the right behind a wall. Had he seen her? Could he now work out which room she was in? She edged her way behind the curtain to the side of the window. She dropped down onto her knees and peeped out. He was still there looking up. Grace watched him from behind the gauze curtain. Suddenly he looked left and right before crossing the road towards the hotel. He disappeared out of sight concealed by the window-sill. Was he coming into the hotel?

Grace checked that her door had locked behind her and sat on the bed. Surely she was safe. Then she started to imagine him bribing a cleaner to open her door. No surely not! All went quiet and she collapsed on the bed and turned off all the room lights from a panel of switches beside her bed. Gradually she started to relax and tell herself not to be so silly. Then she heard it. It was a sort of scratching noise. It was coming from her door. Was it him? She crept around the corner of the bathroom. All went quiet. Grace froze waiting for the sound to start again. Silence. The light coming from a clear moon was illuminating the room to her dark-adapted eyes. She tiptoed up to the door and then bent down to look through the little spyglass in the door. She was puzzled by the almost total darkness. Surely the corridor lights must be on. She moved her eyes around to get a better view. There was light and she was met by a returned stare from one enormous eye. He was looking into the spyglass from outside. Grace jumped, terrified by what she had seen. Realizing that he could not see anything that way through the spyglass, she looked again. Then he moved back. She could see him clearly now. The door handle rattled. He was trying to get in. Grace stood up to check the door lock and gently slid the little chain into its slot to prevent the door opening. She plucked up the courage to look through the spyglass again.

There was no sign of him. Had he given up? She waited for several minutes. There was still no sign of anyone. Then she saw a figure striding across the field of view down the corridor. It was pulling a roller case. It was just another guest. Grace stood tall and returned to her bed collapsing half out of jet-lagged tiredness, part out of the sheer terror she had felt.

Grace fell asleep. She and Drake were being pursued around a baroque church by a man wearing a mask with a long crooked snout. The pews looked more like huge bookcases each holding a copy of The Bible and Hymns of Praise. They could dodge behind these pews in what became an eternal exhausting chase. From time to time Drake would stop her and point out some interesting feature of the architecture, which was not terribly helpful. She made it to a bedroom but her pursuer was prizing up the sash of her window.

Grace woke. Her room was full of silence. She was momentarily confused as to whether she was still in a nightmare or fully awake. She had fallen asleep on the bed without closing the curtains. There was a light flashing somewhere. She checked the window. It had casements not sashes. She was not in her nightmare. She checked her watch but she could not remember if she had changed it to the local time. She checked her phone. It was an hour ahead so it was now four in the morning. She slowly stood up and crept up to the window. He was not there. She was sure that the street lighting was good enough to see him. She scanned upwards and there was the lake in its full nighttime beauty. There were gently rippling coloured reflections everywhere. Grace felt easier after her sleep but she was still tired. She pulled the curtains and got into bed. Sleep came easily.

Grace sat eating a splendid breakfast and trying to plan her day. She checked her ticket. Her return flight was just after lunch. She needed to be at the airport by twelve. There were trains at frequent intervals and the journey was less than half an hour. To get to the station she could either take a taxi or walk. Her route would take her past 5a. Yes, she would just check on 5a again. She checked out and began a pleasant walk along the shore of the lake. She consulted her map and found the correct street off to her right to get back into the old town pedestrianized area. After a few minutes, she began to see familiar things. There was the church she had pretended to photograph.

She slowed down. There was the coffee and wine bar with the bookshop opposite. She stopped and looked carefully into the window just near where she had sat the day before. There was the moustachioed waiter at the back of the shop. The shop was empty. She checked the notice in the window. It was not due to open for another hour. She couldn't stand here all that time. There was nowhere she could sit down and keep an eye on the entrance to 5a. There seemed little point in waiting here. She looked back into the coffee bar. The waiter was talking animatedly to another larger man with his back to her and a huge bag around his neck and held behind him. It was like the bag her postman used. He delved into it and poked around. He pulled out one of the cardboard tray boxes and gave it to the waiter. He turned and headed directly toward her. A shock flowed through her body. It was the man who followed her the previous evening. She could not mistake him. He was not to be messed with, she thought.

Grace stepped back and looked into the window of the shop next door keeping an eye on the coffee shop door. There he was, coming out into the street. She hid her face as if shielding the low morning sun from her eyes. He set off down the street in the direction of the railway station. That made up her mind. It was easy to follow him and keep well back. They progressed along Oberdorfstrasse. Soon there was a sign on a wall. Now they were in Niederdorfstrasse still heading towards the railway station. Then suddenly, he turned left. She reached the same junction. Ahead, she could already see the station in the distance. She rounded the corner carefully and followed. They reached a bridge across the Limmat river. This area was too open so she had to wait and let him cross the river. By the time she reached the far bank, he had disappeared. She walked on under a bridge. There was still no sign of him. Then to her left, she saw it, a post office. Surely that was it. He was going to post all the cardboard boxes.

She climbed a short flight of steps and went in. There were shafts of sunlight slanting through the tall windows and her target was illuminated by one. He was standing at a counter right in front of her. She hurriedly walked to the far end of the spacious post room and looked back. Specks of dust and small insects were picked out in the shafts of light falling across the room. But sure enough, there he was putting the boxes on the counter one after another and the assistant was tapping on a computer, tearing off stamps and sticking them on his parcels. She watched as one after another, the cardboard boxes got dispatched. It appeared to her that each one had to be dealt with separately. They were all going to different places. She edged a bit nearer while hiding behind the queue for the next desk. Then she could just make out airmail stickers on the boxes. They were going overseas. Was one on its way to Evinka Whyte by any chance? Grace slid out her new iPhone with its telephoto lens and snapped her target. So occupied was he that she managed to get both side and front shots. Drake would be pleased after all. If only she knew who he was. For now, he would have to remain Mr Zurich.

Suddenly all was done. Mr Zurich swiped his credit card on the machine in front of him, gathered up his now empty bag and left. Grace walked out slowly behind him. He turned right back down Uraniastrasse towards the river bridge. On reaching the far bank he turned right heading back towards the coffee shop. There was no point in following him further. She could not learn anything new by watching a closed coffee shop. She would get a train to the airport and have some lunch.

16

As the plane taxied to its runway, Grace settled back in her seat and took out her notebook. She wanted to get her facts in order and be able to make a presentation to Drake. As her pencil hovered over the page, she reflected on how she would have to do twice as well as any man in the police force to impress. She no longer had Martin around to support her; she was on her own with Drake. It was not that she didn't like him and she admired him enormously. Who would not? This man was known throughout the force for his instinct, for his ability to see the key facts that cracked a case.

It was not that he looked down on women in general. He was demonstrably proud of his daughter's achievements as a ballet dancer. He had taken compassionate leave to be with his wife during her long illness. Now he was desperately trying to understand the architecture she had loved and through that to appreciate what drove her through such a stellar career.

Grace realised that Drake had given her a major opportunity denied to thousands of others. To watch him work and be known as his sergeant was a real step forward in her career. Most of all, she enjoyed every minute of working with Drake. But he could be grumpy. There were times when to interrupt his train of thought was a high misdemeanour. To extract a compliment she would really have to excel. It had been her idea to come to Zurich and she had hoped to return with a real understanding of what NmN did. She had failed in that through no fault of her own but she believed they were on to something. There was little doubt that NmN had been important in Evinka Whyte's life but the strange set of monetary transactions could not be understood now that her brother Dalibor was also dead. Yes, she would need some notes to describe what she had uncovered in a way that grabbed Drake's attention.

There was a peremptory tap on the case room door and in walked the pathologist, Professor Cooper.

'Good morning Prof,' said Drake. 'I've been trying to contact you.'

'Yes, I got your message. I just wanted to get one test back from Toxicology before I came.'

'You were lucky to catch me as I was just going out actually so it's best to call us first.'

'OK, have you got five minutes?'

'Yes. We have been doing some research, or Grace has. That young lady is going a long way. You mind my words. She's chasing a line of enquiry in Zurich right now.'

'She seems awfully efficient and she always looks smart,' laughed Prof Cooper.

'I've started making the coffee and doing the washing up,' said Drake. 'Let her get on with the good work. Anyway, the main thing I wanted to tell you is that there is a body of evidence that suggests Evinka Whyte's work is tailing off. She is doing less and the critics have started to round on her. They criticise her performances. The more complimentary ones say she lacks the precision she was famous for. The less kind ones just call her sloppy. So I wondered if you have managed to find any signs of some illness?'

'That is a remarkable coincidence, or perhaps not,' answered Prof Cooper. I may have the answer. At least what I have now found could be consistent with what the critics have identified. There are some signs of minor damage to the liver and kidneys.'

'Oh dear,' said Drake. 'That sounds bad. What was her prognosis?'

'I couldn't tell you what would have happened had she lived but I can tell you what has caused it. No, wait a minute. I can't say that but I can say that something else we have found is quite likely to be responsible. Do you remember on the first day I thought I had seen a syringe mark?'

'Yes, you asked if anyone knew she was taking drugs. Nobody did of course.'

'Well, there are some marks on her upper left arm that suggest something rather more than holiday inoculations. Furthermore, we have identified the presence of some opioid substance.'

'I see,' said Drake. 'I'm no medic but I would guess that doesn't make for precise and quick fingering of a flute.'

'Correct. It might well have that effect. The presence of opium or an artificial opioid compound could cause the damage to the organs that we have found. This suggests that the habit has been going on for some time. However, I estimate that it was not advanced. The slowing down of communication between the brain and muscles is characteristic of this. Before too long people would notice it in everyday life.'

'Hmm,' said Drake. 'We have had a couple of discussions with her sister, Renata and she hasn't mentioned anything.'

'Let's provisionally assume the habit is fairly recent then.'

'What do you mean by recent?'

'My best estimate would be months or maybe a year or two at the most, depending on the amount of substance being consumed.'

'Is it possible then that she died from a drug overdose and that therefore it isn't murder at all?' demanded Drake.'

'Possible, yes. However, there is one more thing I can say that might not be consistent with either an accidental self-administered overdose or even suicide. The marks on her upper arm are in a position that gives the game away.'

'Why?'

'Self-administering drug takers do not habitually perform gymnastics when they inject. The positions of the needle punctures are much more consistent with someone else performing the injection. You know how your doctor or nurse gives you a jab, perhaps one for flu or something nastier before you go abroad on holiday.'

'Yes, of course, I get the flu jab every year now that I'm so old. I always have to yank my shirtsleeve right up my arm,' chuckled Drake.

'Try doing that and using the needle yourself. It just isn't natural. They tend to use the forearm as a site.'

'So let me get this straight,' said Drake. 'You think she has a drug problem, opioid of some kind, and that someone else is giving it to her.'

'Correct but I am making some inferences here that could be wrong. What I see is consistent with what I have suggested. Somebody may be injecting her with opioids.'

Drake walked along the Eastgate rows in Chester. He had been fascinated and captivated by these high level covered walkways the first time he came to the city. They were like some medieval shopping mall allowing for two levels of shops both served by pedestrian access. Since the city had pedestrianized Eastgate Street and restricted traffic in Bridge Street and Watergate, the whole city centre had become one outdoor shopping centre free from traffic and yet enriched by black and white half-timbered architecture. On this occasion, Drake was ambling along enjoying his surroundings but with a purpose. George Marshall had told him that members of the new orchestra were going to hold free concerts in the new concert hall. To advertise these, three groups of musicians had been dispatched to play on the Rows at the Cross. Here, as the upper-level walkway turned the corner from Eastgate Street to Bridge Street, there was enough space for a small group to play. They would be heard and, to some extent, seen from the streets below and of course from the upper-level Rows themselves. The idea had appealed to Drake and he was here to see and hear how it went.

As he arrived, a string quartet had started to play. To attract a wide audience, they began with some rather jazzy pieces. From some distance away he could already hear the strains of tunes from the musical Cabaret. People were standing around, some tapping their feet on the wooden deck to good effect. In the street below, a crowd was gathering with people swaying to the rhythms and some even singing the missing words. The performance was greeted with enthusiastic applause when it finished. They immediately struck up again and Drake recognized some sections from Shostakovich's Jazz Suites in an arrangement he had never heard before. George Marshall and his colleagues were dotted around handing out leaflets about the forthcoming concerts in the concert hall.

Time seemed to fly by and the gathered group of listeners grew with every piece. Cleverly, a wind quintet had established itself on the other side of the open steps and they immediately took over, playing a variety of film music as well as tunes from musicals. Down on street level by the Cross, a small band drawn from the orchestra's brass section had assembled. They alternated with the wind quintet but their more substantial sound drifted right down Bridge Street, Watergate Street and Eastgate. People were also coming down Northgate to see what was hidden from their view but audible from some way up towards the market.

Drake ambled around listening and watching the reactions of the passersby. The whole event seemed well-conceived and, as it concluded, George Marshall and his colleagues had run out of leaflets. Drake joined him to congratulate the players.

'I haven't enjoyed a concert this much for as long as I can remember, George. Do congratulate them all for me.'

'Yes,' said George Marshall. 'It's gone better than we could have dreamt. I think people are keen to see inside their new concert hall so we hope the slightly more serious concerts there will now bring them in. We want the citizens of Chester to own their new facility and hope they will come to love it.'

'Well I must get back to work,' said Drake.

'Before you go,' said George Marshall, grabbing the young lady next to him by the elbow. 'Perhaps you would like to meet our Professor of Music here, this is Professor Laura Weeks who has been helping me. She is Head of the Department of Music at Deva

University. She introduced the opening concert for us.' The professor gave a small bow and shook Drake's outstretched hand.

'Pleased to meet you, Professor Weeks,' said Drake. 'As it happens I would like to come and have a few words with you if I may.'

'Detective Chief Inspector Drake,' said George, 'is investigating the awful death of Evinka Whyte.'

'Oh my goodness,' said Laura Weeks. 'Everyone is talking about it. What a terrible tragedy and an awful way to open the new concert hall.'

'Indeed,' said Drake. 'I understand that Evinka was a visiting professor with you.'

'Yes,' said Laura Weeks in a manner that struck Drake as rather short and snappy.

'Well,' continued Drake. 'If you can spare me, perhaps half an hour one day, I would be grateful. You might be able to fill in background material. One never knows in a case what might prove relevant in some way.'

Laura Weeks nodded her head. 'Yes, I'm sure,' she said.

'Right,' said Drake. 'This is neither the time nor the place. I will get my sergeant to call and arrange for us to come up and see you.'

Grace arrived back at the station from Manchester airport late in the afternoon. Drake had already gone leaving her a cryptic note that he was taking a walk along the Chester Rows. Grace read it several times and began to feel unsure whether or not that was a good thing. Dave, the technician was sitting poking away at a computer.

'Hi Dave,' said Grace. 'What are you doing here? I thought you were still on that forensic science course.'

'I am,' he said, 'but it's not full time so I come into work quite often. Drake says this computer was playing up and asked me to look at it. It's a bit embarrassing really because there's absolutely nothing wrong with it. It must be something he did. He said it just wouldn't respond. I don't know how to explain it to him without embarrassing him.'

'That's no problem, Dave. You just say that sometimes computers get in some sort of mess and all you need to do is turn it off and on again. Tell him that's always worth trying and he'll actually be grateful.'

'Brilliant. Why didn't I think of that?' said Dave.

'Probably because you know too much,' laughed Grace. 'I wish you could help me though.'

'What's the problem?' asked Dave.

'I've been all the way to Zurich to find this place NmN on the Evinka Whyte case. It turns out just to be a letterbox. People there were very hostile. There's obviously something funny going on. They just don't seem to want people to find them but I haven't got very far.'

'How did you know they were in Zurich?' asked Dave.

'Don't you remember finding the address on Evinka Whyte's iPad?'

'Oh yes. I didn't realise it was that important.'

'Then I found a very basic website and the only information about them is the same postal address in Zurich. I found the website just by searching the Internet but it took ages to appear. I went through pages of stuff and, of course, I can't be sure it's actually the people we are interested in. It says almost nothing. It doesn't advertise anything. There are no images, just a more or less blank page with the letters NmN in a huge font and underneath is the same postal address you got on the iPad. It all feels rather strange.'

'Have you checked the IP address of the website?' asked Dave.

'You've stopped talking English,' said Grace.

'OK look, every website and computer on the Internet has what's called an Internet Protocol address. They are all unique. Can you show me the website on this computer?'

Grace dug out her notebook and gave Dave the full Website address.

'This is what we call a domain. I have a cunning little programme I can use here look. It sends the website a message and the website pings back a response with its IP address. Look here it is. Now I have another programme that looks the address up in a huge table and tells me roughly where it is. It's called IP geolocation lookup. Have you ever noticed that you sometimes get responses to searches that appear to know you are in Chester so local businesses might respond to your search? Well, that's how they do it.' Dave tapped away on the computer and suddenly let out a cry.

'Bingo. Look this isn't in Zurich at all. It's not even in Switzerland. It's in the Czech Republic. In fact, it's in Prague.'

'That's amazing,' said Grace writing the various numbers and codes down to tell Drake.

'Perhaps I don't know too much after all then,' said Dave, winking at Grace.

'Touché,' said Grace. 'Have you got the actual address in Prague?'

'Oh no,' said Dave. 'It can only give you a general location. Some are a bit more precise than others but mostly you can't do much better than a town or perhaps part of a town. This only tells me that it's in Prague. It's not a hundred per cent accurate but usually, it is a pretty reasonable result.

17

Drake arrived back from the concert on the Chester Rows humming some of the music. Grace struck immediately while his good mood persisted. She briefed him on her discoveries in Zurich and Dave chipped in while she explained the news about the Prague-based website.

'So why have this complex arrangement between Zurich and Prague?' asked Drake. Grace had her answer ready.

'I can only assume it helps to keep people away from the real centre of their operations,' she said.

'And using Swiss addresses and bank accounts makes it more difficult for us to uncover things,' grunted Drake. 'This whole case is beginning to revolve around Prague. Perhaps we will need to pay a visit to that delightful city.'

Grace and Dave exchanged smiles. Drake was preparing for another of his foreign jaunts. He ambled around his work boards putting up the information from Grace's trip. Eventually, satisfied with his efforts he stood back.

'I have called your pursuer Mr Zurich until we know his real name,' he said and Grace nodded her approval.

Grace tapping gently on her keyboard and the occasional squeak of Drake's chair were the only things breaking the silence in the case room. Suddenly, Drake spoke.

'I understand you still keep in contact with my daughter, Lucy,' he said.

'Yes, we have a lot in common,' replied Grace. 'I got to know her quite well when we were looking for her friend's father in the Opera House case.'

'Has she told you that she is thinking of giving up ballet?' asked Drake.

'She's mentioned it,' replied Grace. 'I went through the same process so I suppose she thinks I might be able to help. I think the outcome will be different, though.'

'Why so?' asked Drake.

'I think she is going through one of those periods that anyone might when following such a demanding career.'

'I'm glad you can help her,' said Drake. 'I'm finding it rather difficult. I don't know what to suggest to her.'

'If I may be as bold as to advise, I wouldn't suggest anything. Just listen,' said Grace.

'I see,' said Drake. 'You know, I think you might be right.' The two continued in relative silence until there was a loud bang on the door and Sergeant Denson came in huffing and puffing.

'Those stairs will be the death of me,' he gasped, mopping his brow. 'Why they never put a lift in, I'll never know. No, that's not true, I do know. They were saving money at our expense.'

'Perhaps they were trying to keep you fit,' growled Drake, looking up from his scribbling.

'I've got this young lady downstairs,' said Sergeant Denson. 'She insists you would want to see her, but she won't give her name. She says it's to do with the Evinka Whyte business and she's from the orchestra. I've got a feeling she isn't going to take no for an answer. What do you want me to do?'

'Bring her up then, Tom,' said Drake.

'That means I've got to climb all those stairs again,' groaned Sergeant Denson.

'Don't worry Tom,' said Grace. 'I'll come down with you.'

As the two sergeants left, Drake climbed out of his chair and pulled all the blinds down that had just been fitted to his work boards. He had insisted they were necessary for when he saw visitors. There had been quite an argument about the cost but

Drake had won. He had just finished when Grace appeared with a short and quite stocky young woman. She looked to be in her late twenties, thought Drake, and she was carrying one of those leather music bags with a rod with small balls on each end that flips over the handle. She had closely cropped almost black hair and was wearing sensible shoes, a tartan skirt and a white blouse under a black jacket.

'Please come and sit down,' said Drake to the anonymous visitor. 'Grace here will make you a cup of tea or coffee. We have a clever machine over there,' Drake pointed vaguely in the direction of his newly screened work boards.

'Thank you, black coffee please. I've never been in a police station before!'

'There's nothing exciting about this one,' said Drake. 'I'm afraid that I missed your name.'

'I was hoping not to give it,' she said, 'but now that I think again, it's a bit silly as you could identify me from what I have to tell you anyway.' Grace delivered a black coffee and a milky one for Drake who pushed it aside to cool. The visitor took a gentle sip and began again. 'I am one of the orchestral players, as you know, I suppose. Oh, how silly of me. I play the flute, second flute and piccolo. My name is Sheila Brompton. I'm sorry that I didn't speak up after your meeting the other day. I wanted longer to think about whether or not I should talk to you. If I'm honest, I also didn't want anyone to know that I had contacted you. It's all a bit difficult and, if the person I want to talk about knew, this would cause terrible problems. In an orchestra like ours, there is a lot of banter but it is nearly all in good spirits and we have a strong sense of community. In this case, it is even more of a problem,' she stopped and stared across the room as if looking for permission to continue.

'We understand,' said Grace. 'Continue when you feel ready.'

'It's about Anders Hagen, who is first flute. We hadn't met before joining this orchestra, so I hardly know him but I feel I should say something. I just hope I'm not talking out of turn. Oh dear, this is so difficult.'

'Anything you tell us here will remain completely confidential,' said Drake. 'We shall not need to make this public. If your evidence gave rise to someone being charged, then it's possible you might have to testify in court. However, even then it is possible to appear but remain shielded from the accused and not have your name used.'

'Well, it was the first time we rehearsed. Our associate conductor rehearsed us through the concert pieces the week before the opening day. It was our first time together so there was a lot of getting to know each other.'

'Let me just be clear,' said Drake. 'What does associate conductor mean?'

'For us, he is semi-permanent on a contract for several years. He will typically rehearse us especially on difficult or new pieces a few days before any visiting conductor comes. Usually, they only arrive on the day of the concert. Because we are a totally new orchestra, we have yet to find our collective voice as it were. Our associate will probably conduct us in a fair few concerts especially to begin with. On this occasion, we did an early Mozart Symphony for a start. That sort of thing is fairly straightforward for people like us, so we rattled through it pretty quickly. Then we tackled the Mascagni Intermezzo, again standard repertoire really. Then the conductor asked Anders Hagen, who is first flute if he would stand in as soloist just for practice. The first concerto was straightforward again but the second involving the harpist needed more work. Anyway, Anders who's from Holland stood up and got quite stroppy. He said that the first players of each instrument were guaranteed the opportunity to play concertos as soloists. It was in their contract. He said he was quite happy to stand in for rehearsal but he thought he should also play the part in performance. The conductor said that he couldn't deal with that and suggested he should take it up with Mr Marshall. I hadn't met Anders before but I was aware that he had a reputation for being a bit bolshie. Anyway, we rehearsed and Anders was fantastic. I was a bit miffed not to get the first position myself but he's definitely a good bit better than me and full of confidence. He didn't seem to be at all nervous and everyone applauded him afterwards.' Sheila paused and fiddled with her coffee cup. Drake and Grace waited for her to continue.

'When it came to lunchtime, we ended up having a sandwich together. It was then that he really let fly. He pulled his contract out of his bag and showed me. Of course, my contract didn't have that clause in it so it was news to me. It is quite normal for this to happen in orchestras playing a standard concert. I tried to point out to him that it was a coup for Mr Marshall to get Evinka Whyte and this wasn't just any old concert. But he wouldn't have it. He said it might be years before we played these pieces again and then he would have missed his chance. He claimed that he'd already spoken with Mr Marshall. It all got rather angry and Anders said he was going to see Evinka Whyte to tell her that she should step aside. We all thought it was a bit silly and a few people laughed at him. A famous soloist like Evinka Whyte would never step aside that way. The laughing made him angrier and he said he would take action against her. I assumed there and then that he meant legal action. But you can see ever since the awful business I have been wondering. I thought I had to let you know. I think he's an ambitious man and with good reason given his talent. As I said I don't really know him but...' Sheila Brompton let her sentence tail away into nothing.

'So do you think he might have actually gone to see Evinka Whyte?' asked Drake.

'Well, that's the thing,' said Sheila. 'On the day of the gala concert, he was still going on about it. After the pre-concert rehearsals finished, he turned and asked me if he was better than her. I had to agree. Of course, we didn't hear a lot of her, just snippets. Her intonation wasn't spot-on in the higher register and her phrasing seemed a bit sloppy. I was quite surprised. I've never heard her live but her recordings are wonderful. Maybe she wasn't bothering much and would have given a perfect performance. We'll never know now.

Anyway, after the rehearsal, Anders said she was awful and he was going to see her and ask her to stand aside. I thought that was all rather silly and he stood no chance. When it was announced that she wouldn't be playing, I began to wonder if she'd agreed. The usher came and asked Anders to come backstage. He gathered his things as if he expected to go and winked at me as he left.'

'I see,' said Drake. 'So do you think he killed her?'

'Oh no. I can't imagine that. I thought maybe they argued and he accidentally...I don't know what to think. He did play well though.' She gave out a little nervous giggle. 'After the concert, everybody in the orchestra went and congratulated him. They'd certainly all stopped laughing at him then. He was a bit cocky, I thought, but he is good there's no doubt about that.'

'Is there anything else you can tell us,' asked Drake.

'I've probably said far too much already.'

'Thank you for coming in to see us,' said Drake. 'We take everything that people like you tell us seriously. We will follow it up.'

'You won't tell Anders I came in, will you? We have to sit next to each other every day and that would be awful.'

'Of course not,' said Drake as Grace showed Sheila Brompton out.

'So what do you make of that?' asked Drake as Grace returned. He was already busy lifting his blinds and putting notes up about the new information.

'It's hard to imagine that he killed her,' said Grace. 'I think it's unlikely but we've seen murders over less. He sounds brilliant but a nasty piece of work though.'

'One of the things you'll learn about this job,' said Drake, 'is that unlikely things sometimes turn out to be true. So we definitely need to investigate Mr Hagen. See what you can dig up on him, will you.' Drake walked silently around his work boards. Grace thought he was not really looking at them. His eyes were fixed on the floor about a yard in front of him. Grace remembered Martin saying that Drake walked as if he was apologising to the ground in front of him for treading on it.

Grace looked up Anders Hagen on the Internet. She quickly found his web site. It listed a few recordings and several competition wins, all in Holland. It had his details and contacts. It listed his latest appointment in Chester.

'Look at this, sir. He's quick off the mark. He has a sort of news blog thing here. It already has an entry about his performance. It rather cleverly says he substituted for Evinka Whyte. It doesn't say she was dead or even indisposed. The way it's worded you'd think he was preferred to her. Sheila Brompton was right about how ambitious he is.'

Drake looked over Grace's shoulder and grunted. 'Lady Macbeth was ambitious,' he said. 'I wonder. I wonder.' Drake wandered off across the room muttering Shakespeare to himself. 'To catch the nearest way thou wouldst be great. Art not without ambition...' Grace continued her browsing of the Internet.

18

'Hello, Grace,' said Drake as they met at one of the concert hall doors. 'They seem to have security working pretty well here. There's somebody doing a baggage check at every door. Sergeant Denson has several uniformed branch wandering around rather conspicuously. Short of frisking the citizens of Chester as they come into their concert hall, I'm not sure they could do more. Let's go inside and find our seats. They are at the back just in case of any trouble.'

As soon as Drake and Grace cleared the security they stood watching the crowds milling about in the foyer. Some were already booking tickets at the box office to their right.

'Look,' said Grace, 'what you were telling me the other day. I can see now what you mean. The box office and the auditorium look like solid things inside the glass enclosure.'

'Excellent,' said Drake. 'I wasn't sure I was that good at explaining. I wish Cynthia was here.' With that, he took his handkerchief out and dabbed his eyes. Grace gently touched him on his back. Then she almost recoiled. It had been an instinctive gesture but she suddenly realised she had not previously ever touched him before and she wondered how he would take it. All was well. He stuffed his handkerchief in his jacket pocket, turned and nodded his head with the slightest sign of a smile. They stood for a few moments in silence. Grace felt she should respect that rather than try to engage him in conversation. A small group of musicians, high on one of the balconies that wrapped around the auditorium, struck up and filled the foyer with sound competing with the murmur of chatter.

'Ah, Chief Inspector,' said a voice from behind them. Drake turned to discover George Marshall standing with a man almost as tall as himself but thin to the point of looking ill. He was entirely dressed in black and wore circular lens glasses. 'We are so glad you could come. This is our architect, Ivor Halliday. Ivor, this is Chief Inspector Drake who is in charge of the Evinka Whyte investigation.' Grace wondered why she was not included in the introductions. She thought perhaps she had suddenly become invisible.

'Pleased to meet you,' said Ivor Halliday, shaking Drake's hand. He turned to Grace, holding out his hand. 'Hello,' he said, 'are you in the police as well?'

'This is Detective Sergeant Grace Hepple,' said Drake. 'We were only just admiring your handiwork. I was trying to explain to Grace what my wife, who was an architect, would have said about it.'

'Really!' said the architect. 'What would she have said?'

'Oh dear,' said Drake. 'I'm only an amateur but I do find that taking a piece of architecture apart is a not unlike detective work.'

'Drake,' said the architect slowly. 'I don't suppose your wife was Cynthia by any chance?'

'Indeed she was,' said Drake rising slightly out of his normal stoop.

'Well, we often admire the work of her practice,' said the architect. 'They have an office here in Chester. We are a little bit nervous this evening. Although all the acoustic tests we did before the opening seemed satisfactory, I have still to hear an orchestra in here with a full audience. I shall not be able to enjoy the concert until I have heard every instrument as well as the totality.'

'It was Ivor's clever idea to create all these adjustable panels on the flanking walls and the ceiling,' said George Marshall. 'As a result, we have been able to create a truly wonderful acoustic.' George Marshall slapped Ivor Halliday on the back. 'There is a display of Ivor's drawings over there. Do go and look at them.' With that, he nodded and directed his visitor over to a small crowd nearby.

'Hmmm,' said Drake to Grace, 'that was nearly embarrassing. I'm not sure how he would have taken to my poor man's architectural education.'

The audience soon began filtering into the auditorium. The interior was almost entirely covered in wood of one kind or another. The graceful curves of the main space and the outlines of upper-level balconies were all marked out by the joints between the wooden panels. These were spaced slightly apart revealing a sky blue backing. The width of the gaps between the panels varied, resulting in an almost musical rhythm along the walls. Drake explained that these were to allow for adjustment of the acoustics. Grace noticed that he appeared to be admiring the building but she was sure that he was actually looking for any suspicious behaviour. She could certainly see none. They joined the short queue and soon found their seats. Within a few minutes, the members of the orchestra started to appear, some carrying their instruments. Others like the double bass players finding theirs on the platform.

The noise of tuning up began to swirl around the void. Gradually each instrument stopped until there was almost complete silence. The oboist played his tuning A and the woodwinds and brass copied it assiduously. Then the strings had their turn. A few sounds still punctured the air. A clarinettist snapped shut his instrument case. A cellist on the front row persisted with a few tuning adjustments. Someone coughed and cleared their throat. Drake and Grace heard every sound as if it came from the row in front of them. Mr Halliday's acoustics were working. The conductor appeared to applause from all around the auditorium, took his position on the rostrum, bowed and turned to face his players. The clapping stopped and everyone was ready.

That was when it began. He was past Drake and Grace before they were even aware of him. He dashed, or more correctly skipped, his way down the aisle shouting at the top of his voice. He reached the front of the hall before the ushers could even make their entrance. Some said later that they were all playing cards in the foyer. The intruder climbed onto the platform and turned around. There were a couple of gasps from among the seated audience as he revealed a head to toe costume in black with a white skeleton. Grace was astonished to see he was wearing the familiar white mask. It was an upright oval shape in white with a huge black tear down the left cheek. He suddenly produced a flute and pushed his mask up to free his mouth. Drake had no idea where the flute had been concealed. The intruder began to make untutored screeches and squeals on his instrument. By now the ushers were coming into the auditorium mob-handed. Some rushed in from the back and others came in from the side doors. The intruder stopped making his awful racket, pushed his mask back into place and appeared to begin conducting the audience by pointing around with his flute. Each time he pointed another figure would stand up and begin shouting.

By now, the conductor had lowered his baton and stepped back off his rostrum. While both Drake and Grace were in no doubt that the growing band of intruders were shouting, though neither of them could make out the words. The auditorium acoustics were obviously only meant to work for sounds from the platform. Drake counted at least six shouters each in the middle of a row of seats in the amphitheatre. He thought he could hear more in the upper galleries. Ushers rushed down the aisles and began pushing their way along the rows containing intruders. Several side doors opened and police in various uniformed garb came in, one talking to the phone on his chest. By now the first shouter was being escorted back along the row. People started to chatter and some laughed, others were booing loudly. The conductor stood facing the audience with his arms folded. One or two musicians exchanged light-hearted remarks and grinned.

As each intruder was escorted along their rows, Grace could see they were wearing a similar mask. Uniformed policemen arrived and took charge of the shouters as they reached the end of their rows. Drake beckoned Grace and they stood and turned back down the aisle they were next to. Drake led the way out into the foyer and met Sergeant Denson. More police were appearing from their parked vans outside behind the stage. The first shouter to appear had both arms behind his back pushed along by two policemen, one either side. Grace could see that some of the masks were similar to the one she had so alarmingly encountered backstage. These versions came with a gruesome expression. Gradually the foyer began to echo to the sound of pointless noisy shouting, though most of the culprits were soon silenced and their masks removed. They soon found themselves entering the police vans that had by now appeared outside the main doors.

Drake and Grace stood around and generally assisted by opening doors and Grace helped a few shouters up the step into their appointed van. Soon all were removed. Drake was about to discuss events with Sergeant Denson when the orchestra started playing with a full tutti. The audience applauded and the performance settled down.

Drake went to look over the haul of shouters now sitting quietly in two of the vans.

'Has anyone seen the first guy with the skeleton outfit,' he shouted. Each officer shook his head in turn.

'Drat. We've somehow managed to lose him,' groaned Drake. 'What's even more annoying, this is the second concert that I've missed in this delightful concert hall. Just my luck.' Drake got a couple of questioning looks but Grace had seen the twinkle in his eye and she just smiled.

'So how many have we got?' asked Drake arriving back at the police station.

'There's six of them,' replied Tom Denson. 'They've all given names and addresses. Three of them from Manchester were involved in the first demonstration. The other three are new to us. One is from Liverpool and the other two are from Chester. One of the Chester lads is really truculent and not answering any questions like the Manchester and Liverpool lot. The other Chester lad is only eighteen and terrified. I think he's most worried about what his Dad would do to him if he found out.'

'OK then,' said Drake. 'Let's start with him. Sit him in the interview room by himself and let him stew for a while. I've spoken with George Marshall at the concert hall and he doesn't want it to go any further. He doesn't think it would be good for them. However, we can't just have these disturbances continuing.'

'Understood, sir,' said Sergeant Denson. 'My recommendation would be we tell them that we consider this to have been a breach of the peace and that we could charge them. Then we could caution them.'

'Do that with the other five when we are ready. For the time being, we'll see what this youngster has to say for himself.' Drake and Grace left Sergeant Denson in charge of proceedings and went down the corridor to the interview room. On the way, Drake briefed Grace and told her to take the interview. Grace opened the door and a timid lad was sitting at the table in the centre of the room visibly shaking.'

'Good evening. I am Detective Chief Inspector Drake. This is Detective Sergeant Hepple. She is going to ask you some questions. Do you understand?' The lad nodded silently. Then murmured acknowledgement.

'Your name is Gary,' said Grace. 'Is that correct?'

'Yes.'

'Did you take part in the demonstration at the concert hall this evening?'

'Yes.'

'Did you also take part in the previous demonstration at the opening of the concert hall?'

'No. I don't know what you're talking about. I've not been near the place before. I didn't even know it was there.'

'These demonstrations, especially the one this evening could be regarded as breaches of the peace. Do you understand?'

'No. What is breach of the peace then?'

'It's not a criminal offence, Gary but you can be bound over to keep the peace by a magistrate so you might have to go to court.

You might have to pay some money that you would lose if you do anything similar again.'

'How much would I have to pay then?'

'That would depend on the magistrate, Gary. What was the point of the demonstration?'

'Something about the building of the concert hall, I think,' said Gary. 'My friend said it would be a lark so I went along. I didn't think I was going to get into trouble though.'

'Your friend is also from Chester?'

'Yes.'

'His name is Micky. Is that correct?'

'Yes.'

'Did he organise the demonstration?'

'No. It was a friend of his.'

'What is his name?'

'I don't know.'

'Is he from Chester?'

'I don't know. He might be.'

'Was he the one who stood up at the front and had a flute?'

'Yes.'

'Can you tell us any more about him or the point of the demonstration?'

'That's all I know, honest. I just thought it was going to be a lark. I didn't want to get into trouble.'

19

The next morning, Drake, Grace and Sergeant Tom Denson arrived at the concert hall to meet with all the staff to review the protest.

'Despite it all, the concert was a huge success,' said George Marshall. 'We got a full hall with a few extra standing at the rear on each level. The applause was fulsome and seemed genuine. I think we have established a good few customers.'

'This protest was quite cleverly organised,' said Drake. 'They had booked seats in the middle of rows all over the place. They certainly meant to cause a disturbance whoever they are.'

'They must have hidden their masks in their clothing,' said Grace, turning one over in her hands. 'None of the ushers reported finding any in their bag searches.'

'They are clearly a well-disciplined group,' said Drake. 'The question is, are they just complaining about the building being erected here or is there some other objective to this repeated disturbance?'

'Do you think it is just a coincidence?' asked Grace. 'Or could they be connected to the Evinka Whyte case?'

'Good question,' said Drake. 'We got six of them but somehow missed the instigator. Did anyone here see what happened to the guy at the front in the skeleton outfit?'

'I might have done,' said Jimmy Caxton, the caretaker. 'I didn't know what was going on in the hall but I heard a noise in the backstage corridor and by the time I got there I could only see the door at the far end closing. I'm afraid that I didn't chase it up since, at that time, I wasn't aware of what was going on.'

'Ah, of course,' said Grace. 'I'm pretty sure it was the same guy who knocked me over at the previous protest. He was wearing the same mask as one of the earlier guys. It's the only one with a tear on the cheek. If it was him, then he already knew his way around.'

'We've been a little sloppy then,' said Drake. 'I guess we were all responding to the individuals who had to be extracted from the audience.'

'Yes,' said Grace. 'So he just nipped across in the wings and took the door through to the rear stage and out that way.'

'That's twice now that he's got away from us,' said Drake. 'If there's another of these protests then one of us must be dedicated to apprehending him.' Sergeant Denson made a note in his book.

'They all gave their names and addresses without any fuss,' said Sergeant Denson. 'They don't seem all that serious to me. All the way back in the vans they were giggling and pushing each other. I've seen their sort before. I don't think they believe in their cause whatever it is. Anyway, we cautioned 'em and warned 'em. I told 'em I could have charged 'em with breach of the peace. I even laid it on a bit thick and said if they were to get up to the tricks again we could charge 'em on the Public Order Act. I think that made 'em realise that they couldn't go around playing at being a nuisance in Chester. They went a bit quiet then, all except for a couple who showed a bit of bravado. I guess that we won't see most of 'em again.'

'Did anyone hear what they were shouting?' asked Drake.

'One of our first violins said he could hear the mock flautist and he thought it was all anarchist stuff. Property is theft. Building on public land is a crime, especially when it's for the privileged authoritarian minority. That sort of thing,' said an usher.

'Well I'm not surprised that most of them didn't come from around here,' said George Marshall. I know there were real protests about knocking down the nunnery and taking away part of the park but that was all quite civilised. I think all the protestors are hangers-on, shipped in from elsewhere and latching on to any public protest for their own causes.'

'I didn't think the flute was a coincidence though,' said Grace quietly.

'You think it was some attempt to make fun of the Evinka Whyte affair?' asked Drake.

Grace shrugged her shoulders.

'How did he get the flute in?' she asked.

'I think that was easy,' said Drake. 'He came in after all the bag searches had stopped. Fire Regulations require the doors to be open but by then they might not have been manned.'

'I suppose that was our fault,' said an usher. 'As soon as we closed the auditorium doors, we left the outside doors unlocked but you have to do that for the fire regulations.'

'I heard that you were all playing cards,' said Tom Denson. The ushers sat silently. He turned to George Marshall. 'You need to 'ave protocols,' he said. 'The ushers need to remain alert for incidents during the concerts. No skivin' off and playin' cards.'

'OK,' said Drake. 'I really need to get hold of the skeleton guy. We need to find out who he is. I guess that in contrast with these lads we caught, he is a good bit older. He obviously organised the whole thing and roped in all these outsiders. I agree with you, Tom. They probably have nothing at all to do with any dispute over the building and they're a crowd of hobbyist protestors playing at being anarchists with little idea of what it really means. I still have an inkling that we haven't heard the last of Mr Skeleton. He could even be a more dangerous individual. We need all staff here to keep an eye out for anyone hanging around. He obviously had a clear idea of the plan of the building. Grace, will you get onto the people at Met Special Operations and see if they have any knowledge on protestors in this neck of the woods. I suspect he is local. Now, I'm going to walk along the lovely River Dee, take in the fresh air and have lunch with my daughter.'

Drake picked his way down through the tiered piazzas and reached the riverbank with his mood improving at each step. There was something good-natured about the Dee at Chester. It meandered along in a friendly sort of way, splashing and rippling but never getting threatening. He wondered what it was like further upstream and downstream. One day he must find time to explore. He reached his house and stood for a few minutes just watching the river, the birds that lived on it and the boaters who played on it. It had a distinctive smell but Drake could not pin it down. He thought that the Malverns may have been Elgar's England but he was now quite happy to call this his.

'Hello, Lucy,' said Drake opening the front door of his rented house. 'What on earth is going on here?' The kitchen floor was cleared and one of the large mirrors from the hallway was propped up against a wall. Lucy was standing next to the worktop with her crutch on the floor.

'I've set up a sort of make-do barre,' she said. 'I'm just doing some stretches.'

'I thought you had decided to give all that up,' grunted Drake.

'So did I but then I thought I'd better get my muscles going again just in case,' Lucy had a smirk on her face.

'So you've changed your mind then?' asked Drake.

'Let's say that I'm keeping my options open,' said Lucy. 'What about you? Are you still going to retire?'

'Well,' said Drake. 'I can't leave this case just now. We're not a great deal further forward. Perhaps I'll think about it again when I've tied this one up.' They both laughed. Drake thought he should have lunch at home more often as they sat in the garden eating their paninis and watching the river.

That afternoon, Grace was going through all the protestors' details and logging them on Drake's work boards. She was running computer checks on each of the six masked protestors. The masks were all in a pile on a table in the corner of the room. Drake was sat in his chair rocking extremely slowly and, Grace thought, with the sole aim of making a creaking noise to irritate her. Suddenly the door burst open and in walked Professor Cooper.

'I think you guys are going to be interested in this,' he said. Grace stopped tapping at her computer and Drake even stopped rocking his chair. They all gathered around the central table.

'Well I've finally come up trumps with the toxicology people,' said Prof Cooper. 'You remember that we had found evidence of some artificial opioids in Evinka Whyte?'

Drake and Grace both nodded their heads in keen anticipation. Prof Cooper, satisfied that he had their attention, continued.

'The results we had suggested she was taking some opioids but not enough to kill her. We also concluded that it was likely that someone was injecting her. Now the brilliant toxicology boys have come up with a stunner for us. At last, I know almost certainly what killed her. It looks like she suffered a dose of carfentanil. I don't expect you've heard of it?' Drake and Grace shook their heads. 'Well, it's a rather remarkable and highly dangerous drug. It is more commonly found in the States than here, thank goodness, although I expect we'll catch up with them eventually. We do usually when it comes to drugs. I guess you know that morphine is easily extracted from opium. We get heroin from morphine and it is a more powerful drug. Another even more powerful drug we do see here in the UK is fentanyl, which is another opioid-based drug with greater potency than heroin. Well, carfentanil is another of the drugs known as synthetic opioids with a potency about a hundred times more than fentanyl and at least ten thousand times greater than heroin. It is so powerful that it has never been approved for use in humans and was originally synthesised as a veterinary medication. It can, for example, be used to tranquilise large animals including rhinoceroses and even elephants. We are talking about a relatively unknown and rare drug that is extremely powerful and dangerous. It is normally only used by licensed and qualified individuals like specialist veterinary surgeons.' Prof Cooper paused to make sure his little lecture had been understood and continued.

'This means that even tiny amounts can be lethal in human beings and for this reason it is pretty difficult to detect in post-mortems. All the normal immunoassay tests for opiates fail to react to carfentanil. Only recently have we had tests that can reasonably reliably detect it but such tests are not normally included in an investigation of this kind unless there are specific reasons to do so.'

'How is carfentanil administered, Prof?' asked Drake.

'It can be ingested or injected. It is not normally sniffed since the powder is so potent that even a small amount blown up into the air could cause a fatality. The literature does contain references to the use of an aerosol as the weapon of administration in a murder case in the States. Toxicology have tested the coffee mug and the water bottle and found traces of carfentanil. This tells us that she probably drank the carfentanil that killed her. It could have come from either mug or water bottle as her mouth could easily have transferred the substance. She could for example have drunk it in the coffee, felt a bit hot and then transferred it to the water. It's extremely tricky stuff with only the tiniest amount being sufficient to prove fatal.'

'What I am hearing here,' said Drake, 'is that whoever gave her this awful stuff was pretty deliberate and calculating.'

'Yes,' said Prof Cooper, 'I think you are probably correct. They'd probably need good contacts too. It's a heavily controlled drug and not available to those without a licence except through illicit means. It is not the first thing that comes to mind as a murder weapon.'

'How would a victim die?'

'Carfentanil is so potent that a small amount spilt and then touched could cause death since it can even be absorbed through the mucous membranes. I suspect that our poor paramedic might have touched a surface where some had been spilt and then touched his face. I have checked by the way that he is now recovering. I think he might eventually consider himself extremely fortunate to be alive. You might recall the case of the Russian authorities using an aerosol to subdue hostage-takers in a Moscow theatre. It is believed that carfentanil was used in the spray. It acts remarkably quickly. It inhibits breathing and attacks many organs including the heart. This is the first time that I have run across it.'

'So either this was somehow or other taken accidentally, perhaps drunk,' said Drake. 'Or someone, as yet unknown, has given Evinka Whyte an injection or laced a drink with carfentanil.'

'I think the accident idea is pretty unlikely,' said Prof Cooper. 'This sort of stuff just isn't lying around anywhere.'

'Point taken,' said Drake. 'At least, now we know what we are looking for.'

'A vet with a grudge against Evinka Whyte,' said Grace. 'That helps us a lot then.'

20

The windscreen wipers of the Range Rover had been working overtime since they left the police station. It was the first time Chester had experienced rain since the day before the opening gala concert and this was torrential rain. Just as they turned off the main road up the short drive to the gates of the Deva University campus, the rain thought better of it, abated and let the sun take over. It was a classic spring shower, thought Drake.

As they reached the gatehouse, the attendant came out and waved them down. Drake remembered encountering him before. He thought this man was probably meek and mild at home but at work, he donned a peaked cap and became a pompous tyrant. His cap bore the title "parking attendant," which Drake thought was odd since his main purpose in life seemed to be stopping people parking at all. As the man approached, Grace wound down the window of the driver's door and addressed him.

'It's Detective Chief Inspector Drake for appointments with Professor Weeks in Music and the Vice-Chancellor.'

'Oh, yes,' replied the peaked cap. His diminutive frame conveniently put him at the right height to speak directly to Grace but instead, he talked across her to Drake.

'Excuse me Chief Inspector but are you by any chance investigating the murder of our much loved distinguished visiting Professor Whyte?'

'Oh dear,' said Drake 'we would prefer not to have that trumpeted across the whole campus.' Rather than being put off by Drake's caution, the peaked cap was actually encouraged.

'She was a lovely woman, she really was,' he said. 'We all loved her visits. She would always bring me a CD of hers, signed of course. I have a whole collection of them. I made sure to find her a parking space right next to the main door. I didn't want her getting wet and catching a cold if it rained. We all hope you discover whoever did it. They should lock him up and throw away the key, they should.' Drake nodded and smiled as the little man continued. 'I guessed that it was you so I reserved her space for you. Follow me.' With that he was off at a bouncy little jog, holding his cap on with one hand and waving them on with the other. Grace drove as slowly as she could round the little roundabout and past the main door to the space indicated. The peaked cap removed one of those red ropes that was stretched across the space and saluted. He then dashed around to Drake's door and held it open for him. Drake swivelled himself around, dropped his feet to the ground and, holding onto the open doorway, pulled himself out of the car. Grace giggled as the little attendant watched Drake gradually reaching his full six feet, six and a half inches to stand towering over him.

'In through the front door, turn right and follow the signs to the music department,' said the peaked cap. 'I'll come along and let you in.' He waddled off in front of them, pulling out a credit-card type key on a long extending lead attached to his belt. This magically opened one of a pair of heavy-looking oak doors. He pointed to his right and Drake and Grace set off following his instructions. Drake was instantly reminded of the grisly interior design in this part of the campus. There was pink and grey swirly wallpaper separated by a gold painted waist-high dado rail. Above the dado, at intervals along the corridor, were portraits of the senior officers of the university. Paradoxically, all this attempt at tradition did was to illustrate how short the history of the university was. As they got a little way down the corridor, it narrowed and the attempt at interior design gave way to plain white walls and ceilings with dark grey floor tiles. The Deva University of Chester obviously wasn't into wasting money on things that were not needed. The signs took Grace and Drake out through a rather miserly door and down one side of an open space surrounded by four identical three-storey brick buildings. Drake remembered from his last visit that there were several such squares, he supposed that they were meant to be described as quadrangles but in reality, they fooled nobody. Thankfully, the Music Department was allowed to be different. There seemed to be a double-height hall for performance and a series of small practice rooms as well as the usual academics' offices.

They finally arrived at a glazed doorway, which Grace opened. A woman standing at a filing cabinet looked up and greeted them.

'You must be Dr Weeks' visitors,' she said. Grace nodded. The woman turned to a nearby door, tapped on it and poked her head round. 'Dr Weeks is ready to see you,' she said. Drake ushered Grace ahead into Laura Weeks' office. She rose from behind a huge desk and came to shake Drake's hand. She cut a striking figure. Shaking her hand, Drake assessed her height. She was not as tall as him but she was taller than the owners of most hands he shook. He put her height at nearly 6 feet. The long ginger-red hair falling over her shoulders and her slender build both contributed to the effect of unusual height. She turned to Grace.

'Pleased to meet you Grace,' she said.

'The same, Professor Weeks,' said Grace.

'No, no,' said Laura Weeks. 'I'm not a professor. If you want to be formal you can call me doctor but I'd rather you just called me Laura.'

'So how does that work then Laura,' asked Drake. 'You're head of department but not professor.'

'Long story,' replied Laura. 'That way they get me to do all the work but save on my salary.'

'That doesn't seem fair,' said Grace.

'You've put rather more politely than I would,' said Laura Weeks.

'So what else do you have to do to become a professor then?' asked Drake.

'You tell me,' said Laura.

'I can see we've touched on a sore point,' said Drake. 'That really wasn't the reason for our visit. I'm sorry.' Laura smiled as they all sat down on a small circle of easy chairs.

'I'll see if I can get coffee,' said Laura getting up again and leaving. Drake looked around the room. Behind Dr Weeks' chair was one of the standard vertical shaped windows. To either side were bookcases groaning with volumes and files. On the other side of the room was a stool with an electronic keyboard surrounded by loudspeakers and piles of sheet music. It was then that Drake saw it. On the wall through which they had come was the largest collection of masks that he had ever seen. They were all styled in a particular way that reminded Drake and Grace, who's arm he nudged, of the masks at the demonstration. Drake scanned but he could not see one like the leading protestor had worn or the one that Grace had picked up after he fled.

Laura came back into the room carrying a tray with three cups of coffee and a small selection of biscuits. She put this down on a low table between the easy chairs. Drake saw her against the white blinds over the windows. It drew his attention to the whiteness of her skin. Her mouth was narrow and she pursed her lips when thinking. She had a striking appearance. Taken together with the authoritative way she spoke, Drake thought she would be a formidable opponent in academic debate.

'We were just admiring your masks,' said Drake. 'Have you been to Venice by any chance?'

'Yes, and I've lost count of how many times,' laughed Laura. 'My excuse is that they relate to my research.'

'Which is?'

'Oh you haven't come to be bored by my research I'm sure but I study the relationship between commedia dell'arte and early Italian opera buffa. I presume you want to talk about Evinka Whyte.'

'Yes of course,' said Drake. 'Perhaps you could tell us how you managed to attract her here. I imagine it was quite a coup.'

'I didn't. The Vice-Chancellor did. They met at some conference of the leaders of British universities where she had been hired to play for them after dinner.'

'So you feel that was imposed on you then?' asked Drake.

'To a certain extent, yes. The main problem is that I had to find the money for it out of my budget and I wasn't given any extra.

Even that would have been all right except she wouldn't take any steer from me as to what the department needed. We don't have a lot of students here playing flute and certainly, not many who are already so good that would benefit from the kind of master class she wanted to give. At the same time, we are short of lecturers in other vital parts of the course.'

'Couldn't you tell her what to do then?' asked Drake.

'Well, she retained a direct link to the Vice-Chancellor and had dinner with him every so often so she was always giving him feedback on what she thought was wrong in the department. Here, we teach students for a degree in music. This is not a conservatoire where excellent musicians are tutored for a solo performing career.'

'I can see that was difficult,' said Grace.

'Evinka was also rather out of touch with modern thinking in many ways that I think put the students off. For example, most students of the flute today would call themselves flutists, using the English name. Evinka persisted in using the traditional Italian and called herself a flautist. It's a small thing but indicative of an attitude.'

'Oh dear,' laughed Drake. 'I'm afraid that I'm in the old fashioned brigade then.'

Dr Weeks smiled, passed the biscuits round and began again.

'The VC told me what salary to pay her and of course, it was way beyond what we pay full-time lecturers here so altogether it wasn't a brilliant deal for us. All we got out of it was some kind of reputational benefit. I guess it looks good on the web site and so on and may have helped to recruit a few students but real performers are likely to want to go to The Royal Northern College of Music in Manchester for example. There's no way we could compete with them only in flute. It just never made sense.'

'I understand,' said Drake. 'I hadn't thought it out. It just seemed like a real coup for you but I can see the problems now.'

'To make matters worse, because she and I disagreed about what she should do, I'm pretty sure she was giving the VC bad reports about me. She made it pretty clear that she thought my research was a waste of time.'

'Perhaps you could explain more to us about your research,' probed Drake.

'Well I guess you know what the commedia dell'arte was?' asked Laura.

'Only vaguely I'm afraid,' said Drake and Grace nodded in agreement.

'Of course, I'm always delighted to talk about it,' said Laura, 'but only if you promise to tell me when you've had enough.' They all laughed.

'The commedia dell'arte was a form of early Italian theatre. Its heyday was from the sixteenth to eighteenth centuries. They relied on a series of fixed characters. To understand the plays you needed to know who these characters were as well as their personalities. They were indicated by the masks they wore. So if we look at the wall behind you. Looking along the top row from left to right we see Arlecchino, or Harlequin as we would call him, who often uses a lot of pantomime and has a costume covered in coloured diamond shapes. Then comes Pantalone, who is a greedy old man, Il Dottore who was a "know it all" character and a doctor and so on. These stock characters had a series of what we would call running jokes. The whole performance was a combination of a loose script with a lot of improvisation. Parallels to it today and here might be Punch and Judy. You could also see the puppet show Spitting Image as having some similarities. It is thought that the mask-wearing tradition came from Carnival in Venice and, as you rightly recognized, these masks come from there.'

'I see,' said Drake. 'That is really interesting. So what is your research?'

'Well, I analyze comic Italian opera such as from Donizetti or Rossini to show parallels and how the libretti of these operas continue the same tradition. So, for example, Donizetti's opera L'elisir d'amore, first performed in 1832, centres around a character, Dr Dulcamara who appears to know everything, particularly in terms of medicine, and sells his magic love potion.

The joke is, and the audience know this, that he is a complete charlatan and the love potion is no more than ordinary wine.'

'I can see what fun you must have with all this,' said Drake.

'Evinka Whyte had no sense of humour I'm afraid. Of course, the whole point of this is not just to have a laugh but in doing so to explore attitudes in contemporary society. That is a really important point of my work. I suppose it's almost sociology really seen through music. Evinka couldn't see that and briefed the VC that my work was superficial and pointless.'

'Thank you for that interesting discussion, Laura,' said Drake. 'So I suppose you were glad to see the back of Evinka Whyte and have now recovered control of your budget.'

'Well, yes but for goodness sake, I didn't wish her ill. Her death is a terrible tragedy and a waste of a good talent. Our disagreements wouldn't ever become violent. Perhaps I shouldn't have told you all this. Can I ask, am I a real suspect now?'

'Everyone is a suspect until we find the genuine culprit,' answered Drake, laughing. 'Perhaps one question might help with that. Were you at the opening gala concert?'

'Yes, I did all the introductions.'

'Oh, yes,' said Drake. 'I remember George Marshall telling me that. So did you see Evinka during the concert?'

'No. For both halves of the concert I had a seat reserved for me at the end of the front row, so I could just nip up the steps, do the announcing and get out of the way.'

'So you could enjoy the concert as well then?' asked Drake.

'It was rather a predictable pattern of well-known favourites.'

'You didn't approve?' asked Drake.

'It wouldn't have been my choice. I would have liked to have at least one contemporary piece but it wasn't my job to fill the auditorium. I have agreed with George Marshall to write the programme notes for the concerts. I will have the space and time to introduce some ideas about the history and theory of music. I doubt the VC will see this as valuable work.'

'What did you think of Anders Hagen's performance?' asked Drake.

'I'm no expert on the flute but I thought he was really impressive and played with a lot of feeling. From the little I heard of her rehearsal, I think he was probably better than Evinka Whyte actually.'

'Can you remember what time you arrived at the concert hall?'

'Yes, I can remember because I got it wrong. I assumed they would want to rehearse me to an extent so I made myself available and sat in the auditorium while rehearsals were still going on. It is quite a privilege to watch a seasoned conductor like Stransky especially with a brand new orchestra that hasn't even played together once. It was quite impressive.'

'Can I ask what you did between rehearsals and the start of the concert?' asked Drake.

'I went backstage to make sure I knew what to do. We hadn't rehearsed it. Then I went out on the terraces down to the river with a small glass of wine that George Marshall kindly poured for me.'

'Where would Evinka Whyte have been during that time?' asked Drake.

'I assumed that she was in her dressing room. It had a label on the door as well as one for Itzhak Stransky. Some performers like to be sociable and others prefer to be left alone. That reminds me. One other person who was there and knew Evinka Whyte well was our Roger Gayford. He is in charge of all our performance modules and worked with Evinka on the few master classes she gave. Together they also produced a useful resource for students learning to give any sort of performance. It's all a matter of psychology. Just as there are sports psychologists there is now a growing subject of performance psychology. You might try talking to Roger. Now if you would excuse me, I have another university meeting.'

21

As they left the school of music, Drake turned to Grace.

'Did you see anything there?' he asked.

'What sort of thing?' asked Grace.

'Look, we have half an hour before our meeting with the Vice-Chancellor. Let's go and sit on that bench under the tree over there and have a chat.' Drake walked rather stiffly and was soon several paces behind Grace. She turned and apologized.

'Those chairs were too deep and soft,' groaned Drake. 'Not good for my old back at all. This hard wooden seat will be better. He lowered himself down onto the bench and let out a long low moan. 'This job would be a lot easier if cars were bigger and seats were firmer,' he complained. Grace sympathized.

'Surely you are not serious about Laura Weeks as a suspect?' asked Grace.

'Well we seem to be collecting people with some sort of grudge against Evinka Whyte,' said Drake. 'It's the old story of motive and opportunity. She has a motive, she was at the concert and had access to backstage.'

'The conductor, Itzhak Stransky had a motive and the most obvious opportunity. The best opportunity was undoubtedly the PA Jelena Novakova but we have little evidence of a motive. Her disappearance however does cast some possible suspicion at this stage. Then we have all the protestors, especially the leader with the mask. They had a motive, to create publicity for their cause and plenty of opportunities. They could have wedged the corridor door open during the protest and come back in that way when the concert started. Now back to Laura Weeks room. All those masks are surely an amazing coincidence. But you didn't notice as we left and got close to them something that starts to make me even more curious?'

'I'm afraid not,' said Grace, feeling under pressure.

'The wall was painted pure white. As we got closer I could see two tiny pins in positions to suggest they might have supported two more masks. We have seen two more of them already. You saw one far too closely.'

'Oh my!' said Grace. 'Why didn't you ask her where they were?'

'Not wise at this point to alert her to our interest,' grunted Drake. 'We need to tread more carefully. Ah, here we go. Don't look round but Dr Laura Weeks has emerged for her meeting. I thought that might happen. You can't miss her appearance, tall and red-haired. Let's see where she goes.' At that point, the blackbird in the tree above started his most melodic of tunes. Grace hoped Laura didn't hear it and look round. She didn't.

'Ah,' said Drake. 'She's just waved at the far corner of the quadrangle and a man has emerged from the door there. Yes, now she's hurrying to meet him. He's about her height with long black hair, an untidy short beard and looks rather skinny.' Drake half hid behind Grace who lifted up her phone in the trick she had worked out in Zurich. The unknown man went to Kiss Laura but was pushed away and they seemed to start arguing. They walked down the side of the quad and into the door Drake and Grace had come through. Their argument appeared to continue all the way.

'OK, now let's go and see what the sign on that door that he came out of says,' said Drake after the two had disappeared. Drake got up slightly more easily than he had sat down and they made their way across to the corner door. It read "Department of Sociology" with hours of working beneath in much smaller letters.

'Remember,' said Drake. 'How Laura described her work as sociology through music. Isn't that interesting?'

Drake and Grace retraced their steps back to the main entrance to find the Vice-Chancellor's office. Security was quite heavy with huge roller shutters drawn up to the ceiling of a small bay set back in a wall of the main corridor. Drake was not sure if this was a fire precaution or needed in case of student rebellions. Grace tried the door but it was locked so she pushed the doorbell button on the right-hand side. An elaborate chiming ring was heard from deep inside the Vice-Chancellor's realm. They waited. Eventually, a woman in a black trouser suit with gold-rimmed half glasses appeared and opened the door slightly.

'We are here to see the Vice-Chancellor,' said Grace. 'We are from Cheshire Police.'

The door opened fully and the woman, announcing herself as Jaclyn Walker, set off beckoning them to follow. The strength of the door closers caught Drake out and embarrassingly the door closed in his face. Soon the woman appeared again looking as if this had never happened before. Drake thought possibly that it hadn't. Grace and Drake were soon sat skimming through copies of Country Life Magazine, patiently waiting for the man himself to appear. The best part of a quarter of an hour passed before a tall, extremely slender man in a pinstripe suit appeared. Jaclyn Walker rushed across to help the struggling Drake out of his chair. She simultaneously announced that they should meet Professor Alec Sunderland.

'Sorry I'm running a tad late,' he said. 'My life is all meetings and academics always have a lot to say.' Drake let out a tiny laugh and followed Grace into the VC's office. Here leather was everywhere. The chairs and even the top of the polished hardwood desk were all in deep green shiny leather. There were remarkably few books but the walls were decorated with a plethora of somewhat conventional and rather dull landscapes. Drake studied the nearest one, trying with some difficulty to detect clues about where it was or who it was by.

'I see you like my paintings,' said the VC. I've been doing them for years now. It keeps me sane in what is otherwise a rather stressful job these days. The students are more commercially minded now and demand unreasonable quality while HMG tries to reduce our budgets on an annual basis. Sooner or later the concept of a modern university like this will become unsustainable. Anyway, I fight on! Now, how can I be of assistance?'

'We are sorry to interrupt your battle,' said Drake. The irony in his voice seemed to be missed by Professor Sunderland 'As you may have heard, the new concert hall in the city held a gala opening concert last week…'

'Yes. Of course, I had an invitation but I was just too busy to go,' said the VC firmly.

'At that concert,' continued Drake, 'the soloist, Evinka Whyte sadly died in somewhat mysterious circumstances.'

'Yes, yes, awful, terrible,' said the VC. She was a visiting Professor here you know. I recruited her. I thought it might pep things up a bit in the music department but I was too ambitious. I kept in touch with her. Lovely person and so talented but she kept telling me of the problems there. I suppose I'll have to find another approach to the problem now. It couldn't have come at a more inconvenient time' He fell silent but made a note on a sheet of paper sitting all by itself on the leather blotter on his desk. 'Yes, I must have another look at music.'

'Well we are investigating this unexplained death,' said Drake. 'Since we believe that you knew Miss Whyte, you might be able to help us.'

'I'm not sure that I can, but perhaps if you asked me some questions that I could answer we might make some progress.'

'I believe that you got to know Evinka Whyte socially a little.'

'Yes. She and I had dinner every couple of months or so, whenever she was in Chester. I think she enjoyed seeing the running of a university first hand. She was a great dinner guest. My wife loved having her to come over to the lodge.'

'Did she ever mention any difficulties in her life or people that gave her concerns?' asked Drake. 'Perhaps just general remarks that in the light of recent events might trigger some ideas.'

'I think she had her battles in life like all of us but I don't remember anything more than that. She was quite secretive about her personal life. She did once tell me a bit about how she and her twin brother were brought out of communist Czechoslovakia when they were very young. She mentioned her father. She was devoted to him. He had taken mortal risks in getting the family out. It's hard to believe now. She goes back to Prague now quite a lot but her father still has a fear of the state there. I think though that he might be rather old and demented. I think there is some long-running feud with several other families who wrongly believe that her father gave their ancestors away in exchange for his escape. Evinka was certain that wasn't true.' The VC sat and thought for a moment. 'She did occasionally mention her sister, I can't remember the name now.'

'Renata Kubicek,' said Grace.

'Yes. That's it, Renata. On Evinka's recommendation, we appointed her to a visiting chair too. She is a music historian but in recent times Evinka said they had an argument and it was difficult for her to have Renata involved. We wouldn't have dismissed Evinka, so Renata had to go. I think she was a bit sore about it. Came to see me and complained. She was quite a tricky sort of person, awfully PC. Demanded to know on what grounds she had been sacked. I just told her, she wasn't sacked, but that we just didn't have the money to renew her contract. I found her rather abrasive and was quite glad we had got rid of her. I only really appointed her to keep Evinka happy anyway. We had hoped she would publish a high profile biography of their great grandfather Josef Kubicek but she seemed to be taking forever to finish it. Shame it would have given us quite a boost but there it is.'

'Well thanks for that,' said Drake.

'There is one more thought,' said Professor Sunderland 'Her other problem was here. She had a terrible time with Dr Weeks, who is head of department. She can be really awkward that woman. I think she hated Evinka. We have all sorts of problems with her but unfortunately, there doesn't seem to be anyone else in the department who could replace her as head. Her research is really slow and she publishes in the wrong places. She tries to dress her research up as sociology but she isn't awfully good at that. I think the staff like her and I've never really understood why.'

'Tell me, Vice-Chancellor,' said Drake in his most innocent voice. 'Does she cooperate with people in your sociology department?'

'Well that's her other problem,' said the VC. 'She is in some sort of liaison with a character in that department who is a real troublemaker. I have problems with him endlessly. Nothing I do is ever right with the man. He always finds fault. I've only got to issue a memorandum of some sort to staff in general and he takes great delight in taking it apart and accusing me of chauvinism or even racism. Somehow he got onto Senate. He'll always stand up there and complain about some aspect of university policy. He calls himself a post-modern anarchist.'

'I think we might have seen him,' said Drake. 'What is his name?'

'Peter Sostre. Dr Peter Sostre. Even his PhD examiner had trouble with him.'

'Does he by any chance take part in protests and demonstrations?' asked Drake.

'Oh yes, anything like that. He loves it. He'll travel miles just to shout at some poor blighter over something. Talking of Senate, we had trouble with him over Evinka's appointment. He got up in Senate and claimed she was bringing the university into disrepute because she was just a populist performer with no intellectual programme. Dr Weeks and Dr Sostre have written papers together. I tried reading one once. I understood all the words but not many of the sentences. I hate to have to say it but I could well believe he might kill somebody. He believes in the right to violent protest.'

'The VC doesn't like Dr Laura Weeks much, does he,' muttered Drake as they got back into the Range Rover. 'I think we need to track down Dr Peter Sostre. I have an inkling that he might be your favourite masked man.' Drake laughed to himself. Grace was busy negotiating some heavy traffic. 'You might try getting hold of his address from the VC's office and setting up a tracking.' Drake started writing in his notebook and they drove in silence until Grace's phone announced itself with a bright and insistent ping as it sat nonchalantly on the central console.

'Have a look, sir,' said Grace. Drake picked up the phone at the very moment the screen chose to fade. After several abortive attempts at understanding Grace's passcode, Drake managed to get the message on the screen.

'Oh this is turning into an excellent day,' he said.

'Message from Tom Denson. They are just about to receive a visitor at the station. It is none other than Jelena Novakova, Evinka's PA. She was detained at Manchester Airport after arriving on a plane from Prague.'

22

'Miss Novakova,' said Drake as he and Grace entered the interview room. 'We have been looking for you everywhere.'

'I went to Prague for a few days. My mother is not well. When I was there I heard on the television that Evinka Whyte had died at the concert. The news said she might have been murdered. Whatever has happened?'

'Why did you leave the concert so quickly?' demanded Drake.

'It was getting late for my flight. Evinka had promised to let me go earlier but then she needed me there.'

'Why did she need you?' demanded Drake. Jelena shuffled in her seat, reached for a handbag, pulled out a handkerchief and dabbed her eyes. Grace noticed the handbag was Gucci and probably worth several thousands of pounds. She was taking in this new character. Jelena spoke with no accent and perfect English. She was immaculately dressed but in a rather ordinary sort of way. Even across the room, Grace could smell her perfume. Grace was building an impression of a confident person used to high society but also happy taking a back seat.

'She always needed me just before a concert,' said Jelena. 'It was one of my duties.'

'What other duties did you have?' asked Drake.

'I helped with organizing concerts. Evinka could be terribly particular about that. A few concerts are organized quickly like her previous one in Milan but most take months and often, years. This Chester concert started to be planned a couple of years ago. George Marshall must have come to the house at least four or five times, probably more. Evinka seemed to like him and often told me about her interesting conversations with him. Evinka thought he might be a useful contact. He seems to have had a really interesting career and deserves a better job than he's got now. So Evinka met with him and handled most of the organization in the gala concert but I don't know how she let him invite Itzhak Stransky as conductor!'

'Why not?' prompted Drake.

'The two families, Kubicek and Stransky don't like each other much. Evinka told me she even argued with him after rehearsal.'

'Perhaps you could explain the whole process of you going to a concert?' asked Drake. 'Do I take it that there was a fairly standard procedure?'

'Oh yes,' said Jelena. 'We always followed precisely the same process.'

'Which was?'

'We would normally get a cab to the concert hall. Evinka would carry her instrument bag with two flutes, just in case one got damaged. Usually, they were OK but occasionally a pad would stick and Evinka would lose confidence so we would change instruments. We always carried two Nagaharas. I would carry a small case with her concert performance dress, makeup and so on. I also had my own case. Evinka was extremely superstitious and we always had to carry the same bags. She once bought me this Gucci handbag, duty-free in Singapore. I had to carry the most important items in it every time.'

'We understand you both checked in at the concert hall,' said Drake. 'What happened after that?'

'Evinka had rehearsals with the orchestra. She did a small amount of preliminary warming up first and then Itzhak Stransky called for her.'

'What did you do while she was rehearsing?'

'I usually go and sit, just in case Evinka needs something.'

'How long was rehearsal?'

'About twice as long as usual with such concerts. Amazingly, she had agreed to do two concertos. The second one with harp took more rehearsing to be sure everyone knew how it would work.'

'What happened then?'

'We went back to her room and got things ready for the concert. They had given her a warm-up room next door and she went in there and played through parts of both concerti. I got a light meal ready. In such cases, we always take our own food so that Evinka knows what she is eating. You can't afford to have the wrong food before performing on a wind instrument. We had a salad and orange juice. Evinka went out for a bit of a walk. She wanted to see what the concert hall looked like from the riverside.'

'So surely your job was done by then?' asked Drake. 'You could have left then to get your plane surely?'

'Evinka likes some company before a performance.'

'How long have you had this job?'

'About ten years now.'

'What did you do before that?'

'I tried to make my own way in music but I wasn't good enough. Then I trained as a nurse.'

'So how did you meet Evinka Whyte?' asked Drake.

'I've known her since childhood. I was brought out of communist Czechoslovakia with her sister Renata. Nearly all those children have kept in touch.'

'So you were a nurse before working for Evinka,' said Drake. 'So you would know how to give someone an injection?'

'Why do you ask that?'

'You were giving Evinka Whyte regular injections weren't you?' Jelena Novakova sat silently looking at her hands resting on the table.

'No comment.'

'What were they for?'

'No comment.'

'Why have you suddenly clammed up?' asked Drake. 'Are you worried that what you did was wrong in some way?'

'No.'

'Are you worried that this one went wrong and killed Evinka Whyte?'

'No that's not possible,' snapped Jelena.

'So what was it that you injected her with?'

'I can't say. I don't know.'

'So you did give her injections?' demanded Drake. 'All we are debating now is what was in them. Is that correct?'

'Evinka made me swear never to talk about it.'

'Evinka Whyte is dead now,' said Drake.

'Yes, but she has a reputation.'

'This conversation of ours is hardly public. We need to know what happened to Evinka Whyte before the concert.' Jelena sat quietly looking more assured.

'Did you kill Evinka Whyte, Jelena?' asked Drake softly.

'No, of course not.'

'As far as we know, you were the last person to see her alive. We need you to answer these questions. Something went wrong didn't it? Something went wrong and you gathered up your things and dashed out.'

'No. That's not true. She was fine when I left.'

'Maybe now it's time to think about your reputation rather than Evinka's,' said Drake. 'You could be facing a charge of murder.' Drake paused and got up. He walked slowly around the room and sat down again. 'So the last thing that happened to Evinka was that you injected her. Was she a drug addict of some kind?'

'No. At least I don't think so. I don't know.'

'So she might be. Is that what you are saying?' demanded Drake. Jelena shook her head and started to sob. 'OK we will leave you now and I'll organize a cup of tea.' Drake got up and signalled to Grace to leave the room. They walked down the corridor exchanging thoughts. 'I think we are near the truth in some ways,' said Drake.

'She is on the edge of telling us something,' said Grace.

'Perhaps a softer approach from you might do the trick,' said Drake. Grace went off to get a cup of tea. Drake paced haltingly up and down the corridor pondering the situation.

Grace entered the interview room with two cups of hot tea, putting one on the table where Jelena Novakova had been sitting.

She was now standing behind the table and stretching. She was of medium build and height with fair, almost blond, hair cut in a collarbone length bob.

'We couldn't find any keys on Evinka Whyte,' said Grace. 'How would she have got back into the house?'

'I always carried a set of keys,' answered Jelena, sitting down again. 'She couldn't take them on stage and didn't like leaving them in the room. She was always conscious of security. Actually, she was rather obsessive about it.'

'Have you still got those keys?'

'Yes.'

'So you can get back into the house?'

'Yes, I have a room there,' said Jelena.

'Can you produce those keys now please?' asked Grace.

Jelena fumbled around in her Gucci bag and pulled out a sizeable ring of keys that she put on the table. Grace picked them up and flicked them across her fingers one at a time.

'I recognize the house keys,' said Grace. 'We have of course been there. This is obviously a car key. We haven't seen Evinka's car. Where is it kept?'

'It's in a lockup just down the road. I go and fetch it when Evinka needs it. She didn't use it much. It's a real problem because Evinka is away so much the battery is always going flat, so she often uses taxis.'

'So this small key here. Is that to open the lockup garage?' Jelena nodded her head. 'And would this be the key to the car?' Jelena nodded again. 'What number is the lockup? I've seen where you mean and there is a whole row of garages.'

'It's number 4,' said Jelena in little more than a whisper.'

'Tell me Jelena. What is this large key for?'

'I've forgotten,' snapped Jelena, recovering her composure.

'Is it by any chance for the safe in the music room?' Jelena sat motionless for a while and eventually gave a single short nod of her head.

'What will we find in the safe Jelena?' asked Grace quietly.

'I can't remember.'

'Look,' said Grace. 'Obviously, we are going to the house and will open the safe. You might as well tell us now to save you having to sit here waiting for us to return.' Jelena sat silently looking down at the table. Drake came back into the room having watched the CCTV next door. He sat down next to Grace at the table. Jelena Novakova took a deep breath and began talking.

'For a number of years, I think it must be about five, Evinka Whyte has suffered from increasingly bad nerves. I suppose you would call it stage fright. She was friendly with a man called Bohdan Pelech. He started a company called No More Nerves in Prague who were selling what he claimed was a cure. We knew him because he was one of a group of Czech children who were secretly evacuated from communist Prague. That is how I came here along with Evinka's sister Renata. The three of us got out together. Bohdan had gone back to Prague in later years and started a company making this stuff. Evinka had always kept in touch and so she brought some back from one of her many visits to Prague. We have been using it ever since.' Jelena paused and shook herself as if a huge weight had just left her shoulders.

'She recruited me partly because I could give injections as well as helping her with musical matters. I give her an injection a couple of hours before a live concert. She has become entirely dependent on it. I don't know what is in it and strictly speaking, I feel I shouldn't be giving injections without knowing what they are and I'm not sure they do her any good.'

'So why continue to give her the injections?'

'I suggested that we stopped and she said she would sack me. So my only alternative was to lose my job and I love this job and working with Evinka. It brought me as close to music-making as I have ever been.'

'So you gave her one of these injections before the concert?' asked Drake.

'Yes. I've been frightened that there is something that she shouldn't be taking.'

'So you think that might have killed her?' asked Drake.

'I don't know what to think. Maybe eighteen months ago the NmN company moved to Switzerland and brought out a new version and I think there has been a change in her since. I don't know why. She gets more edgy and cross with me. I have been worried that her playing is not what it was. Some critics have noticed. Part of her anxiety is the worry that she might get to a concert and not have any ampoules to inject so she had accumulated quite a lot. She usually prefers to take the earlier version but sometimes she insists on one of the new ones. That happened at the concert. When I went back to Prague I stayed in the Kubicek family house. Some years ago, Evinka gave me a key and said I could always stay there. Apparently, Bohdan was in some difficulty at one stage and couldn't afford to pay for his laboratory. Evinka was worried he might stop making NmN and let him have the top floor of the family house. When I was at the house, I went up there. It was like some movie laboratory almost like Frankenstein. Then Bohdan arrived one day. I demanded that he tell me what was in these injections. Bohdan just got nasty and told me it wasn't any of my business. He demanded to know what I had seen on his floor. I had no idea what I'd seen. I couldn't understand it. I thought I knew him but he had changed. I left the house right away and stayed with a friend.'

'Where did Evinka Whyte keep all these accumulated ampoules?'

'In the safe.'

'So,' said Drake. 'Let us be absolutely clear. You gave her one of the new injections several hours before the concert.'

'Yes,' said Jelena. She collapsed sobbing. 'I have been so frightened,' she said between gasps. 'I didn't know what to do.'

'Jelena,' said Drake firmly. 'I'm afraid we need you to stay here in Chester for a while. I am taking possession of these keys. Where were you intending to live now?'

'My home is in Evinka Whyte's house. I will go there.'

'I'm afraid not,' said Drake. 'The house is still under investigation. It is a potential crime scene.'

'I have a couple of friends who might put me up for a few days,' said Jelena.

'Are they in Chester?' asked Drake, Jelena nodded.

'That's fine. Please let Grace have the addresses and your phone number. Then let Grace know where exactly you are staying.'

Drake and Grace arrived at Evinka Whyte's house and made their way to the music room. Grace put on her rubber gloves and offered up the key to the safe. It turned with a satisfying clunk. The door swung open. Inside there were three shelves. Grace instantly recognized the cardboard trays that she had seen in Zurich. She counted six trays on the bottom shelf and five more on the middle shelf. Grace pulled one out from the bottom shelf. It had a small label on it saying NmN. Those on the middle shelf had the characters "v2" printed under this name. The top shelf was empty save for a small USB memory drive.

'Right,' said Drake. 'Get the memory drive to Dave to see if he can decipher whatever is stored on there. Tell the locksmith we've opened the safe and get two vials, one from the middle and one from the bottom shelf to toxicology. We might be making some progress here.'

23

'Thank you for coming in,' said Drake as he entered the interview room where Roger Gayford was waiting. 'We understand from Laura Weeks that you worked quite closely with Evinka Whyte at the university but I didn't want to embarrass you by having a couple of police officers arriving at your office.'

'It's not a problem at all,' said Roger Gayford. 'I'm happy and willing to help in any way that I can. It's just awful what has happened. None of us can quite believe it. She was a lovely person to work with and I found it a privilege.'

'So what form did your collaboration take?' asked Drake.

'Well, she did some master-classes for us to start with. We have just a few students who play the flute and she began with them. Typically they would choose a piece to learn and work up. They would then usually play it for Evinka with an audience of interested students. Sometimes she would let them play all of it. Other times she would stop them at various points. She would then show them by playing herself and suggest some improvements. Sometimes these would be of a technical nature, perhaps how to attack a certain note and how to maintain tonality. This is a problem on the flute. It doesn't necessarily play perfectly in tune through all its registers. The player has to make subtle changes in their embouchure. In simple terms that is how they form the shape of their mouth. I learned quite a lot about the flute myself. It is a curious instrument in that the player does not put it into their mouth or even actually blow into it. They blow across the opening in the mouthpiece. She was full of clever technical advice about all that. Mostly, she would discuss matters of musicality, for example, how to phrase a section, use dynamics and so on. The students were so keen on these classes that she extended them to other woodwind instruments, clarinet and saxophone, oboe and bassoon. Although she didn't claim to be an expert on these other instruments, she could play the single reed ones like clarinet and sax. But in these cases, she mainly concentrated on musical interpretation. She was particularly good at advising on how the composer would have expected their work to be played depending on the history of their period and so on.'

'Oh,' said Drake. 'That is so interesting. I wish I could play an instrument.'

'It's never too late to take it up,' said Roger Gayford. 'There is now good evidence that learning and playing an instrument can have health benefits. Especially, it is thought that this can help to stave off dementia. It requires every department of the brain to play. It's a good hobby to have.'

'Yes, perhaps I'll try to learn,' said Drake, laughing. 'But I think it is probably too late to teach this old dog new tricks.'

'There was another thing Evinka did with me,' said Roger Gayford. 'We developed a series of talks and exercises to help with the psychology of performing. I'm not sure that I should tell you this but Evinka had suffered badly from performance nerves so she was full of advice on how to deal with that.'

'That all helps to give us a better feeling for her work at the university,' said Drake. 'We understand that perhaps she didn't get on terribly well with your head of department.'

'Oh dear, no. They just didn't hit it off,' said Roger Gayford. 'I think Laura was a bit upset by the VC just imposing Evinka on our budget when we are quite short of resource in other areas. Laura is a great head of the department and takes all her duties seriously. I think she was quite offended.'

'Understandable,' said Grace.

'I think there is another problem too,' said Roger Gayford. 'People who make their living from playing like Evinka probably studied at a conservatoire and don't quite understand what a university school of music is trying to do. We also teach composition, advanced theory, the psychology of music, history. I could go on. Evinka was a bit dismissive of all that.'

'Thank you Mr Gayford,' said Drake. 'That has been helpful as well as interesting. Is there anything else you could tell us?' Roger Gayford sat for a moment and then shook his head. Then he spoke again.

'Actually, there is something but it's not easy and I don't know if it's at all important.'

'Go ahead,' said Drake. 'Sometimes things that seem unimportant in an investigation turn out to be central.'

'Well, it's to do with a man called Peter Sostre. He's in sociology and, as it happens is Laura's partner. They seem quite close these days.' Roger Gayford paused. 'Peter has campaigned unrelentingly to have Evinka's contract terminated. He stood up in senate and gave a long and complicated argument as to why Evinka was just a pop musician with no intellectual background. He was even nastier about Evinka's sister Renata. He called her an amateur historian and a musician who couldn't even play. Everyone thinks that it is all because of his relationship with Laura. It's rather difficult and sensitive in the department.'

'We have heard a bit about him already,' said Drake.

'What I have to tell you is certainly highly confidential and probably I shouldn't know at all.' There was another long pause. Roger Gayford took a deep breath. 'My brother, Simon, is in the computing department. They look after all our computers, the university network and so on. A big part of what they do involves keeping our network safe from hackers and malicious cyber attacks of all kinds. That is quite a big job these days.' Roger Gayford paused again. 'Well a couple of months ago, Simon had to work on Peter Sostre's computer. It had got infected with some awful virus and was almost unusable. Eventually, Simon managed to fix it without losing Peter's data. The silly man had not been backing it up so was in a real mess. In doing his work, Simon found Tor and Torch on Peter's computer and then uncovered a lot of evidence that it had been used to search for all sorts of illegal things. They included illegal drugs and cyber theft. He'd apparently been using BlackBook. I'm afraid I don't totally understand all these things but Simon says they are all really dodgy if not illegal. Simon didn't know what to do. It is of course, against the rules to use university computers or our network for such things. He really should have told someone. However, we both know that Peter Sostre is out of favour with the VC and other university bigwigs so there's a real possibility he could get dismissed. So in the end, he just warned Peter Sostre and told him to take these illegal tools off his computer and that if it was found that he was accessing the dark web from the university network he would have to report him.'

'So what did Peter Sostre say about all this?' asked Drake. 'Well, he didn't try to deny it, in fact, the opposite. He attacked my brother for being part of the corrupt establishment and how the dark web is the Internet of the people. He has a lot of views on modern society that one.'

'Ah Dave,' said Drake as he arrived back in the case room. 'I see you're still tapping away on that computer of yours.'

'Yes, sir,' said Dave. 'I've got some coursework to do on my cybercrime module for the course you sent me on.'

'Excellent,' said Drake. 'We've just had a really interesting talk to a man at the University of Deva. He starting saying things that we think could be quite important to the Evinka Whyte case. But he stopped speaking English so we need you to interpret. He was talking mainly about what he called the dark web. I've heard about it before and my instinct tells me it could be rather naughty.'

'Not necessarily, sir,' replied Dave. 'It isn't in itself illegal but a lot of what happens on it is.'

'Grace,' said Drake, 'tell Dave what else Mr Gayford said. It just goes in one ear and straight out of the other for me.' Grace opened her notebook and started to scan her latest pages.

'He talked about things called "Tor", "Torch", "BlackBook" and several other things. I'll read this more carefully.'

'Well,' said Dave, turning around and folding his arms in a rather important sort of way. 'The dark web is actually just part of the Internet. It consists of resources like the web sites you normally see when you use a browser like Internet Explorer or Safari.'

'Ok,' said Drake. 'I can follow that but it's rather disappointing.'

'That's because there's a lot more to it,' replied Dave.

'You know how you search the Internet with Safari on your iPad or computer?'

'Yes,' said Drake cautiously.

'Well, you remember that all the sites or domains as we call them have a postscript like ".com" or ".co.uk" and some other less common ones?'

'Yes, I'm with you still,' said Drake, 'but I've got my fingers crossed.'

'Well, for example, ".gov.uk" is used for all our government sites and so on.' Drake nodded. Well, the search engines like Google that you use to find those sites also know about all these subscripts. So the range of subscripts you can use is limited and our search engines trawl through all these sites continuously indexing them and creating a layer of information that they use when you do a search. But there is a whole bunch of other sites with a ".onion" subscript. Google won't search them and Internet Explorer and Safari won't display them. You have to use a special browser and that is what "Tor" is. This is what's called the dark web because our everyday tools won't shed any light on it. It's there all the time but we just can't see it. To search this stuff you need to use Tor instead of Safari and a special search engine. One of the most used is called "Torch" and "BlackBook" is a bit like an equivalent to Facebook.'

'So what is the point of all this then,' asked Drake.

'Well one of the most significant uses of it is when people want to keep things secret,' said Dave. 'It's a bit like the black economy. So it attracts a great deal of crime. We have special police units dealing with it these days. Right here, I'm the best you've got.' Everybody laughed including Drake.

'Everything on the dark web is highly encrypted. There are many layers of it, which is why the files are called "onion" and they are difficult to disentangle. They also disguise their IP addresses. That was what Grace and I used to discover that the NmN web site is in Prague. You just can't do anything like that on the dark web. So it is almost impossible to know who is posting what. This is rather attractive to, say a drug dealer who can advertise and sell without the buyer ever knowing who they are. Of course, the seller also doesn't know who the buyer is with one exception. That is that almost all drugs sold in the dark web are then sent by ordinary mail. Often, people can use mailboxes to disguise themselves. It's a paradox that illegal drugs are bought and sold on the dark web and yet are sent in plain sight through the mail. The Met Cybercrime Unit chases all this stuff amongst other things. Incidentally, the secrecy is further compounded by the common use of Bitcoin and those transactions can also be anonymous. Nearly all the web sites use long complicated sequences of random letters and numbers making it extremely difficult to find things unless you know the name you are looking for.'

'So,' said Drake, 'are you telling me that someone like our Dr Sostre could buy illegal drugs this way?'

'Absolutely,' answered Dave. 'It's also the way people carry out other kinds of cybercrime like malware, Trojans and DDoS.'

'Hang on Dave,' said Drake. 'You've stopped talking English again.'

'DDoS means Distributed Denial of Service,' said Dave. 'It's when masses of other sites make a demand on say a commercial website so that it cannot take any more and thus appears to go offline. It's a simple tool of cyberwar. We can expect to see much more of that as time goes on. Some people argue that we no longer really need our armed forces and certainly not tanks and warships. They say nations will conduct a war on the Internet. Imagine what would happen if say the NHS web sites were put out of action. If you could put other government web sites out then it might do far more damage to a country than a conventional invasion. In theory, for example, you could bring the national grid down and the whole country would lose power. It's all more than naughty it's downright dangerous. Our cybercrime unit spends a lot of time tracking down organized crime on the dark web. The criminals can use BlackBook to communicate and organize events.'

'Oh dear,' said Drake. 'I knew about all this stuff but I didn't understand how it was done. It's the dark web that conceals things. So as well as organizing a protest demonstration at the concert hall, our friend Sostre could also buy drugs like Carfentanil. Grace, I think you need to track him down in the good old fashioned way and see if we can get the Met boys to help on the cyber side.'

24

Grace had dropped Drake by the river. He walked slowly under the Queen's suspension bridge along the Groves passing the concert hall to his left. He stopped to watch some swans being fed by a small boy who's mother held a loaf of sliced bread. He reflected on the parallel between these swans, a ballet dancer and Evinka Whyte. There must be some tricky crossword clues to be got out of that, he thought. All three shared an ability to look calm and graceful while behind the scenes, out of sight, they were actually working like the blazes. It was then that he saw someone waving frantically but otherwise sitting still at a riverside table outside The Moorings cafe. He looked around to see who they might be waving at. There was no obvious candidate. He walked on several paces until he realized it was Lucy. He quickened his pace as far as possible. Lucy was laughing.

'What are you smirking at?' demanded Drake as he reached the table puffing.

'You, Dad. You always look so funny when you try to run. You look as if you're going to fall forward because your legs can't keep up with your brain.'

'I'm sorry, I didn't recognize you at first,' he said 'but the crutch propped up against the table was a giveaway. Maybe I need to get some glasses. I'm getting old, Lucy. Things are starting to go wrong.'

'Don't be daft, Dad. You've always walked like that. If you like I'll do a barre class for you to stretch those leg muscles.'

'Do you know,' gasped Drake, slumping down onto the seat next to Lucy. 'I'm beginning to get an insight into the world of professional performance.' Lucy waved at a waitress to bring another cup for her father while he continued. 'Evinka Whyte was always happy, smiling and appeared to find playing no more difficult than breathing. We now know that was an illusion. I'm beginning to think that neither her talent nor her money really gave her contentment. I suppose it's the same for you is it?'

'Yes, in a way,' said Lucy thoughtfully. 'Even so, I'd like to bet she couldn't have given it up. It's a sort of drug. Maybe it's the adrenalin. I don't understand the science behind it but you do become addicted to it. It can be hard to give up.' Drake thought of asking her if that meant she was going to carry on dancing but then he remembered Grace's advice just to listen. So they both sat looking at the swans and drank their tea.

The following morning, Grace was sitting at her desk in the case room keeping an open line to the three cars following Dr Peter Sostre. For the last four days, he had left home in the early morning and gone straight to the university where he had stayed all day and then returned home. Grace was beginning to wonder if they were going to get anywhere by following him. PC Katie Lamb had broken the news that this morning he was headed out of town along Hoole Lane. Katie was currently the most forward car and she had taken delight in the fact that Sostre had one of the latest all-electric cars in an extremely shiny black finish.

There was so much traffic along Hoole Lane that Katie was worried she was going to lose her target. Then someone stepped onto a zebra crossing at the last moment and she had to jam on her brakes and wait. A lorry turned out of a side road to the left and caused her to lose sight of Sostre's car altogether. She was beginning to get just a touch anxious. She had been on the driving course covering following but this was no longer theory or practice, it was real life in all its messy complexity. Thankfully, the lorry stopped and she could safely overtake it. Then the car in front of her turned right. She had to wait again but this time, the road cleared and she saw the black electric car straight ahead.

'Hang on guys,' said Katie. 'I'm pretty sure he's going to take the M53 at the next roundabout. It might be easier to swap over then.'

'OK,' said PC Redvers. 'I'll come right up behind you as soon as I can.'

'OK got him,' said PC Redvers. The question is are we taking the M56 at the next junction or are we going straight along the M53 to Ellesmere Port? OK, it's the M56 East and we are headed for Manchester.'

Grace resumed her task. Of course, Sostre could turn off the motorway earlier but Grace's instinct was telling her he was going to Manchester. So it would be at least half an hour before anything more happened. She turned back to reading Peter Sostre's papers that she downloaded from the Internet. It was pretty heavy going. Long words and complex sentences were the norm. On several occasions, Grace thought that what she was reading could easily be submitted to the Pseud's Corner of a well-known magazine she enjoyed every fortnight.

A howl from PC Redvers woke everyone up. 'He's leaving at the M6 junction. We're going around this complex set of roundabouts here. Maybe he's going to Birmingham. No, it's the services.'

'Oh, I know this. It's a weird place,' said PC Katie Lamb. 'Let's hold back here. The team parked up and kept apart as they walked in under a glazed roof. They passed between a coffee bar on their left and a convenience store to their right and arrived in a large brick courtyard. To their right were the toilets and washrooms. There was a weird sight indeed. Several full-sized wooden cowboys were assembled in the far side of the courtyard.

'Whatever are they all about?' asked Constable Redvers. 'I didn't know we were going to the wild-west.'

'They've been there for years,' said Katie. 'Actually, I think there used to be even more of them. I've got absolutely no idea why they are there.' Ahead, in the far right corner of the courtyard, was the entrance to a canteen type affair.

'I bet he's in there,' said Katie. 'I'll go in, give me a couple of minutes. She spotted their target at the far end, edging along the counter with a tray of cups and saucers. He paid at the desk and came back down to the entrance end of the canteen but on the other side away from where Katie had found a table. The clients were almost exclusively middle-aged men. She guessed they were mostly lorry drivers. Sostre had joined one other person at his table. Both soon had laptops out and were engaged in deep conversation. PC Redvers came in and was dispatched to fetch coffees. Just as he returned, a third member joined the table with Sostre and one other. He also pulled out a laptop and joined the animated conversation.

Katie was soon clicking away with the telephoto camera, waiting for each person to turn either full or half face. 'Should be good enough to get to the rogues' gallery with,' she said. After nearly an hour, their targets began to flip the lids of their laptops down. They carried out an enthusiastic high five gesture. Sostre sat back down and the other two left.

Forty-five minutes later, PC Katie Lamb arrived back in the case room and flopped down in front of Grace.

'I'm exhausted,' she said. 'That needs such concentration. I had no idea how tired I was going to feel. One car headed off along the M56 east towards Manchester and one went south down the M6. Sostre came back to Chester.'

'Job well done,' said Grace, looking at the pictures. I'm going to get these down to the Met and see what they make of it.' Drake looked up from his Times crossword.

'Well done Katie,' he said. 'Good effort. Next time we need a car chase I'll call for you.'

'I've been doing some research on our new friend Dr Peter Sostre,' said Grace. 'He's published a lot of papers in various places and they are full of grisly stuff. I can't understand a lot of it. It's all academic-speak to me. He makes a lot of reference to some

Russian character by name of Mikhail Bakunin. He was a nineteenth-century revolutionary anarchist. Most of what he says seems to be pretty extreme socialism to me. Given our interest in Prague. I was fascinated to see this Bakunin character was involved in the Czech rebellion of 1848 but got caught and sent back to Russia. Sostre doesn't believe in religion or political systems like democracy or even Marxism, though at times what he says feels like socialism. Sostre argues for collective anarchism. He believes in what he calls "liberty" and defines it as "the revolt of the individual against all divine, collective and individual authority" and he goes on a bit about all that. The most worrying thing is a paper in which he argues in favour of violent revolution. He says that the democratic system is one in which people choose between a series of ways in which the political body is given authority over them. This system cannot by definition be broken using democracy so anarchists claim a right to use violent insurrection.'

'Good grief,' said Drake. 'You've been back to school.'

'Not the sort of stuff I learned at school,' laughed Grace.

'So do you think Sostre is dangerous?'

'Difficult to say but he could easily seem attractive to younger followers who see themselves as disadvantaged in society. I think the latest protest is an example. What we've seen is a group of pretty young minds bent to believe in his stuff and in the end, he exploits them to do the dirty work and cleverly escapes. The Met boys actually have some stuff on him and keep a wary eye out for him. They say his favourite trick is to latch onto an innocent protest of some kind and then bring in his followers to take over and distort the original objectives of the protest.'

'Well that seems to be exactly what we've seen here.' grunted Drake.

'The Met boys say he uses several aliases,' said Grace. 'But they say their new computerized face recognition system should pick him up at a demonstration.'

'I thought so,' said Drake. 'This mask business looks part of the scene but in reality, he needs to keep his face out of the game or it will get shut down rapidly. Grace, now we've got that set of keys from Jelena, perhaps you might go and look at the garage lockups and see if you can find Evinka's car? It's a long shot but it could contain something that might help us. Take Katie with you. She can drive it back to the station. Then our forensic boys can crawl all over it.'

For once, Grace was sitting in the passenger seat. She gave Katie instructions on how to get to Evinka Whyte's house.

'Yes I know where it is,' said Katie. 'I think I can remember. We go round the inner ring road and out towards Boughton.'

Grace watched out of the window for a few minutes before opening her notebook. She looked up as Katie drove off the main road to the right. Two turns later, they were in front of a row of lockup garages.

'We want number four,' said Grace. Katie parked up immediately outside and they took the bunch of keys that Jelena Novakova had given them. Grace pointed to the small flat key and sure enough, it unlocked the garage door. Both police officers put on their disposable rubber gloves. With one substantial push on the top part of the door, it moved and Katie bent down to pick up the bottom and pulled it up. There inside was a rather posh sort of car; a German model in shiny silver. There was a notice in the rear window about some musicians' charity. Grace pointed to it.

'Looks like we've got the right one,' she said. Katie unlocked the rear door of the hatchback, pressed a button just under the window and the door swung sedately up. The boot was empty. There were no tools, no bags or umbrellas, just large empty open space. Grace stood staring at it as Katie edged down the garage to the right-hand side and opened the driver's door as far as it would go up against the wall of the garage. She sidled her way into the driving seat and pressed the start button. The dashboard lit up with a cheerful but refined ping and various needles dutifully moved into place on their dials. The mileage indicator was showing only 13,326 miles. The registration plate had indicated that it was three years old so this car had not had to work too hard. Katie waved Grace out of the way and pulled the automatic lever. It stuck momentarily and Katie gave it an extra shove. It ended up in drive and the car lurched forward. She hurriedly hit the footbrake and pushed the lever back into reverse. The car obliged by rolling silently out of the garage. Grace went round to the front. That was when she saw it.

'Come and look at this Katie,' she said. Now the car was out in the daylight, Katie was already pointing to the bonnet in front of her. She put it in neutral and joined Grace at the front. The nose of the bonnet was pushed right in. The nearside headlamp was hanging out on its cabling. The radiator grille was a complete mess with bits of trim hanging off all over the place. The front registration plate was trailing along the ground.

'Oh dear,' said Katie. 'I'm sure I didn't do all that.'

'No way,' said Grace. 'I would have heard it if you had. Anyway, just look at the damage. This vehicle has been in a major incident. It's a wonder it's capable of being driven.'

25

'This is beginning to come together,' said Grace as Drake flopped into his favourite chair with his freshly made coffee. Look I've got an email from the people in the Cybercrime Unit. They have identified Peter Sostre from Katie's pictures. They say he is known to them and is on a sort of watch list. They won't say why, of course. They also know the two characters that he met at the motorway services place. One comes from Birmingham and one from Manchester. Katie told me that one headed towards Manchester on the M56 and the other turned south onto the M6 so that all makes sense.'

'Hmmm,' grunted Drake. 'Our friend Sostre becomes more interesting at every twist and turn. So far we know now how he could have got some carfentanil from the dark web. He might have a motive in his argument with Evinka's appointment all waged because of his association with Laura Weeks. I wonder how much Laura knows about it all. She seemed genuinely upset at the appointment of Evinka but I didn't feel there was that much animosity, more frustration with the Vice-Chancellor. If Sostre did poison Evinka then he was being quite clever and thought he could cause a major collapse of the inaugural concert. If so he didn't reckon with Anders Hagen stepping in and, by all accounts, playing a blinder.'

'Well I've been trying to read some of his published papers,' said Grace. 'I think you might take a look. You might be able to understand them better.' Drake grunted and waved his arm dismissively. Grace continued. 'There's one paper actually about the dark web. He conducts an elaborate debate as to whether it is a genuine anarchistic concept or actually part of the established order.'

'Which argument wins?' asked Drake, finally sipping at his lukewarm coffee.

'He doesn't come to a conclusion, which might itself be an act of anarchy,' laughed Grace. 'But I think he accepts that it might be a new order but still a useful tool for anarchists.'

Drake laughed. 'Typically academic,' he said. 'If we get back to the meeting of anarchists at the motorway services, I've looked at Katie's pictures. They are obviously looking at each other's laptops. My guess is they are plotting another demonstration of some kind. Look, in this picture, one is pointing to his screen. I think Tom Denson's lot need to be on the lookout for trouble. I wonder if we should keep some sort of presence at the concert hall for now anyway.'

'OK,' said Grace but we've got some news for you about Evinka's car.'

'Ah,' said Drake. 'I thought there might be something useful in it.'

'No that's not it,' said Grace, nodding at Katie who had just come in. 'Why don't you tell him, Katie?'

'Yes sir, it's not what was inside the car. It's the car itself. It's in a terrible state. It's been in some sort of accident. The front is badly smashed up. It turned on all right but it looks like there's quite a lot of damage. I could possibly have driven it but we thought it better to bring it down on a low loader to avoid disturbing any possible evidence.' Drake tried to get out of his chair and made it at the second attempt. He set off prowling around his work boards.

'I guess you are thinking what I'm thinking,' he said. 'Was it the car that smashed into Dalibor Kubicek?'

'Exactly,' said Grace. 'If so, was it Jelena who was driving and what sense does that make?'

'Is it possible?' Drake asked and then went silent. 'Is it possible there was some awful dispute between Evinka and Dalibor? Did Jelena go to his house on some sort of revenge mission? She made a mess of his otherwise tidy house. He came back and tried to stop her but she ran him over.'

'Does she think that Dalibor killed his twin?' asked Grace slowly.

'But she claims to have flown to Prague on the night of the concert,' said Drake. 'Maybe she didn't after all, and that is some sort of attempt at an alibi. OK get onto Manchester Airport, check the airline and get them to look at the passenger list. Before we see Jelena again, I want to know if she was really on that flight. The other thing we need to do is to get Forensics down to look at the car. Prof Cooper may be able to tell if the damage is compatible with Dalibor's injuries. There may even be some shreds of clothing on it. Grace, one more thing. I've been looking back at our interview with Karel Whyte or Kubicek, whichever name you want to use. I'd like to talk it over with Renata. See if you can persuade her to come and meet us again at Evinka's house.'

Grace made notes of all her new tasks. She had just been checking the diary for the upcoming concerts at the new concert hall. Sure enough, the web site proudly announced the first in a series of evening concerts. It was to be the following evening and conducted by Itzhak Stransky.

'Look at this,' said Grace. 'Perhaps we can see both Itzhak Stransky and Anders Hagen tomorrow.'

'Good thinking,' said Drake. 'Last time, Stransky stayed at the Grosvenor Hotel. It's the best option and only a short walk down to the hall. Why don't you check with the hotel to see if he's arrived yet? I could go and see him there. Tomorrow he will be busy rehearsing.'

PC Katie Lamb dropped Drake by the Roman Amphitheatre. She watched him as he walked up St John Street to the far end where it opened onto Foregate Street. His usual hobbled gait seemed even more pronounced than usual. He had intended to climb up to the top of the City Walls and go that way but, she assumed, he thought better of it. Drake turned into Foregate Street and passed a couple of beggars sheltering under the overhanging upper storey of the black and white timbered building that abutted onto the great Eastgate. He paused for a moment and looked up at the clock. It not only told the time but also the year it was erected, 1897. It had watched down over millions of pedestrians since the street had been cobbled and pedestrianized. If only it had been able to record all that it would have been a hugely useful tool for the police. He passed the jewellers on his left and found himself at the Grosvenor Hotel. He had a soft spot for the old place having stayed there while on the Singapore affair. He stood and recalled the awful events at the end of the Singapore Case. How he wished that could have turned out differently. But his cases rarely finish as they begin. He stepped onto the black and white diamond paving under the entrance colonnade acknowledging the salute of the doorman in his smart grey-frocked coat, who greeted him like a long lost friend and opened the door wide.

'I have a meeting with Maestro Itzhak Stransky who is staying here,' he said to the receptionist. The manager has arranged for us to use the library.'

'Yes sir, Mr Stransky is already there with a tray of tea,' she said. Drake thanked her and turned into the library to see Stransky already seated. He was pouring over a music score. Drake wondered if he could hear the music in his head.'

'Drake,' said Stransky, rising and holding out his hand. Drake shook it and they both sat at the low coffee table. Stransky poured another cup of tea for Drake and one more for himself.

'Is that the score for the next concert?' asked Drake.

'Yes,' said Stransky it's an old copy that I've had for years. It has all my notes on it. I haven't conducted Brahms One for several years. It's a wonderful piece of work. You know he was so worried that he had been unduly influenced by Beethoven that he kept altering it for years before eventually allowing it to be played. Of course, he was so in awe of Beethoven that he had studied his works. Some people have unkindly called Brahms' first symphony Beethoven's tenth. I shall need quite a bit of rehearsing to get it the way I want it.'

'Do you actually hear the music when you read a score?' asked Drake.

'Good question,' replied Stransky. 'I suppose so in a way. But I am much more aware of the various parts and the instrumentation than one is when listening to a performance. It's a more analytic experience I suppose.'

'When we met after your previous concert,' said Drake, choosing a ginger nut biscuit from the tray of alternatives, 'you said that you had not seen Evinka Whyte between your rehearsal and the start of the concert.'

'Correct,' said Stransky. 'I left her in peace. At the start of the second half, I waited for the usher to bring her to the stage door. He came with the terrible news. I think he, first of all, said she wasn't well and had collapsed. This would have been bad enough. But to discover later that she was dead was a terrible shock.'

'You also told us that you had conducted her on at least two previous occasions. They were concerts in Prague, I think.'

'Correct again. I think they were at the Smetana Hall. It's a wonderfully florid building with beautiful acoustics. I love conducting there.' Drake made a note in his book and sat looking at it for a few seconds. He was anxious not to rush this.

'When you said that you hadn't seen her, that seemed a little odd to me. Your room and hers, are interconnected by a little practice room. It would have been easy to just tap on her door.'

'Yes, but I prefer to leave a performer to make any approach if they have anything else to discuss. We didn't. The rehearsal had gone well.'

'So did you by any chance see her outside?' Stransky sat silent for some time. Drake wondered what he was thinking. He was soon to discover.

'I see,' said Stransky. 'Someone has told you.'

'Told us what, Maestro?' asked Drake in his most innocent tone.

'Yes, we did meet accidentally outside on the way down to the river.'

'Why did you not tell us about this in your first interview,' asked Drake.

'I was trying not to complicate matters.'

'It seems an odd way to try to simplify things,' grunted Drake. He sat in silence waiting for Stransky to say something else. Eventually, he spoke again.

'I think a young woman from the orchestra passed us. I suppose she told you,' said Stransky. Drake kept quiet and motionless. He was sure Stransky would say more. He did.

'We were having a bit of an argument. It was silly. I thought it best not to tell you about it. It had no bearing on the awful events that followed.'

'Perhaps it would be best if I decided that,' said Drake. 'Perhaps you could tell me what the argument was about.'

'As I said, it was rather silly. We were arguing about her cadenzas.'

'Her cadenzas!'

'Yes,' said Stransky. 'They are passages where the orchestra stops and lets the soloist play some extemporized bars.'

'I know what a cadenza is,' growled Drake, 'but why would you argue about it?'

'It was silly of me. In reality, they are almost always written out. Mozart wrote cadenzas for all his piano concertos because he was a pianist and played them himself. He didn't play the flute so he left just an instruction in the score to devise a cadenza. There are some excellent ones for the flute concertos. Evinka had chosen the ones written by Emmanuel Pahud, which are quite good but, I feel, too long. I think they interrupt the flow of the music. I had suggested to her that she find some shorter ones. She reacted badly and accused me of interfering. I got a bit cross myself and so it developed. She was right really. It was silly of me.' He stopped and sipped his tea. Drake thought it was time to push things along a little.

'Are you sure that this was what you were arguing about?'

'Of course.'

'It sounds a silly sort of thing to get as heated as apparently you both did' said Drake.

'Yes. It was childish and silly,' said Stransky.

'I thought perhaps you were arguing about the feud between your families,' said Drake.

'I see,' said Stransky. You have been doing your research Inspector.'

'That's my job,' grunted Drake. 'It is your job to tell the truth.'

'I'm sorry about that. It was silly of me.'

'I'm struggling to believe you,' said Drake. 'From the description we had, it seemed much more serious than a silly squabble over a cadenza.'

'What you call the family feud is even more silly really,' said Stransky. 'It was all a long time ago and it has got blown up out of all proportions. I think neither of us knows what it was all about originally.'

'You say neither of us, so you have discussed the feud with Evinka Whyte?' demanded Drake. 'I put it to you that it got mentioned and you argued about it. The argument continued as you walked together back into the building and then into Evinka Whyte's dressing room. It got more heated and then somehow, perhaps accidentally, you killed her.'

'No.'

'Or perhaps you were so angry that you meant to kill her in a fit of temper. You went back to your room and brought her something to drink. You pretended that you were apologizing and it was best to drink to it. You had however laced her drink.'

'No that's just not true,' said Stransky angrily. 'We didn't even mention the feud this time.'

'You had discussed it previously then?'

'Well, yes,' replied Stransky slowly. 'As I have told you, we have played together before so it has come up naturally. We have both agreed not to talk about it any more.'

'These previous times you played together,' said Drake. 'Would they be the concerts you gave in the Smetana Hall in Prague?'

'Yes.'

'I put it to you that the disagreements had festered since then. Perhaps you came to this concert intending to kill her?' said Drake. 'Or perhaps you intended to drug Evinka Whyte to embarrass her. Perhaps she would play so badly that her reputation would be destroyed but you overdid the drug and she died more or less instantly.'

'No. This is nonsense. It is all a figment of your imagination,' said Stransky.

'I suggest that you might be trying to avoid complicating things again,' said Drake. He stood up and trying to do it suddenly, embarrassed himself by nearly falling. He saved himself with a hand on the table between them.

'Perhaps if you remember anything else, we could talk again after the next concert,' said Drake. 'I shall be there. I intend to enjoy your interpretation of Brahms. He turned and left. As he set off down Eastgate, Drake tried to assess what his provocation had achieved. Somehow, he felt, there was something still not out in the open about Stransky. He had not originally intended to go so far with his invented scenarios. He had allowed it to get slightly out of hand. However fantastic they seemed, perhaps they had not been so far from the mark. He would contact Professor Cooper again to see if there might be some other possible explanations for Evinka Whyte's death.

26

PC Katie Lamb was continuing her surveillance of Peter Sostre. In order not to give the game away, she had to park well away from his house in Egerton Road. At least his car, parked right outside his house, was instantly recognizable. At his usual time of eight-thirty, he emerged with a rucksack thrown over one shoulder. The bag went on the back seat and he set off. This was different. He was not going to the university, Katie's heart missed a beat. She needed to concentrate. They headed along Egerton Street over the humpback bridge on the canal, turned left onto St Oswalds Way and set off out of town. He took the Tarvin Road and before long was signalling left to go into the supermarket. Katie waited across the car park keeping his car in sight. About a quarter of an hour later, he emerged with his knapsack bulging, got in the car and drove back to Tarvin Road. They went further out of town and through Tarvin village. Then he braked almost urgently to take a left turn, which soon became little more than a country lane. It was a dead-end and there stood two houses. The first was clearly inhabited. The second, right at the end of the lane, was a rather dilapidated but quite sizeable house. A for sale sign outside was hanging half off its post. Sostre stopped right outside and grabbed the bag from his back seat and went round the side of the house out of Katie's line of vision. Katie turned around and drove back to almost the start of the lane, wound down her window and waited. They were several miles outside the city of Chester. There was an unmistakable smell of the countryside. Katie sat watching the birds squabbling in a nearby tree. About fifteen minutes later Sostre's car came past and turned right onto the main road. Katie followed him back into town.

Grace drove Drake up to Evinka's house again for a meeting she had managed to arrange with Renata Kubicek. They had only just entered the house when Renata appeared. Grace showed her down to the music room, where Drake was waiting.

'Renata,' thank you for agreeing to meet us here again,' said Drake as they entered. 'We have a couple of things that we may need your help on.' Renata nodded abruptly.

'After you gave us details, we went to visit your father, Karel Kubicek, at his care home. He is a lovely man but as you warned us, tragically struck down with dementia. However, he did play his violin for us and gave a charming rendition of Massenet's Meditation from Thais. It was quite moving.'

'Good gracious,' said Renata. 'I am so glad to hear that. I didn't know he had started to play again.' She pushed her hair off her face and dabbed her eyes.

'Indeed,' said Drake. 'As you warned us, he is now rather confused but one thing he said made me think. Do you remember telling us about the feud between the Kubicek and Stransky families?'

'Yes,' said Renata slowly. 'I do hope he didn't start talking about all that nonsense again,' she said. 'He was obsessed with it at one time but I thought he had forgotten about it all by now.'

'Well, he called the Stransky family "scallywags" and said they had tried to take his violin. Does any of that make any sense to you?'

'I'm afraid it does,' said Renata. 'He once had a lovely violin. When he played it, people would almost swoon. In his time he was a wonderful musician. But he hadn't played seriously for many years. By the time I was brought out of communist Czechoslovakia, my father had got a job as a history teacher. He always loved history, especially European history. He had stopped playing the violin professionally. It was all part of his lifelong fear of the Czech authorities finding him and dragging him back to the country of his birth. I call it that because it is now called the Czech

Republic and nothing like the old country. He thought that he was so well known as a violinist that if he gave performances here in England he would attract publicity and they would come for him. That may have been true when we all first arrived here but it hasn't been the case since what we call the Velvet Revolution in 1989. His mental health was so damaged by his earlier experiences, both of the escapes and the disappearance of our mother. I don't think he ever really recovered from all that. When we were small children, if we were lucky, he would sometimes get his violin out and play for us. Occasionally I would accompany him on the piano. He would make me swear not to tell anyone. Once we had all left home, I don't believe he ever played again.' Renata pulled out a handkerchief and dabbed her eyes.

'More recently, his mental health deteriorated and he couldn't really look after himself any more. I was in Australia, and Evinka was touring. Dalibor would have been absolutely terrible as a carer. So Evinka and Dalibor sold dad's house in Chester and they found this lovely care home for him. He has been there for several years now. I worry about how it is all paid for but Dalibor told me that Evinka has paid most of the fees for it. They only realized later when he had moved that they hadn't found his old violin. He would go on about it, which was odd because he hadn't played it for years. He was always accusing the Stranskys of stealing it. He used to get so upset and the staff in the care home had no idea what he was talking about. So I found an old second-hand instrument and bought it for him. I hoped that would stop him worrying. I hadn't expected him to actually start playing it. I think part of the problem is that I don't think he knows who I am. He certainly doesn't use my name. I suppose it is because I was away for such a long time in Australia. He still recognizes Evinka and Dalibor. I'm so glad that he has started to play again but it is a shame he was still worried about the old violin. There is nothing more I can do about that now.'

'Thank you, Renata,' said Drake. 'That clears that one up well enough for us, I think. Renata nodded and suddenly burst into tears. Grace got up and went round to comfort her.

'I'm sorry,' said Drake. 'I didn't realize we were upsetting you.'

'You were not to know,' Renata choked the words out one at a time in between sobs. Drake waited while she recovered herself.

'We were not to know what?' asked Grace.

'I had a call from the care home yesterday,' said Renata. 'My father died in the night. The doctor said it was a heart attack. I'm sorry it has just overwhelmed me. I'm the only one left now so I will have to organize everything. I feel a stranger here having lived mostly in Australia and Prague. I don't know what to do.'

'We have a really helpful document that tells you everything and it is a simple step by step guide,' said Grace. 'People have told us they find it a great help. I'll email you a copy right away.'

'Thank you,' said Renata. 'I've lost all my living relations and I feel so alone. I had got cross with Evinka about losing our father's violin. Then we argued about silly things. She died before we could make friends again. Of course, the violin is neither here nor there but he loved it and I think it somehow helped him to remember his past life. Neither Evinka nor Dalibor could see why it mattered to him. Now if you will excuse me, I have a plane to Prague I must catch.'

Back at the police station, the team met in the case room. Drake took control of the discussion. 'We've got a report back from forensics. They have managed to match threads found on the front of Evinka Whyte's car with clothes being worn by Dalibor Kubicek on the night of the hit and run. They say that there was a proliferation of clothing threads and that they could make matches with both his trousers and his jacket. So we need to know who was driving. From what we know so far, the most obvious candidate must be Evinka Whyte's assistant, Jelena Novakova. But was she even in the country?'

'We have the data back from the airport,' said Grace. 'She did indeed fly out to Prague late on the night of the concert as she claimed. However, she came back again before the day that

Dalibor was knocked over and killed. While the motive isn't entirely clear, I think we should bring her in.'

'Agreed,' said Drake. 'Do it straight away, Grace and get me the first flight you can to Prague. It has increasingly become important in this case. I wonder why?'

PC Katie Lamb arrived at the estate agents in Lower Bridge Street. She showed her ID and asked about the empty house. She was handed a flyer about it. It told her that the house had been empty for some time and was in need of much renovation. No price was fixed and offers were invited. An auction was originally fixed for this month but had now been delayed. The estate agent said that it would probably go to a builder for demolition and rebuilding. There was a delay caused by builders and developers wanting to get planning permission to construct several houses on the plot. The owner of the nearby house was objecting to any such development. Katie set off back to Tarvin with the keys.

Katie arrived back at the house that Peter Sostre had visited earlier. There was no car to be seen and she was fairly sure the coast was clear. She stopped right outside the house by the for sale sign. It was a short path through the small garden to the front door. The key opened it immediately, the door moved to be ajar but then stuck. It was badly in need of some oil and let her know this in no uncertain terms. Eventually, the door opened in installments and Katie was in the rather dingy hallway. She went down the passage beside the stairs to a large kitchen. It had a further door to the outside at the rear of the house. Her other key opened it. This must have been the door Sostre was using. She shut it and turned to explore further. That was when she saw all the provisions. On the counter beside the old-fashioned gas oven was a cardboard box and a large loaf of sliced bread. The box contained various tinned foods, a can opener, a jar of instant coffee and some tea bags. Lying on the counter alongside was a small collection of cutlery.

Katie stood back wondering who all this was intended for. She looked in the front and rear rooms, which were just an extremely dusty shambles. She negotiated the creaky staircase and checked out two bedrooms. They too had seen better times. She finally came to a third door. She pushed at it instinctively but almost immediately saw the padlock that was holding it firmly shut. It was then she realized that if this was the third bedroom, there was no bathroom. Katie retraced her steps back to the kitchen and then out into the rear overgrown garden. She looked up at the back of the house. There was clearly a bathroom with obscured glass in the window. Alongside that, another much larger window was obviously the third bedroom. It appeared to be boarded up from the inside.

It was then she realized that the padlocked door was across the upper landing and must have given onto both the bathroom and the third bedroom. Was this all meant as some sort of hideout? It wasn't until she got back in the car that it struck her. Why did she not see it before? She was cross with herself for being so slow. This was surely a place to imprison someone. Who and why?

As Katie walked back to her car, a man appeared in the front door of the nearby house.

'Can I help you?' he enquired.

'Maybe you can,' said Katie holding out her ID. 'We are interested in the man who has been visiting this house in the last few days.'

'Oh him. Yes, he's been here a lot. He's got the key from the estate agents and we think he copied it. He seems to go round to the rear entrance. Sometimes he comes with someone else and sometimes they spend several hours there.'

'This house has been empty for a long time I believe,' said Katie.

'Yes, many years. The problem is there has been a planning application to build houses on the field beyond. They want to demolish the house to create an entrance road.'

'Does that bother you?' asked Katie.

'Yes and no. We don't want to lose our privacy but we would quite like a few neighbours. Anyway, it would be better than this old ramshackle place. It lets the neighbourhood down. This chap who keeps coming, I'm sure the estate agents don't know about it. We think he must have copied the keys. I've tried phoning the agents but they don't seem interested. We think he's up to no good. Why would you want to keep coming to a place like this otherwise?'

27

Drake emerged from terminal one at Vaclav Havel airport and looked for the shuttle bus run by his hotel and quickly found not only the stop but also a bus already waiting. He clambered up the steps and dragged his overnight bag in behind him. As they set off, he looked back at the terminal building. It was about as ordinary as ordinary can be. He pondered the paradox that airports form gateways to so many cities and countries and yet so often look completely dull and uniform. In the case of a delightful historic and unique city like Prague, this seemed even more disappointing than usual. He was happy to be heading right into the centre of Prague. He pulled out his travel guide and started planning his visit. He needed to check up on the concerts Stransky had claimed to play here with Evinka. Something just did not seem quite right about those but he was not sure why. Stransky had tried to deceive them at every step of the way. Next, he wanted to see what Renata was doing over here. She had flown out straight after their most recent interview. She kept coming here and he wanted to know why. He had a job to do but he was also looking forward to seeing the architecture and culture of Prague. The twenty minutes it took to reach the hotel soon flew by. He let others queue down the centre of the bus to disembark and sat back in his seat wondering why so many people did this on buses and planes. As soon as the back of the queue passed his row, he clambered out of his seat and reached his bag off the overhead rack. The small woman in front of him was struggling and Drake used his great height to help her. He smiled smugly to himself. He may have had to sit with his knees pressed against the seat in front, but he could reach the luggage rack with ease. He was soon at the front of the bus, nodded his thanks to the driver and tumbled down the steps with his bag half a step in front of him.

The hotel looked more like it. It was quite a grand pile. Built throughout in buff fair-faced stone and with red banners hanging from upper floors, it was trying to look important and welcoming. It just about managed both. There were seven storeys with the top one built into an attic fronted by Dutch gables. Even more importantly, this was right next door to the best concert hall in Prague. Drake had his work schedule planned out for the next three days but he was also hoping to make good use of the evenings. Surely one could not come to Prague and fail to take in at least one concert.

After a quick stop in his room to unload his bag and freshen up, Drake was hunting for an evening meal. It felt as if the whole day had been wasted at airports and sitting in ridiculously cramped tin cans of one kind or another. He left the peaceful quiet of the hotel, to emerge in the middle of a wide-open cobbled piazza. Dotted around, there were sculptures, kiosks and umbrellas. Nearby, a bus carefully picked its way through the pedestrians. On the far side, a couple of old trams clanked their way along a busy route. Dodging the small amount of traffic, he crossed a street and found himself right in front of the Municipal House. This splendid arts nouveau building accommodated the main concert hall for the city. He scanned the posters but sadly there was no performance that evening. He checked his map and walked on for about five or six minutes before a couple of sharp turns down narrow pedestrian streets brought him into the old town square. Straight ahead was the astronomical clock about which his guidebook had waxed lyrical. It was indeed a fascinating edifice. It reached up through three storeys of a building that Drake thought was otherwise unremarkable. The clock was a different matter. The main dial, over a storey high, had circles within circles as well as multiple hands. It looked impossible to read without help from his guidebook. It showed him how it told the time in several zones as well as the positions of the sun, moon and stars. He was lucky, the hour was just chiming and two windows above the clock opened to reveal a parade of manikins representing the apostles. For some reason that Drake found hard to grasp, the assembled crowd started to applaud.

Drake retired to a nearby restaurant, ate a quick supper and watched the sun go down and the lights come on in the old town square. Drake was both charmed and refreshed but ready for his bed. He had a busy day to follow so he would turn in a little early. He reached the hotel in no more than ten minutes even at his slow pace. The old town was both beautiful and yet compact, a characteristic his ageing legs would appreciate.

The next morning, after indulging himself with rather too much breakfast, Drake had an appointment with the concert director of the Smetana Hall in the Municipal House.

'Chief Inspector Drake,' said the director, 'welcome to Smetana Hall. How can we help you?'

'Thank you,' said Drake. 'I'm researching concerts given here by Maestro Itzhak Stransky.'

'Of course, there are many. He is one of our most outstanding and loved conductors, though it is probably a year now since he last appeared here as he gets more international engagements. I have a register of all our performances and you can search through them on this computer.' Drake soon got the hang of the database and was busy scanning through concerts. Sadly there was no facility to search by performers, so Drake reluctantly accepted that his task would take some time. He would rather be out and about in this beautiful city but there it was. He settled down at the keyboard.

Stransky was a regular, often conducting the resident Prague Symphony orchestra. He was well known for his interpretations of the great Czech composers, Smetana of course and Dvorak as well as Josef Kubicek. Mozart also featured being an enthusiastic visitor to the city. Many of the concerts seemed directed at the tourists rather than local residents. Drake thought there must be a limit as to how many times even the most ardent Czech nationalist can listen to Ma Vlast.

'How are you doing?' asked the concert director, coming into the room where Drake was sitting at the computer. 'You have been here nearly all day!'

'I seem to have gone right through,' said Drake, 'and I think I went back far enough to find all Stransky's concerts. They are indeed numerous.'

'Yes he's very popular here, and the Prague Symphony are always willing to play Czech music for the tourists.'

'What I don't seem able to find,' said Drake, 'are any concerts where he has conducted the flautist Evinka Whyte.'

'Evinka Whyte,' said the director. 'She has certainly played here. You realize she is a descendent of our celebrated composer, Josef Kubicek?'

'Yes indeed,' said Drake. 'I have seen several of her concerts but none with Maestro Stransky.'

'It is extremely unlikely,' said the concert director. I'm pretty sure we have never had them both together while I've been director. It is possible that they appeared together before my time. You do understand that the Kubicek and Stransky families don't seem to like each other much. I can't imagine ever booking them together. It would be too inhibiting of artist collaboration. Is there any other way I can help?'

'No, I don't think so,' said Drake, 'and my eyes are going square, looking at this screen for so long.'

'Perhaps this will help,' said the concert director. 'It's a ticket for the concert tonight. It's not Czech music I'm afraid. It's all Beethoven and Brahms.' Drake nodded his appreciation and left holding the precious ticket. He grabbed a quick meal in his hotel and changed his shirt ready for the concert.

The interior of the hall itself was the height of European arts nouveau. Drake had never seen anything quite like it. There was a huge glazed dome over the centre of the space, which was mainly finished in stone and plaster. High above, where the circular opening of the dome met the square space below, there were murals, some of enormous proportions. Drake sat taking them all in and begging for Cynthia's voice to tell him how to describe these lavishly decorated curved surfaces. As if by magic and unusually cooperative, his brain dug out the architectural terms of pendentives and squinches. He remembered that, although they were both curved, one was sort of rectangular and one effectively triangular. He had to admit that, for the life of him, he had no idea which was which. He sat smugly for a while, casually browsing through the programme while congratulating himself on his growing architectural knowledge. He wondered if these words would ever be useful again in his life and concluded probably not. He watched the orchestra assembling on the three or four low steps of the platform. Behind them was space for a substantial choir and then a grand looking organ. Drake heard all of the Beethoven but snoozed off a couple of times during the Brahms. His brain kept interrupting the music as it wondered why Stransky had falsely claimed to have conducted Evinka Whyte in this splendid space. Brahms reached his conclusion and it was time for bed.

His job the next day was to tour the museums of Prague hoping he might discover where Renata worked. Drake thought she was an increasingly important figure in the investigation and he needed to understand what she did. She had definitely told him that she did curatorial work in some Prague museums. Perhaps that was where she was now. He made a reasonable guess that she must work for one of the musical museums so he would tour them first. He was not sure how he would handle the situation if he did find her. Yet again, he found himself in a foreign country and beyond his jurisdiction. This was always uncomfortable but there was no alternative but to play the situations as they occurred. He set off towards the town square, pleased that he could walk so easily around the centre of the city. He passed through the main square again and turned left along the river to the nearby Smetana Museum. It sat right on the bank of the Vltava looking up at Prague Castle on the hill growing out of the opposite bank. It was a rather stodgy block of a building with the topmost floor behind the now-familiar Prague version of the Dutch gable. In truth, he found the displays rather unimaginative and gave up pretty quickly. He asked at the counter if Renata Kubicek worked there. The receptionist asked her boss who emerged from his office.

'No,' he said, 'sadly not. Perhaps it might be Bertramka where he would find her.' He thanked them both and left. Secretly, he was glad to be going to Bertramka next rather than the Dvorak Museum as he had originally intended.

He sat on the bus that his guidebook told him would get him to Bertramka. This was some way out and much too far to walk. He spent the journey looking up the museum in his guidebook. The street names all seemed a bit of a mouthful but he just about managed to keep track of their progress and stepped off the bus at the correct place. A quick check of his map and he headed up a street with the promising name of Mozartova. It sloped gently up towards a large arched entrance with a pair of open gates. Almost immediately, he was in a friendly cobbled courtyard. There on his left was Bertramka. A pale cream stucco-covered lower floor housed a double staircase that led up to a colonnaded logia under a pink pantile roof. Trees dipped their lower branches down across the façade and the sun came dappling through. It was a charming scene. The building was puffing itself up architecturally to look more important than it was. His guidebook had told him that this was a house owned by a wealthy family in the era of Mozart. It seemed that he had come to stay several times and the claim was that he composed his opera, Don Giovanni, here. Drake climbed the stairs and was soon inside. There was a hushed silence. He moved slowly around the exhibits until he came to an early piano. Was it here that Mozart sat composing and playing? Drake felt the hair on the back of his neck stand out. It was an uncanny feeling suddenly to be so close to the genius that had created much of the music he loved. He reached out his right hand and touched the keyboard. On the one hand, he felt that he should not touch the exhibits but on the other, he just could not resist touching the keyboard that had trembled under Mozart's hands. Regaining control of himself he went to the counter and asked for Renata.

'I'm afraid you've just missed her,' said the receptionist. 'She was here a couple of days ago but had to go downtown to see someone about her work on the Josef Kubicek Museum.'

'Forgive me. I didn't know there was such a thing,' said Drake. The receptionist laughed.

'You are quite right,' she said. 'But there are plans to create one and Renata Kubicek is acting as their consultant.'

'Where will it be?' asked Drake.

'One idea is that it might be in the Kubicek house, which is still in the family's ownership. However, to begin with, it might be in the Municipal House. They might know more about it.'

'You mean where the Smetana Hall is?' asked Drake.

'Yes, of course.'

'Where is the family house?' asked Drake.

'Do you have a map in your guidebook?' Drake opened it up and held it out. The girl marked the location on his map and scribbled the address. It was just across the river from the old town square. He had time to go there before dinner.

Drake got off his bus just outside the old town square. He walked across and through the narrow streets that gave onto the famous Charles Bridge. He made his way under the arch of the tower that marked the end of the bridge. It was a busy sight. All along the pedestrianized bridge, people and statues mingled in his view. To his left was a weir and to his right, he could see a tourist boat reaching the end of its trip and turning back to the far bank. The sky was clear save for some wispy clouds. Ahead and to his right, he could see Prague Castle on its hill and reaching for the sky above it was St Vitus Cathedral. It was a perfect scene and, not surprisingly, there was an artist painting it. Pictures of it had appeared everywhere in tourist material and postcards. Drake stopped for a moment to inspect this view and pondered why it was so popular. He smiled to himself as he saw an interesting architectural phenomenon. As he moved his eyes upward, the buildings got larger and appeared more impressive. From the humble boathouse on the riverbank, he saw quite ordinary houses with more substantial ones above. His guidebook had told him that these would often be occupied by courtiers. Next came the castle, of course belonging to the Kings of Bohemia. Finally, at the very top was their God's house in St Vitus Cathedral. It was a sort of architectural model of Prague society. Drake smiled at his detection of this neat concept and set off again, soon reaching the end of Charles Bridge. Two towers marked this end with an arch spanning between. He duly passed under the arch and began the steady climb up towards the castle. The Kubicek family was well regarded by the Kings of Bohemia so they were important enough to have a house higher up on the hill.

Consulting his map, he took a left and then a right, walked a little further uphill and found the house marked on his map on a short dead-end street. It stood four storeys high right on the street. It was elegant and yet simple with little decoration. Drake took a deep breath and pressed the doorbell to the right side of a heavy solid, panelled door. He heard the bell ring somewhere deep inside the building but there was no reaction. He rang it again and stepped back into the empty street to look up at the high-level windows. He saw a figure move across one and disappear behind a curtain. He thought the figure was male but he could not be absolutely sure, so quickly did it vanish. He rang again to no effect. Whoever was inside the building did not intend to open the door. Tiring a little after the climb, he staggered dejectedly back to his hotel wondering if it was Renata Kubicek who was avoiding him in the family home. She had seemed quick to end her interview in Chester. Was she hiding something?

28

Drake arrived back in the old town square. Somehow he found himself drawn to the place. He thought it was time to relax He wandered around the square and took a couple of side streets before discovering what seemed to be a small opera house. A performance of Mozart's opera Don Giovanni was just beginning. He knew that the premiere was also played here in Prague so guessed they must know how to do it justice. It was not until he was inside that he discovered the theatre was tiny and half empty. He was about to go back to the ticket office when the lights dimmed and the curtain went up. It was a marionette theatre. The entire opera was performed by puppets acting to a recording played over giant loudspeakers. Soon Mozart himself made an entrance and appeared to conduct an orchestra painted below the stage. Drake was transported by the marvellous music as well as roaring with laughter at the occasionally comic capers of the puppets, especially Mozart who conducted a running dialogue with any member of the audience who dared to speak. Drake felt sure the real Mozart would have approved of this delightful performance.

The following morning, Drake woke suddenly. The shutters and curtains in his room left it in almost total darkness. He reached for his watch but succeeded only in knocking it off the bedside table. He shook off his bedclothes and groped his way across the room. Gradually his eyes were adapting and he felt for the curtain. It opened with a ceremonial sort of swish and he was temporarily blinded by the early morning sun. At last, he found his watch, which was warning him that he might soon be too late for breakfast. The day here was an hour ahead of the UK and although he did not feel jetlagged, his body was still running on British summertime.

Having had his indulgent breakfast, Drake emerged from the Kings Court Hotel, determined to explore more of Prague. He had originally intended to visit the Dvorak museum but that no longer seemed necessary. He would have a wander around the old town, have some lunch in the square and head back to the Municipal House. He was soon lost in the maze of narrow streets of the old town. At one point, it seemed as if every other shop was selling puppets of Mozart. He stood and looked at some in one shop and recalled how, when Tom and Lucy were children, he would almost certainly have bought them one each. Those days were long gone and he missed them even more since Cynthia died. He wandered further and found the most marvellous music shop. They sold every imaginable instrument and he entered out of curiosity. He was soon astonished by the price of good instruments. Many thousands of pounds were needed to buy a reasonable bassoon. Idly he shuffled over to look at flutes. Surely these would be cheaper. They weren't. An assistant asked if he needed help.

'Why are these flutes so expensive?' he asked.

'Ah, there is a good reason,' said the assistant. 'Cheaper flutes are just silver-plated but the better ones are made from solid silver. This one here has purer silver in it than any jewellery you would normally buy. Some are even gold. If you can't afford gold you might still get a silver one that has a gold riser.'

'Forgive me,' said Drake 'but what is the riser?'

'It's the tiny piece of tube that connects the lip plate to the main body, look here.' Drake peered into the instrument that the assistant had picked up and saw the glint of gold inside.

'I think if I was spending money on gold I would want it on the outside where it could be seen,' joked Drake.

'Ah but it's on the inside where it makes a difference to the sound,' said the assistant. 'We buy all these instruments from the makers and the cost of these pure silver flutes always changes with the value of silver on the international markets. Right now, the price of silver is low so it is an excellent time to buy one, sir.'

'Oh I wasn't thinking of actually buying one,' said Drake, 'though I have long wished I could play an instrument.'

'Well a reasonable student flute is quite cheap now, look here are a couple that we recommend.'

'Do you really think that I could learn to play at my age?' asked Drake. 'My daughter learned to play the flute when she was little. It sounded lovely but she was much younger.'

'Certainly, sir. There are well known medical benefits to learning an instrument. It is thought to be particularly good for older people. There are some excellent tutor books that I could recommend. Of course, once you've got going, it also really helps to go to a teacher.'

Half an hour later, Drake found his way back to his hotel carrying his new flute and three books, which he was assured, "would get him going." He nibbled hurriedly on a sandwich in the café off the lobby and was soon on his way again. He stepped onto the street that he had to cross to reach the Municipal House. Once inside, he made his way up to the concert director's office and tapped on the door.

'Hello, Chief Inspector,' said the director. 'I wasn't expecting you back again. How can I help you?'

'You referred yesterday to the feud between the Kubicek and Stransky families. Is it possible to explain this to me?'

'Not easily,' replied the director. 'I believe it goes back a long way and many generations before the current ones. We Czechs live in a complex country. In its current form it has only really existed since the so-called velvet revolution in our lifetime. However, long before this, our part of the country, Bohemia, was ruled over by a long line of Kings. We were then absorbed into the Austro-Hungarian Empire. Later, we had an unhappy period under communist rule and so on. Sometimes people found themselves on the other side of one of the many arguments about our country. I think this true for the Kubicek and Stransky families. Josef Kubicek, as our museum will show, became a favourite of Emperor Franz Josef when we were part of the Austro-Hungarian Empire. The Stransky family members were also well-known musicians and composers at that time and would have given performances of many of Kubicek's compositions. However, they were not supporters of the Emperor and were critical of the way he ruled Bohemia. Then the two families were briefly united by a marriage that ended in acrimony. The two families would describe this period of our history differently. The Stransky version held that the Kubiceks stole precious items during the marriage. I cannot describe it to you any more clearly as there are so many variations of the story.'

'Thank you,' said Drake. Talking of history, you mentioned that you might be working on the idea of opening a museum to Josef Kubicek here. Is that true?'

'It certainly is. Such a thing is long overdue. We have museums for Smetana and Dvorak but so far we have neglected Josef Kubicek. He was, of course, from the same era though a little later and every bit as important to us. Again, the feud raises its ugly head. I have already been lobbied by Itzhak Stransky who believes that his ancestors were every bit as worthy of a museum as the Kubiceks. At the very least he wants them celebrated in the Kubicek museum. That is nonsense of course.'

'Is it also true that Renata Kubicek is helping you?' asked Drake.

'It is indeed. She is a great help. Not only is she a good historian but she is preparing a biography of her illustrious ancestor so she has everything at her fingertips, as you might say.'

'I went up to the Kubicek family house yesterday because I thought she might be there. I believe you have plans to open the museum in that building.'

'Well that is less sure,' said the director. 'It is still owned by the family and there are three children involved. Renata has told us that there are other people there at the moment but she is hopeful they can find other accommodation eventually.'

'Sadly you might find your task has got a little easier,' said Drake. 'I'm afraid to say that both Evinka and Dalibor have died recently and in somewhat odd circumstances.'

'Really?' said the director. 'I'm astonished that we haven't heard about that. Renata was here only a couple of days ago and she didn't mention it.'

'That seems odd. I wonder why,' said Drake.

'Our current plans are to open a small museum in this building first of all,' said the director. 'A lot depends on just how much material we can get hold of. Renata is helping us to write the text of a series of display panels and she has a good range of early photographs. However, we have some extremely exciting possible acquisitions that Renata is investigating for us. She thinks she might be able to get some of Kubicek's original manuscripts. This would be remarkable as none of them has ever come to light. According to Renata, a couple appeared just recently at a well-known auction house in the UK and she was rather surprised and even a bit angry. She said that she would follow that up and see if they are still available. Of course, acquisition depends on funding but we have now also got a benefactor who wants to remain anonymous at this stage. I am very hopeful. I try not to let myself get too excited but it is a wonderful possibility.'

'I went to Bertramka yesterday,' said Drake. 'I felt the presence of Mozart there. It was a wonderful experience.'

'Oh well, be careful,' said the director. 'While it is almost certain that Mozart visited, there is some doubt about the extent to which he stayed. Some of the claims they make seem exaggerated, to say the least.'

'Really?' said Drake.

'We think it almost certain he visited not least because we are sure that he knew the owners of the house. The usual story is that he completed his opera, Don Giovanni, there. We know that it was completed in Prague and first performed at the Estates Theatre. He would have been much occupied by putting on this performance and he would likely have been at the opera house most days. Bertramka is well outside the old city walls and in those days getting from there to the opera house would not have been as easy as it is now.'

'Oh dear,' said Drake. 'I thought I was touching Mozart's' piano yesterday.'

'Don't worry,' said the director. 'It would seem likely that when Mozart visited Bertramka, he was asked to play. We must be careful with the Kubicek museum only to have accurate material backed by scholarly research. That is where Renata can help us so much. No one in the world knows more about Josef Kubicek than her. I should not tell you this but I am so excited that I will just make a few comments. Renata says the family may have some of Josef's belongings. We think that we can prove he wore some of the clothes still in the family house. Renata has hinted that she may be able to produce even more interesting items that belonged to him. At the moment she is trying to put her hands on these items, one of which would be extremely exciting. She tells me not to worry because she can find plenty of good things to exhibit. I should say no more. It will of course be quite a feather in my cap, do you say? I hope we can pull it off. Please however, do not say anything outside this building. I believe some deals have to be done and Renata does not want any publicity.'

Drake was preparing himself for an early night when his phone rang. It was Grace Hepple.'

'I'll try to be brief,' she said. 'Sorry to disturb you so late, I know you are an hour ahead of us over there. However, I have just got the chemical analysis back of the vials found in Evinka Whyte's safe. 'They have awfully long names so I'm going to text them to you. I'm told that there are three main components that seem harmless. However, the vial marked "v2" also contained a small amount of an opioid compound. My chemistry isn't good enough to tell you what all this means except that I suppose the addition of opium in the second version is possibly rather suspect and potentially illegal in this country and would probably result in some addiction.'

29

Drake had his now customary lavish breakfast before setting off from the Kings Court Hotel. He was headed for an appointment with his opposite number in the Prague City Police. They were due to meet at ten o'clock in the Old Town Police Station. Drake worked out a route that took him past his favourite music shop. Somehow he now felt as if he was a musician and he enjoyed window-shopping. His fondness for jazz was only bettered by his fondness for classical music. There was a window full of saxophones that caught his attention. He had not realized before just how many different sizes they came in. He had been told that the saxophone was a fairly simple instrument to learn but he was not so sure that he could manage to make the reed sound easily. He wasted ten minutes wandering around inside the shop, some of them scanning the sheet music for flute beginners. Several albums of easy versions of classical excerpts were soon in his possession before he set off again. He was headed for Rybna. It took another ten minutes of plodding along and enjoying the old buildings that often crowded in along the narrow streets. All of a sudden, there it was, a street called Rybna just as his map indicated. The police station was in a delightfully civilized building.

After checking in with the receptionist, he had only a couple of minutes to wait until a large and rather portly man with a small moustache partly obscuring a welcoming face appeared.

'I'm glad to meet you, Chief Inspector. I am Kapitan Alexej Havlik. I'm rather pleased that you have come. I think we may both be chasing the same fox. I was wanting only to communicate by telephone as we think they may be hacking into our computers. Please tell me what you know about them.'

'I sent you an email about a man called Bohdan Pelech,' said Drake. 'We believe he makes the substance that a murder victim was injecting. Otherwise, we don't know much about him. My sergeant went on a wild goose chase to Zurich since the only address we could find on their, almost blank, website was in the old town there. They obviously like historic quarters.'

'This would be the NmN website I presume?'

'Yes, that's right,' said Drake.

'We know of another website that points to it. Here let me show you.'

Drake peered over his host's shoulder at the desktop computer screen that flicked into life somewhat reluctantly.

'Forgive us. Our technology is rather old now,' said Alexej Havlik.

Eventually, the computer decided to cooperate and its screen showed a site named "Put an End to" in rather jazzy lettering. The site offered a variety of products all aimed at putting an end to some common problem. There was "An End to being Fat", and "An End to Smoking" Other less ambitious products helped with smeared glasses and computer screens, one item was designed to put an end to blocked ears. But Drake's eyes went straight to "Put an End to Performance Problems" which he guessed might be the one he was most interested in. It assured the reader that stage fright was a common complaint amongst actors, singers, dancers, musicians and sports professionals. It described a "simple easy solution that has many satisfied customers" and there was a button to press. His host pressed it and, sure enough, the website that Drake was familiar with appeared showing the address in Zurich. Kapitan Havlik pointed to it and continued.

'We have many people complaining about this lot. Some are owed large sums of money. Others complain of a failure to deliver reliably. We also believe these products may be there to get customers to enter their bank details. Many complain about mysterious debits appearing on their accounts. It seems to be a cybercrime organization fronted up by a company selling a variety of chemicals. They are secretive. Mostly, they use sophisticated methods of concealing their whereabouts. Occasionally, they make mistakes. On one occasion, we have discovered an IP address that we can trace to the Prague 1 district, but that is too vague to enable us to find them. They only allow people to communicate by email and you cannot purchase anything directly from the websites. Customers email them and are then given bank account numbers and names to transfer money into. Of course, these are not real and there is some clever redirection going on to make the actual transfer. In any case, they now use Swiss bank accounts so it is not possible to follow the money.'

'We have a murder case,' said Drake. 'The victim was a famous flute player, also known over here, called Evinka Whyte. She had been using the NmN injections. We have some of her vials and are having them chemically analyzed. However, something confusing and abnormal has occurred. NmN have been paying her a monthly amount of significant proportions.'

'Really, that is odd!' exclaimed Alexej. 'Well, I have more news for you. When you first contacted us, you mentioned that Bohdan Pelech owned the company. We have tracked him down. I have got him coming here this morning.' Alexej looked at his watch. 'In fact, he should be here by now. One of my constables has gone to collect him. Apparently, he doesn't like to be seen coming into a police station. I'll go and see if he has arrived.'

Inspector Alexej returned to the room where Drake was sitting looking at the website on the rather old computer. He brought with him a larger, somewhat intimidating, man wearing a worried expression. On the end of his nose, were ridiculously small glasses with perfectly round steel frames. He had dark hair worn long at the back in an old-fashioned mullet style. Drake saw that he was large all round. If British, he might easily have been a front-row forward in a rugby team.

'Perhaps it would be good to start with,' said Alexej Havlik, 'if you told us what you told my sergeant the other day.' Bohdan Pelech nodded his head and took a deep breath. His substantial chest heaved.

'I am trained as a pharmacist,' he began. 'I studied in Nottingham in England before I returned to Prague. I worked for other people and, at the same time, began a small company of my own selling an anxiety-reducing compound. A really old, childhood friend of mine in England, Evinka Whyte, began suffering from dreadful anxiety attacks and I first dispensed it for her. It is based on a chemical known as GABA, which stands for gamma-aminobutyric acid. This exists naturally in the human body and it has many effects. It has also been prescribed for anxiety reduction. It is actually a neurotransmitter in our brains. It does not occur normally in our diet but can be taken as a food supplement. It reduces feelings of anxiety, stress and fear. I take it myself nowadays. There are also some claims that it relaxes muscles. I combined it with Taurine, which again occurs naturally within our body. It reduces blood pressure and helps the GABA to fix on proteins. Finally, I added Theanine, which is supposed to improve mental function. It is sometimes found in tea. Evinka Whyte started to use it and became enthusiastic about it. I found some research that recommended injections rather than using it as a drink significantly increased the speed and effectiveness of reaction. So I created two types, one to be taken daily as a drink supplement and the other to be injected before an important occasion. That was all quite a few years ago. I called it No More Nerves. Evinka said she would endorse it but later decided that this could adversely impact on her reputation. It spread through word of mouth and eventually, I had a going business, which I have since lost.'

'How did you lose it?' asked Kapitan Havlik.

'I'm afraid that I got into deep water with my gambling. I got into trouble in a casino I used. I thought they were tolerant but I was wrong. They had just waited until I was in far too deep to pay my debts. The man who owned the casino, which has since closed, threatened me. He told me that I might just disappear one day and nobody would bother.' Bohdan stopped as if that was the end of his explanation. Drake could not imagine anyone disposing easily of this large man who noisily blew his nose and started to speak again.

'Eventually, he took the business off me and started to combine it with other rackets he was involved in. I later tried to track him down but I think that he had been using a false name and I couldn't find him. That is all I know. I think he has people following me, which is why I was too nervous to come here on foot. I am sure they have hacked into my emails as well. So please don't contact me that way.'

'I think we might already know about this man,' said Kapitan Havlik. 'We have been interested in him for some time. He uses several names. Is the name you have Milan Schelling?'

'No,' said Bohdan Pelech cautiously. 'No, I don't know his name.' Drake thought he shuffled his feet nervously.

'I can also tell you something of interest,' said Drake.

'I had a phone call last night from my sergeant. She has been in charge of chemical analysis. She has emailed me the results and they confirm what you have just told us. However, they now supply a second version and that has opium added to it.'

'I didn't do that,' said Bohdan Pelech. 'I cannot think of any reason to do that. It might even impair the effect of my compounds, as opium will act as a depressant. It certainly would not be good for performers like Evinka. Perhaps, Inspector Drake, you could warn Evinka for me. Please tell her to not to get involved with these people. They are dangerous.'

'So do tell us what you are doing now,' said Kapitan Havlik.

'I'm trying to develop some new products. You could say I'm starting all over again. So far I'm not having much luck.'

'Is there anything else you could tell us, Mr Pelech, that might help with either our inquiry here or that of Chief Inspector Drake's back in England?'

'No I don't think so, but if I remember anything else, I will call you. I do hope you both catch these people. I'm sure they operate in many countries. So that would make the world a safer place.'

'If you follow me,' said Kapitan Havlik, 'I will arrange for my sergeant to take you back to wherever you would like in a blacked-out van.' Bohdan Pelech shook Drake rather too firmly by the hand and left. Drake resumed his inspection of the new website until Kapitan Havlik returned.

'Well our friend Bohdan must have done extremely well out of his potion,' said Kapitan Havlik. 'He lives in a rather posh district of Mala Strana.'

'Really?' said Drake pulling out his notebook and opening it. 'I'm afraid that I don't know how to pronounce it. This isn't by any chance the address, is it?

'Yes,' said Andrej Havlik. 'How do you know it?'

'That,' said Drake, 'is the house where the composer Josef Kubicek once lived. I understand the family still own it.'

'My goodness, he does move in high society. Perhaps then he is a guest there,' said Kapitan Havlik making a note. 'I can tell you that we do believe this is an international racket and my guess is that we have not uncovered it all by any means. Of course, I must now ask you to leave all enquiries here in Prague to us. However, we clearly may benefit by keeping each other informed about progress.'

'Understood,' said Drake. 'Because of the nature of many of my cases, I am used to working outside my jurisdiction and with other international police forces.'

Drake sat looking out of the window of his aircraft as it took off and circled over Prague. It had been an interesting three days. He promised himself to come back and explore Prague at his leisure. Perhaps the retirement that he was wondering about would create the opportunity. For now, he was totally immersed in the Evinka Whyte case. It seemed to be getting more complicated by the hour but he dreaded the thought of not having his brain challenged by such puzzles. There were several new questions.

Why did Itzhak Stransky keep telling lies? What was the point of saying he played two concerts with Evinka Whyte at the Smetana Hall when these never happened? Was his memory really so bad or was he trying to create some obscure alibi? This hardly seemed likely. Why say something untrue about the distant past that confused the issues? When faced with this, would he yet again claim he was trying to keep things simple? Drake could only conclude that he was trying to obscure the true nature of his relationship with Evinka Whyte. Drake recalled how George Marshall had described Evinka Whyte's initial horror at having to work with him.

Drake moved on to consider the revelations about the proposed museum for Josef Kubicek. It was clear that Renata Kubicek was a major player in the enterprise. If it all came off, Deva University would look pretty silly for having discontinued her post. What were the items that she thought she could produce that were so exciting the concert director? Did any of this have a bearing on the death of Evinka Whyte?

Was it perhaps Bohdan who deliberately refused to answer the door at the Kubicek house? If so, why? This latest discovery of the illegal drugs trade and other scams here in Prague offered perhaps the most promising line of enquiry though Drake was not entirely clear yet how to follow it up.

Drake was trying to hold all these questions in his head and failing. His brain kept roaming around between them rather than considering them as a whole. Was he missing something that tied them all together and gave a bigger picture? He needed to get all this on his work boards. They were even more essential on this case than ever before. Was there a lesson here from his beloved crosswords? When things got tough with these, he sometimes found himself just circling around, looking at each clue in turn and then moving on. He had been trying to teach himself not to do that and concentrate more on one at a time. He also recognized that so often he would leave the crossword altogether for perhaps an hour or so and do something else. It was frequently the case that, when he went back to the crossword, he saw one or more answers almost immediately. He knew that sometimes, his brain preferred not to be bothered. The lesson seemed to be to just let it rumble around in the background for a while. He shuffled his knees and tried unsuccessfully to stretch his legs. He irritably snapped his notebook shut, glanced at the formations of clouds passing by his window and opened one of his flute tutors.

30

The next morning, the others were all waiting for Drake to arrive. He had sent an email suggesting they should set aside some time for a discussion about his discoveries in Prague.

'Good morning,' said Drake 'I thought I was dreadfully late but I hadn't set my watch back, so I'm only moderately late. I badly need a cup of coffee. He went over to the coffee machine but Grace followed him.

'You go and sit down,' she said. 'I'll make one for you and the others can make their own.' There was a little gentle smirking and eventually, they all sat around the table in the middle of the room. Drake pushed his coffee away to cool.

'First things first,' said Drake. 'I had a long and rather tedious time going through decades of the concerts in the Smetana Hall. There was no concert involving both Evinka Whyte and Itzhak Stransky. Grace would you just do a triangulation on this by going through all those posters in Evinka's music room to cross-check. We can discuss what this tells us about Stransky after that but it does appear that he keeps on telling lies. Why?' Grace made a note and nodded her head.

'Next comes the question of Renata Kubicek. In Prague, they already have museums for Dvorak and Smetana but not yet for Kubicek. They are planning one and it may start in the Municipal House, which is where the Smetana Concert Hall is. The concert director there seems to be in charge. It may later move to the Kubicek family home, which I found but couldn't get in, though a moving curtain indicated somebody was there. I watched and saw what I think was a man, and now I think it may have been Bohdan Pelech. However, the important thing is that Renata Kubicek is doing all the research for the museum and is promising them material that she says she should be able to get her hands on. The concert director was clearly extremely excited about it all but wouldn't elaborate. We have now searched both Evinka's house and Dalibor's house and not found any evidence of material that would be so central to a museum of Josef Kubicek. So where is this material? Is it in the family house in Prague or does Renata have it somewhere else? From what was said, I don't think that she actually has it yet but thinks she can get it. She hasn't mentioned any of this to us. Puzzling. Does this have any bearing on our case?' Drake took a sip of his cooling coffee.

'We need to make contact with Renata again and see what we can get out of her. Presumably, she was in contact with Evinka and Dalibor over the proposed museum but we don't know how involved they were, if at all. She has sort of indicated to Grace and me that she sees herself as the odd one out because the other two were twins and consequently rather close.' Drake took another couple of appreciative sips of his coffee.

'The other news I have relates to NmN or more properly No More Nerves. We have a new person in the case. We know that Bohdan Pelech was brought to Chester in the same cohort of escapees that included Renata and Jelena and of course Evinka's, father, Karel Kubicek. Karel had adopted his wife's name, Whyte and was still playing beautifully on his violin in a care home but otherwise probably too demented to help us any further and has since sadly died. I met Bohdan Pelech in Prague and he told us that he studied and qualified as a pharmacist at Nottingham. That university is famous for being the home of Boots and the University is heavily indebted to Jesse Boot for a large donation, which still makes it the place to study pharmacy.'

'Bohdan told me of his continued contact with Evinka. It is now clear that the cohort of escapees from communist Prague have understandably remained close right up to the present day. Bohdan Pelech dispensed the original injection vials for Evinka but then went on to sell them more widely. He's a big fellow but the poor chap is a nervous wreck and needs his own medication. He told us that he accumulated a huge gambling debt with people it would be better to keep clear of. It is them we need to investigate next. Bohdan claimed he had nothing to do with the second version and seemed astonished when I told him of the addition of opium. Of course, that would have the effect of forming a habit, which would keep users hooked on his drug. He claimed the opium addition was after these nasty people had taken the company off him in exchange for his gambling debts. He confirmed what Grace's chemists had told us about the composition of the first set of injections. It appears they are entirely legal.' Drake pulled out his notebook and pushed it across the table towards Dave.

'Try getting this website up Dave,' he said. Dave went over to his computer and the others gathered around. Suddenly the website for "Put an End to" appeared for all to see.

'Why didn't our searches find this?' asked Drake.

'Well if it isn't registered as a domain that gets trawled by the search engines it is possible not to see it at all or for it only to appear after probably hundreds of others when the search engine thinks it might be of interest.' Dave started playing around with the site. He pressed the button for "contact us" and it went to the page they were familiar with.

'On this new web page it doesn't seem to mention NmN or even No More Nerves,' said Dave. Here it is called "Put an End to Nerves" so it isn't likely to be found when searching NmN which was all we had to go on.' There are several more products here and they all go to similar pages. There doesn't seem to be any way of contacting them other than by letter to the Zurich address or by email to this address on the new site. It's all rather odd. There doesn't seem to be any way of ordering any of these products.'

'What happens if we send an email?' asked Drake. Dave typed away on his computer using a disguised email address asking how to get Put an End to Nerves. There was an immediate response.

'This looks like an automated reply,' he said. 'It gives you another button to press to get information.' Drake and Grace crowded around Dave's shoulders as a whole page of material suddenly appeared. Dave studied it and pressed another button. An email now appeared in his inbox. Dave read it.

'Ah, I see,' he said, after what felt like an age to Drake.

'Come on Dave, tell us what you see,' he growled impatiently.

'It is telling you how to download Tor onto your computer and giving a great long list of odd characters to type in. This is obviously a dark web site as it uses the ".onion" postscript. Luckily, because of the research I was doing on Peter Sostre, I have Tor already loaded. He typed away again.

'Here it is, look. You can order NmN from here and it gives an account name to transfer money into. Look it uses the CH country code which is Switzerland and the BAN code 00762 which I think is the prefix for Swiss accounts.' Dave pulled up another page on his computer. 'Yes, I'm right. It's a Swiss bank account. You won't get the Swiss police to allow you to get any further information. They are nothing like as secretive as they were but they still allow a great deal of privacy and anonymity.'

'This lot seem to try to erect a great wall of secrecy, which only goes to make one feel they have things to hide,' grunted Drake.

'Well, in this country they need to,' said Grace. 'For a start, they are guilty of not observing the Misuse of Drugs Act (171).'

'Oh I'm impressed that you can quote that,' laughed Drake. 'More importantly, are they or their agents guilty of murder?'

'I have something else to report,' said Dave. 'I think Grace might have emailed you, sir. She gave me a USB memory drive that she found in the safe in Evinka's music room. I've had a devil of a job opening the folders and files on it. They are all extremely heavily encoded. One document that I have been able to open is a pdf of some chemical analysis. Here it is look. You may not be surprised to hear now that it is of the No More Nerves vials. It reveals just as we have discovered that the second version is laced with opium.'

'That is a really important discovery, Dave, well done,' said Drake. 'So this tells us that Evinka Whyte knew she was secretly being injected with opium. Does it have a date on it, Dave?'

'Yes. From memory, it's about a year ago.'

'Grace, when did Evinka start receiving payments from NmN in the accounts we found in Dalibor's house?' Grace looked over Dave's shoulder at the date at the top of the pdf on his screen.

'About two months later, is when the first sum appeared,' she said.

'So our provisional conclusion might be that she must have suspected something,' said Drake. 'She had the fluid analyzed and discovered what had happened. She was outraged and did what you might expect. She confronted her supplier and threatened to go public. She got a pay-off and has been pocketing it until recently. Jelena told us that she preferred to have the original version in her injections but occasionally, as before the gala concert, decided to take the second. Perhaps she even realized that she was dependent on a drug that was responsible for impairing her performance. We can also assume that she thought she was still dealing with her old friend Bohdan Pelech, but she wasn't. The new owners now knew the reason for the payments and decided to stop them. Perhaps they also intended to take further action. They sound like a pretty determined lot. It may not have been wise to cross them. I wonder if Evinka did?'

'So they somehow organized for her to be killed,' said Grace.

'We know the drug carfentanil that killed her is readily available on the dark web,' said Drake, 'so it would be no problem for this crowd to get hold of it.' The team sat in silence. Drake took the final sip of his lukewarm coffee.

'It's an attractive theory,' he said slowly, 'but we also need to be critical of it. We have jumped to several conclusions here.'

Grace was the first to say something. 'Would they really choose to do this at the concert? If so why?'

'Perhaps it somehow offered a way of getting to her. I imagine Jelena is quite an effective gatekeeper,' said Drake. 'Another question is who actually did it. Did they send someone over or have they got contacts in the field who they call on to do this sort of thing?' Drake clambered up out of his chair and started prowling around his work boards.

'Perhaps Evinka Whyte was killed by a professional hitman,' said Dave.

'I think they are more likely to use simpler methods on the whole,' said Drake from behind his boards, 'but it's a possibility.' The room went quiet until Drake suddenly let out a shout.

'Bingo,' he said. 'Grace, come here and check this for me.' Grace rushed over to find Drake looking at the board where her Zurich trip was itemized. 'These pictures,' said Drake. 'They are of the man that trailed you in Zurich. Is that right?'

'Yes,' said Grace and I followed him to the post office. I think he was probably the same man who was packing up the NmN ampules the day before he posted them.'

'You have called him Mr Zurich. I think we have another name for him. This picture is of Bohdan Pelech who started the whole NmN business in Prague. If I am right here, Kapitan Havlik has been partly taken in. He referred to a man they are interested in as Milan Schelling. Bohdan Pelech denied knowing him but I think he was fooling us all. I believe that Milan Schelling is just the name Bohdan uses when in Zurich. He hasn't lost the NmN company at all. He is still running it. I thought I saw him through a window in the Kubicek family house in Prague. He dispenses everything on the top floor there. Jelena told us about that and she was obviously frightened of him. I must email my friend Kapitan Havlik and tell him. This changes everything. Grace you might have had a lucky escape in Zurich. I suspect this man is both dangerous and ruthless.' Drake stopped and looked into the air for a minute as if trying to recall all of his adventures in Prague.

'OK,' he said suddenly. 'What has happened here? Have you managed to get Jelena Novakova in to see what she has to say about the hit and run on Dalibor Kubicek?'

'Nope,' said Grace. 'We've tried all the contacts we have and drawn blanks. I got back to the airline to see if she had flown back to Prague but they couldn't find any sign of her.'

31

Drake and Grace were sitting about halfway back in the auditorium watching the rehearsal for that evening's concert. Maestro Stransky was taking the orchestra through Brahms first symphony.

'Before we begin,' said Stransky to the orchestra. 'I'm sure you know that Brahms took many years to complete his first symphony. Historians tell us that he spent fourteen years revising before he allowed it to be performed. Though Brahms himself claimed that from his first idea to completion was actually 21 years. It will take us three-quarters of an hour to play it this evening. The conductor Hans von Bulow described it as Beethoven's Tenth. I think Brahms was torn and in two minds. On the one hand, he was so in awe of Beethoven that he wanted the work to be a homage. On the other hand, he was desperately trying to find his own voice. We now know Brahms' voice from his other symphonies and concertos. It is Brahms voice I want to hear this evening. Please play it as Brahms and not as Beethoven.'

Stransky picked up his baton and opened a huge score on the desk in front of him. 'We start with the second movement. There are passages here where we need to hear the oboe and the leader's violin. We will play these first to get the balance right.' He conducted several excerpts and eventually, signalled his satisfaction. 'Good. While we are doing this I will take the Bach second orchestral suite. The badinerie. This is effectively a flute solo throughout. We will play it through to get the balance right here and to exhaust poor Anders Hagen.' They played and Anders Hagen flew across the notes at a rate beyond Drake's belief.

'I didn't know it was possible to play the flute that fast,' he said to Grace. 'It's all I can do to get one note to follow another.'

Maestro Stransky took the orchestra through several other minor sections of the rest of the programme and then announced lunch. George Marshall was sitting just in front of them. Grace asked him if they could use his office for an interview. Drake thanked him and went backstage while Grace climbed onto the platform to ask Anders Hagen if he could join them briefly upstairs in George Marshall's office after the concert.

'I'm full of amazement,' said Drake as Anders entered the room. 'I've no idea how you manage to get all those notes in without tripping over.'

'It's very simple,' replied Anders. 'I just practice a lot.'

'Well I'm still struggling to get a sensible note,' said Drake.

'You have a flute?' asked Anders.

'Yes,' replied Drake. 'I stupidly bought one in Prague. 'I don't think I can actually learn to play it at my age.'

'That's wonderful,' said Anders. 'I should be most happy to give you some lessons if you wish.'

'Thank you that is a marvellous idea and please take a seat,' said Drake. 'We would like to talk to you about the day of the opening gala concert. How did it go from your point of view?'

'Better than I had expected,' said Anders. 'Of course, I'm terribly sad about what happened to Evinka Whyte but it gave me the opportunity of a lifetime. I was able to play in a concert that was being recorded for broadcast all over the world. I have had several enquiries about my availability since then. It may be that my life has changed.'

'From what I heard, you played extremely well,' said Drake. 'But I heard that previously you had been rather critical of Evinka Whyte's playing.'

'Correct,' said Anders. 'I was rather surprised. Of course, I have heard her records. While on the one hand, she has mostly made her name playing popular music, on the other hand, I did not doubt her ability. At rehearsal, she was frequently off the beat and at times lost perfect tonality, especially in the high register.'

'Did you say anything to her?' asked Drake.

'Ah,' said Anders. 'I think perhaps people have been talking. You think I saw her after rehearsal. I did intend to go and ask her if she was unwell and would prefer to let me play. However, I never got the opportunity and anyway thought better of it.'

'Why didn't you get the opportunity?' asked Drake.

'Well, I left her for a while. That seemed polite. Then after maybe twenty minutes I came down the stairs by the stage entrance and walked along the corridor. But a woman came the other way and beat me to it. She knocked on Miss Whyte's door and went in. I stood around for maybe ten minutes and she was still in there so I went back and got some lunch.'

'Who was the woman you saw going into her room?' asked Drake.'

'I've no idea.'

'Can you describe her?'

'Oh, dear. I only saw her for a moment and I'm not much good at recognizing people.'

'Was she tall or short?' asked Drake.

'I'd say she was fairly tall but not unusually so. She was certainly a little taller than me.'

'How tall are you?' asked Drake.

'I'm one metre eighty,' said Anders.

'Sorry,' said Drake. 'What is that in feet and inches?'

'About five foot eleven I think.'

'What colour hair did she have?' Anders paused and looked up at the ceiling as if the answer to the question was up there.

'A light colour,' I think,' he said hesitantly.

'Thank you, Anders,' said Drake. 'Is there anything else you could tell us that might help with our enquiries?'

'Well, there is something a bit odd now I think of it. During the two days before the concert when we were rehearsing and they were adjusting the acoustics, we had a break and Itzhak Stransky came up to me. He congratulated me and asked if I would like to play the solo part in the concert. I said yes of course. At the time, I thought he was just making idle chat and that it wasn't a serious question. He would not have heard Evinka Whyte play. Now looking back, it might have been because somehow he was already worried about her performance.'

'Do you have time to come to the station so Grace can take you through what everybody calls a photo-fit session? It's all done on computers now so we call it E-fit'

'Yes, I could make it in the morning. We are free until lunchtime.'

'What did you make of that?' Drake asked Grace as Anders Hagen left.

'It's all getting rather confusing,' said Grace. 'Itzhak Stransky's behaviour seems to get more confusing every time we hear about it.'

'True,' said Drake. 'The other piece of information may be even more important. We seem to have a new character. A woman with light coloured hair who is fairly tall coming from the fire escape end of the main corridor and going in to see Evinka Whyte. This is after rehearsals and before the concert began.'

'I'm not sure if she is new,' said Grace. 'That description could cover Evinka's personal assistant, Jelena Novakova.'

Drake finally got his wish to hear an uninterrupted concert. He knew that he had to work again afterwards but he could put that to the back of his mind for now. The orchestra was superb, the acoustics worked beautifully and Itzhak Stransky conducted with the confidence that comes with experience. At the end, there was a standing ovation for Maestro Stransky and the orchestra. He was brought back to the platform to receive more applause three times. After a little charade in which he looked impatiently at his watch he finally gave in and, it just so happened, that he had rehearsed an encore. It was the Pas de Deux from Tchaikovsky's Nutcracker ballet. The harpist had her moment of glory, playing arpeggios throughout. The strings were at their smoothest sweeping best and the brass, timpani and piccolo heralded the final crescendo. This generated even louder applause as Stransky brought the orchestra to their feet, bowed once more and finally left the platform not to return.

'I think we should give him a few minutes to recover,' said Drake.

'Has Lucy ever danced that?' asked Grace.

'Yes last Christmas,' said Drake. 'I don't mind admitting that I cried. If only Cynthia had been there to see her.' He fell into one of those reveries that Grace knew not to interrupt.

'Right,' said Drake, breaking the silence. 'Time to go and see what Stransky comes up with this time.' By now the auditorium had emptied and George Marshall came over to see why they had remained.

'We are just going to have another word with Maestro Stransky,' said Drake.

'Ah yes,' said George Marshall. 'I thought he might be your chief suspect.'

'I couldn't possibly comment on that,' snapped Drake. Grace smiled at George Marshall who made way for them to go through the stage side door into the main backstage corridor.

'Come in,' called the voice from inside as Grace knocked on the conductor's door.

'Ah Inspector Drake, Grace,' said Itzhak Stransky, standing and bowing slightly. 'I think we have two chairs. Please sit down. How can I help you?'

'We have a few little inconsistencies with things various people have said about the night of the opening concert,' said Drake. 'Our first problem is with this argument about the flute cadenzas that Evinka Whyte had chosen to play.' Drake paused to let this introduction sink in and have its effect.

'As I understand it, Anders Hagen played the same ones. He had checked with Evinka some time before so that he could help the orchestra to rehearse its re-entries and so on. Is that correct?'

'Yes,' said Stransky.

'So didn't you also have an argument with him?' probed Drake.

'No. He said it was her choice and I couldn't disagree with him in rehearsal,' said Stransky after a slight pause that both Drake and Grace noticed.

'I don't think your argument with Evinka was about anything so trivial as the choice of cadenzas,' said Drake. 'I put it to you that you had a much more substantial issue and that is why it got so heated.' Stransky paused and was obviously thinking.

'No,' he said eventually. 'That is not correct.'

'Well let us discuss a more serious issue then,' said Drake. 'You said to us that Evinka Whyte was on form. You said you would have noticed any problems.'

'Yes,' said Stransky hesitantly.

'But members of the orchestra have told us that they thought she performed rather poorly in rehearsal. So why didn't you notice this?'

'I can't explain that,' replied Stransky.

'I put it to you that somehow you came here expecting a poor performance from her. You asked Anders Hagen if he was prepared to stand in for her. You did that even before rehearsals.'

'It is true,' said Stransky. 'I had seen many critics recently writing about her performances. I was worried. I was right to be worried.'

'So you did notice her poor performance?' Stransky sat silently as if making up his mind what to say.

'Yes, of course. No one could miss it. Musically, she was but a shadow of her former self.' Stransky leant back in his chair and looked at himself in the large mirror on the wall at the back of his counter. Drake waited. It seemed he was reflecting and making some sort of a decision. Drake was right.

'You are right, Drake,' he said eventually. 'I can't remember who. One of your great writers wrote "What a tangled web we weave, when first we practice to deceive," who was that?'

'Robert Louis Stevenson,' said Drake.

'Ah yes!' Stransky stopped again. As he looked in the mirror, he patted down the remnants of what, in his youth, had been a full head of hair. It had inevitably been ruffled by the sheer physicality of conducting.

'Perhaps I had better go back to the beginning and start again,' he said.

'It had seemed an odd invitation to conduct here and with Evinka Whyte,' he said. Everyone in the world of music must have heard about her fading performance. Then there was the troublesome relationship between our two families. Why would anyone book us together? My first reaction was to turn it down but the more I thought about it the more curious I became and somehow I got involved. Then they said she was unhappy and asked if I would step down. Me, step down! Certainly not. If anyone was stepping down it was not a Stransky. Other members of the family had heard about it. I couldn't step down. When I heard Anders Hagen play, I knew he was a great musician and he just needed a break. So many excellent musicians don't get a break in our world. At first, I couldn't see the way forward. Then I met Evinka. We had met many years previously. Her eyes told me. She wasn't the same person. I had to persuade her to be indisposed – a lovely understated English word – and to step down without losing face. Once we rehearsed I realized the whole orchestra knew. She couldn't do the work justice. So, after rehearsal, I went to her room. Our rooms interconnected. She was angry and abusive. She got up and left the room. I followed her. That was the angry discussion that got reported to you.' He paused as if reluctant to describe the next sequence of events.

'When later, she didn't turn up for the Mozart, I assumed she had changed her mind. Surely she must have known that she couldn't perform. I had given her a way out. She could just be ill. Not one of the fans in her home city would know. It was only later when I heard she was dead and that police were involved, that I worried. Our interconnected rooms, the angry argument outside, our family feud; it would all point to me. Perhaps I had been the last person to see her alive. I had no idea. It seemed easier to say I hadn't seen her than to explain all this.'

'I think I have said before,' said Drake. 'Telling the truth is always simpler in the end. You realize that giving false evidence to a police officer and wasting police time are criminal offences?'

'I can only apologize,' said Stransky.

'One last thing you might be able to help me with,' said Drake pulling out his phone and scanning through the pictures. 'I ran across this again this morning.' He was looking at a picture of the wooden wedges found with Evinka Whyte. 'Is there any chance they are musical in any way?'

'Probably,' said Stransky. 'They look rather like blanks to make bridges for string instruments. Many people are particularly careful to use the right kind of wood for this. It must be capable of being cut, drilled and carved without splitting. These are almost certainly for violins. A craftsman luthier will take one of these, carve holes in it designed to make it flex ever so slightly and make notches for the four strings. It is a highly skilled process that begins with a good blank made of the right kind of wood. He will leave one face flat and the other ever so slightly curved. The flat face is always inserted facing the toe of the violin. Two feet are left when the luthier has cut away the centre section at the thick end. These two feet must be cut in such a way that they precisely follow the curvature of the belly of the instrument otherwise the bridge may move when under pressure.'

32

The following morning, Anders Hagen arrived at the police station as agreed. Grace took him to an interview room and led him through the E-fit process. They arrived at a picture. Drake came in to look at the result.

'Interesting,' he said. 'Anders, could you give us a little longer please?'

'Yes, sure. I'm free until lunchtime.'

'Grace, can we have a minute please?' asked Drake. He turned and left the interview room.

'I've been reviewing all our personnel on my work boards,' said Drake. 'There are two women who stand some chance of being a match.'

'I was wondering about Jelena Novakova,' said Grace.

'Yes, so was I,' said Drake. 'If it is her, then we have nothing new. We know she was with Evinka so she could have left the room and was returning when Anders Hagen saw her. But there is another possibility. That is Laura Weeks. She is taller but not a great difference and she has red/blond hair. On the work boards, there are a lot of images that we dragged off the Internet. We took a photo of Jelena. Let's try showing them both to Anders and see what happens.'

'Yes, I'll go and make a couple of copies straight away,' said Grace. 'Just give me ten minutes.' She went to the case room, took some pictures off the boards and photocopied them. 'Ready,' she said coming back into the case room. Drake checked the pictures.

'Yes, these are worth trying out on him.' They went straight down the corridor to the interview room. Drake had brought Anders a mug of tea that he gratefully drank.

'Anders,' said Drake. 'There are two women we know of that could have been in the main corridor during the time in question. Please look at them and see if either triggers something in your memory.' He put the two pictures down on the table in front of Anders who shuffled them around several times.

'It could be either of them,' he said slowly. 'This one is more likely. I know I said fair hair yesterday but now I think about it, the hair could easily have been more ginger coloured. There is something else about her that makes me think it could be her. It's the length of hair. Her hair is longer than the other one. That seems to ring a bell with me. That could be her.'

'Anders,' said Drake. 'The one you have picked is the woman who did the introductions to the music at the concert. Does that help your memory?'

'Well, I only saw her from behind in the first half when I was playing in the orchestra. The flutes sit pretty much in the middle of an orchestra so it was a fairly distant view but she definitely had longer hair. The other woman has it cut to her chin. This one, her hair just covers her shoulders. If it is either of them it is her.'

'Thank you for your time and patience,' said Drake. 'You have been really helpful. If you do think of anything else please contact Sergeant Hepple. She will give you a card.' Grace pulled a card from her pocket and showed Anders Hagen out. When she came back, Drake had returned to the case room and was sat looking at the pictures on his table.

'I think we might need to speak to Laura Weeks again,' he said. She admitted being around the backstage but claimed not to have gone in to see Evinka Whyte. I wonder if she is hiding something. It's a long shot but we need to speak to her carefully. Let's get her to come in. Organize it, Grace.' Drake collapsed back into his favourite chair and studied his half-completed Times crossword.

PC Katie Lamb came into the case room looking for Drake.

'I've collected Dr Laura Weeks and put her in interview room one with a cup of tea,' she said.

'Thanks,' said Drake, 'We'll just leave her to stew along with her tea for a few minutes. Are you free, Grace? I could do with some female backup in this job.'

'Just finishing this little search on the Internet,' replied Grace.

'Good afternoon, Dr Weeks,' said Drake as he entered the interview room. 'I'm sorry to keep you waiting. I hope you've been made comfortable.' Laura Weeks nodded and took a sip from her mug of tea.

'Last time we spoke to you in your office, you told us about the day of the opening concert,' said Drake. 'I think we established that you were present in the auditorium though not involved during the rehearsals. You were of course in the auditorium during both halves of the concert. Can you just go over the period between rehearsals and the start of the concert again?'

'Sure. I went backstage and checked with George Marshall what they wanted me to do, he poured me a glass of wine and I took it outside.'

'Are you sure that was all that happened at that time?'

'Yes, as far as I can remember.'

'We now have some conflicting evidence about that,' said Drake. Laura sat silently, so after a pause, Drake continued. 'Is it possible that you have forgotten to tell us something?'

'No, I don't think so.'

'We have information that suggests you approached Evinka Whyte's dressing room, knocked on the door and went in. That evidence suggests you were in her room for some time.' Drake paused. Laura Weeks shuffled her feet got a handkerchief from her bag and blew her nose.

'You do realise the significance of this if our other evidence is correct?' said Drake. Laura remained silent. Drake tried again. 'If you are found to have given false evidence to a police officer, this is an offence. You could be tried, and if found guilty, you could be imprisoned for up to six months under the Criminal Law Act 1967.' Laura remained silent. 'I don't want to have to charge you but if necessary I will,' said Drake. 'I will leave you to think about it. Would you like another cup of tea?' Laura nodded her head silently and perceptibly gulped. Drake left the room.

'Ah, Grace,' he said, as she arrived outside the interview room. I think we have her. I'm sure she is hiding something. Get her another cup of tea. I wouldn't mind one myself. I'm leaving her to think about it.' Grace went and collected three mugs of tea. She gave Drake one and took one to the interview room for Laura Weeks. She came straight out again.

'She's ready to talk,' said Grace.

A few minutes later, Drake and Grace entered the interview room.

'I understand that you are now prepared to change your original statement,' said Drake. Laura Weeks nodded her head.

'I don't see why I should shield others and get a criminal record of my own,' she said. Drake waited for her to speak again. 'Your information is correct,' she said. I did go in to see her. I asked her to speak up for me with the Vice-Chancellor. She more or less refused. She didn't deny giving him a bad assessment of me but she said they always had a frank conversation. I explained all the difficulties I had in the department and she listened. I think she understood, for the first time probably, but she wouldn't give me any assurances. Eventually, I left and did what I had been asked to do.'

'You had been asked to do something else by somebody?' asked Drake. 'Yes. I am thoroughly ashamed of it now and disgusted.'

'Perhaps it would be helpful if you told us all about it,' said Grace. Laura smiled.

'You are right,' she said. 'Why should I put myself in trouble for someone else who doesn't deserve it?' Drake and Grace waited patiently while Laura dabbed her eyes again.

'I had agreed that I would wedge open the fire escape door so they could get in while everyone else was in the auditorium in the first half. They gave me a rubber wedge to hold the door open.'

'Who are they?' asked Grace after Drake nodded to her. Laura remained silent.

'Perhaps I can help you,' said Drake. 'We happened to notice in your office that two of your masks were missing. Did you perhaps lend them to someone?' Laura looked over Drake's head and sat motionless, apparently thinking.

'I think you know, don't you?' she said slowly. I lent them to Peter Sostre, Dr Peter Sostre. He is a lecturer in sociology. He has helped me a great deal with the sociological aspects of my research. He promised me that they would take Evinka somewhere pleasant and make it clear to her that she wasn't going to be harmed. Then they would release her after the concert. They wrongly assumed that the concert would fall apart. They didn't reckon on Anders Hagen. It was all just to make a point about the concert hall being for the privileged few. But then she somehow got killed. That wasn't in the plan at all. I had almost decided not to play their game. If Evinka had been more reasonable with me I wouldn't have wedged the door open but she made me so angry that I suppose I thought it would serve her right. I hadn't expected them to kill her. Please believe me.' She started to sob.

'You talk about them,' said Grace. 'Are there two of them?' Laura nodded.

'Who is the other person?'

'I don't know his name. He comes from Manchester. He's part of a group that Peter belongs to. They specialise in causing trouble. Peter isn't a bad person really. I thought we had a good close relationship but now I realize that he was just exploiting me. I've been very silly.'

'So why did you agree to help them in the first place', demanded Drake.

'I didn't. I just said that I'd help Peter. It seemed fairly harmless. I thought he and I had something. I was wrong.'

'So do you know what they did to Evinka?' asked Grace.

'Peter claims they didn't do anything. He claims they decided not even to go to the concert hall. I don't believe him I'm afraid. I suppose he will be charged with murder?'

'That is possible,' said Drake. 'It all depends on other factors.' Laura sobbed again.

'What an awful mess I've made of things,' she said. Drake rose slowly out of his chair, grimacing slightly and levering himself up against the table. Laura watched his face rise all the way up. He was wearing a grim expression that must have terrified Laura Weeks. She sobbed again.

'Do you know where Dr Sostre is now?' he asked. Laura shook her head. Drake beckoned to Grace and they left the room.

'I think we will eventually have to charge her with aiding and abetting. Take over while I get some others to go and bring Sostre in.'

'Katie' there you are,' said Drake, entering the case room. 'You know where Peter Sostre lives don't you?'

'Yes, sir. We've been following him. It's quite tricky actually because Egerton Street is really narrow and sort of paved over. It's almost pedestrianized. It's hard to find somewhere to park for surveillance.'

'Good. You needn't worry about that this time. I want you to bring him in. Take care; he may be dangerous. Take another constable. If you can find his computer bring that in for Dave to look at.' Katie nodded.

'Yes, sir. Straight away.' She beckoned to PC Steve Redvers, who did not need a second invitation.

PC Katie Lamb returned to the case room empty-handed.

'Got him?' asked Drake briskly.

'We tried his house in Egerton Street,' said Katie. 'Then I rang the university and they told me that he hadn't been in all day. So we trailed right out to Tarvin and searched the house there; still no sign. Oh, by the way, I went out to the university to collect his computer. Dave is already playing with it.'

'Ah,' said Drake, 'he's gone to ground. Perhaps he knew Laura Weeks was going to talk to us today and guessed she would let us in on his little plan. But, thanks to Katie, we're not without a plan of our own. Katie, get the addresses in Birmingham and Manchester where the Met people told us his friends live. Then get onto the respective police forces and see if they can check him out there for us. '

33

Grace was back at Evinka Whyte's house yet again. She let herself in and went straight downstairs to the music room. She took off her coat, got out her phone and notebook to start on her task. She looked at the long array of concert posters that Evinka had framed and stored with obvious pride. They took up the space between the floor and the lowest shelf on two sides of the room. They were housed vertically and slid in on runners. She had already established that they were in chronological order so she began on the far left side. She took out the first poster. It was neatly housed in a slim back frame. She doubted it would be possible to frame them any more neatly. She laid it on the floor, stood up, photographed it and noted the place and date in her notebook. Happy with the procedure, she decided to work on three at once to save time. She slotted the first frame back and took out the next three. All photographed and noted, she stacked them on the floor before taking out the next three. She could then put the others back without losing her place. It proved to be tedious and exhausting work and, by the time she had completed the first half, her back was beginning to complain. She took notice and retreated to an upright chair, sat down and checked her notebook.

It was then that she heard a noise. She froze and listened carefully; it could have been a door slamming. It could have been something dropped, perhaps on an upper floor. It was difficult to locate but it seemed to be from inside the house. As far as Grace knew, she was alone in the building. She took a sip from her water bottle to relieve her suddenly dry throat. Walking as carefully as she could, Grace tiptoed out into the hall. She could see up into the hallway at the ground floor. She climbed up a few steps so she could see the front door. It looked firmly closed. She glanced at the staircase going up to the bedrooms. There was no sign of anybody or anything that could have caused such a noise. Perhaps it was from outside. Could it have been a car door slamming or some other event in the roadway? She went back into the music room and looked out into the landscape. There were rowers on the Dee and a few people walking along the far bank. There was no one in the gardens running down behind the terrace to the river. Grace was reassured that nothing was happening inside the house. She would have known about it by now.

It was nearly lunchtime when Grace reached the end of her task. She could confirm to Drake that there was no evidence of a concert in the Smetana Hall in Prague with both Evinka Whyte and Itzhak Stransky. Job done. The list of places and dates could be useful as a record of where and when Evinka had been. She stood up and stretched her aching back. It was then that she noticed that in each batch of posters there seemed to be two missing. She looked around and there, on the wall behind her, were two posters. The first was for a concert in Venice. It had been mainly work of the local man, Vivaldi. She photographed it and noted its place and date in her book. The second poster was in Berlin. Where, she wondered were the third and fourth missing posters?

It was then that she noticed that the first three posters in the second batch had not slotted neatly all the way in and were protruding untidily. She pushed one but it refused to go any further. The next two were the same. She pulled the third one out again and squatted down to see what was causing the problem. It was too dark so she pulled out her torch. She could not see any obstruction so she removed the next two. Shining her torch in now she could see a shiny silver strip across the space right at the back. She reached in right up to her shoulder and could feel it. She could put her hand around it. It moved slightly. It felt like the lever of a door handle. She tried pulling it out but it remained obstinately in position. Then she tried pushing it down and it gave for a few centimetres and stuck again. She changed arms and somehow managed to pull the lever down into almost a vertical position. She let go and it sprang back. She repeated the procedure and then pulled.

She stumbled backwards as the whole set of shelves suddenly swung out. Now it was obvious that the shelves were effectively mounted on a door, which she could open to ninety degrees. Then she saw it. There was no doubt that the door of what looked like a huge safe occupied the whole space from floor to ceiling and about a meter wide. Standing up again she could see a small brass sign plate on the door. It was the maker's name and it was the same as the one on the safe in the fireplace that they had already opened. Below the sign was a large keyhole. She tried to peer in but all was black. She shone her torch but couldn't look in at the same time. Then she remembered that the key to the other safe was in the bunch they had discovered at Dalibor's house. That bunch had another large key. It surely must be the one she needed. She called PC Katie Lamb and asked her to find the bunch and bring it out. The day was going a lot better than it had looked earlier. At least, if her hunch proved correct it could reveal something else of value to the investigation.

While she was waiting for Katie to arrive, Grace began to worry about the earlier noise. She started wandering aimlessly around the house. Perhaps the missing posters would be in another room somewhere. Katie returned to the ground level and opened the door straight ahead from the entrance. It was a reception room, sitting room, living room. Whatever you wanted to call it. Sure enough on the side wall nearest the river, was another poster. She went across to photograph and take its details. She turned to explore the room.

She went to the top floor and poked her head into all the bedrooms and bathrooms. One, particularly spacious room was obviously Evinka Whyte's. She walked around the large double bed and into the en-suite bathroom. Back on the landing, she noticed that one room was labelled for guests, with best wishes for their stay. She explored it. There too was an en-suite bathroom. It was on the street side of the house and had blinds on the windows. Finally, she came to Jelena's room. She had told them how she had a room in the house that was effectively her home. It was a bed-sit with a bed at one end and a large sofa and armchair at the other. It was then that she saw it.

Lying on the floor behind the bed was the body of a woman. Grace rushed over and checked for breathing or a pulse. She found neither. The skin felt cold. The body looked as if it had fallen, mostly face down but rather awkwardly. Alongside having apparently fallen separately or maybe dislodged from the outstretched right arm, was a pistol. Grace recognised it as a Glock 19 semi-automatic 9mm handgun. She had trained with one at the police range. Now she could see enough of the face of the fallen body. It had a bullet hole in the right temple. There was a small pool of half coagulated blood on the carpet. She looked around and found the empty cartridge case several metres away. She eased the body over slightly to see the face more clearly. It was Evinka's personal assistant, Jelena Novakova.

By the time Drake arrived, the room was buzzing. The scene-of-crime-officers were everywhere recording the scene and checking for other pieces of evidence. Drake left them to their work and went down to the music room to check what Grace had done. The shelves normally covering the huge safe door were wide open. He idly tried to pull at the safe door but it stubbornly refused to budge. He returned to Jelena's room just as Professor Cooper was arriving.

'We're gradually running out of living suspects on this case, Drake,' he said. 'You must have terrified the poor girl. She appears to have committed suicide.'

'We think she may have been responsible for the hit and run incident the other day,' grunted Drake. 'At first, we thought she was out of the country but the airline has confirmed she arrived back in time to have been responsible. She had the keys to the car and the garage. We don't have a motive unless she thought we were going to charge her, but even so,' Drake's voice trailed off into a mumble. Prof Cooper nodded and resumed his task.

At that point, the door opened and in came PC Katie Lamb with a big bunch of keys. 'I wasn't quite sure which one you wanted,' she said so I brought the whole bunch. Grace took them and a small train of people trudged down to the music room. The others stood back while Grace tried the largest key of the bunch. The safe gave out an enthusiastic clunk as if it had been waiting patiently for this very moment. The door swung open in the opposite direction to the shelving that had covered it. Drake peered in over Grace's shoulder. There was a shelf about a third of the way up. Above that was just empty space. Below were a series of leather-bound volumes standing vertically. Everywhere was covered with a thin layer of dust but the leather spines looked in good condition. Drake counted quickly. There were twenty-three. Some had what looked like year dates on the back, while others were blank. Drake scanned them. If they were indeed years, they were all from the late nineteenth century. These were not Evinka's but came from a past era.

'Oh my goodness,' said Drake. 'I think I know what you have found, Grace. Slide one out carefully.' Grace pulled on her rubber gloves and eased one out from near the left end. It was not a book but a folder that was larger than today's normal size, perhaps about 400 millimetres high. It slid slowly and dipped a little as she reached its whole depth.

'It's heavier than I expected,' she groaned. She took it across the room to a small table. She laid it on its back and opened the leather cover. There was another board cover inside tied with a red ribbon. She gently pulled the loose end of the ribbon and it came free, shooting a tiny cloud of dust up into the air. She opened it and beneath was a handwritten musical score. It was labelled in blue ink. "Overture IV" was scrawled at the top of the score. To the right was the date 1892 and quite clearly the name of Josef Kubicek and the simple word "Praha" shed any lingering doubt as to where it came from and what they were looking at.

'Look it's a full orchestral score,' said Drake. 'See down the left-hand side are the names of the instruments in Italian, as was the practice, with flauti at the top followed by oboi, clarinetti, and fagotti. Those are the bassoons. Then come the brass and finally the strings. From memory, I don't think Kubicek composed an opera but I'm pretty sure there's a ballet in amongst his work. I wonder if this is the overture to it.' Drake patted the back of his neck where his short hairs were standing on end. 'We are looking at history here and I think we are among a handful people who have seen this. Unless I am much mistaken, this is a collection, made at the time, of Josef Kubicek's original manuscripts. I would like to sample a few more carefully now but my suspicion is these represent the life's work of a great composer as archived by himself. It's no wonder the world has seen very few of his original manuscripts. They have been guarded by generations of the Kubicek family.'

'Would these be valuable?' asked Grace.

'I'm no expert,' said Drake, 'but I would hazard a guess that they might each be worth a pretty penny but as a collection, they might almost be priceless. I'm going to suggest an unusual procedure here for the SOCO. We will need to review all this as important material and probably relevant evidence in our cases. However, we need to take expert advice on how to handle them. Grace, can you find someone who can help us, please. However, the existence of all this must remain a secret until we have cleared up these cases. I think we have no alternative but to take all these and lock them up at the station.' The others stood around and looked at each other in awe of what they had found. Drake was revelling in the discovery. He pulled himself back to the present.

'We don't have time now to sit looking at these wonderful manuscripts. So we have yet another death to investigate, that of Jelena Novakova. It looks like suicide or was she murdered? We'd better get back to work.'

34

'Hello Love,' said Drake as Lucy appeared for breakfast.

'Good morning, Dad,' she replied. 'You were working late again last night. I was a bit tired and went to bed. You work too hard.'

'No such thing,' said Drake. 'It just isn't nine to five in this job. Anyway, things are developing on our Evinka Whyte case and I've got something to show you before I go out. Grace will collect me in half an hour.' Lucy peered over her father's shoulder as he pulled some papers out of the bag by his side.'

'Have a look at this. What do you make of it?'

'It's obviously handwritten music. It's quite scratchy and hard to read. It's called Overture IV.' Lucy started to hum. She stopped and started again and then yet again.

'OK, I've got it now. I know it but I can't quite place it. It's certainly familiar.' She hummed intermittently.

'Shall I tell you what it is?' asked Drake.

'Yes,' said Lucy you're going to have to. I can't remember now but I definitely know it.'

'It's the original manuscript in the composer's hand. I've photocopied it obviously but we found the original yesterday in Evinka Whyte's house in a huge safe that was hidden behind a bookcase. It's by Josef Kubicek.'

'Yes of course. It's from his ballet. We danced it a couple of years ago. I thought it sounded like Tchaikovsky at the time but he was actually Czech wasn't he?'

'Yes, he was Evinka Whyte's great granddad.'

'It says overture IV at the top,' said Lucy. So it must be the overture to his ballet. I'm desperately trying to remember what it was called. If I recall correctly from our pre-rehearsal briefing, he wrote four overtures to it before he was happy. The other three have never come to light so the assumption is that he destroyed them. I'm sure this was the one we had.'

'So he was copying Beethoven then,' said Drake.

'Why do you say that?' asked Lucy.

'Beethoven didn't compose a ballet and he only wrote one opera, Fidelio, which is wonderful,' said Drake. 'He changed its name from Leonora to Fidelio in the end. He wrote three overtures called Leonora and one called Fidelio. At least Beethoven published all three rejected overtures. So Kubicek seems to have copied him or at least had the same level of indecision.'

'Good gracious,' said Lucy. 'It's amazing what you know, Dad.' At that moment, Drake's phone rang and he went through the usual ritual of hunting it down. It was under the music on the table.

'Hello, Drake here.'

'Drake, this is your friendly pathologist.'

'Hello. Have you made some progress with Jelena Novakova's body?'

'Yes. That's what I'm calling you about. I think I've got some important findings for you. But, as a result, I need to get back into the house. I think you've got someone on guard there now, is that right?'

'Yes,' said Drake. 'I'll make sure they will let you in.'

'Actually, I think it would be better if we met up there so I can explain what I've found.'

'OK. I'll get Grace to drive me up there. We should be about half an hour.'

'Excellent. It will probably take me half an hour too.'

Grace pulled the Range Rover to a halt right outside Evinka Whyte's house. Drake slid himself out of the vehicle, stretched and yawned.

'Are you OK, sir,' asked Grace.

'Yes, just rather tired. I didn't sleep much last night. There were too many ideas competing for attention in my mind. Hopefully, Prof Cooper can tell us something that gives us a push forward.' Grace acknowledged the constable on duty and held the door open for Drake. She thought he was not on his usual form. They arrived in Jelena's bedroom and Drake went round it all again. He started talking but not addressing anybody in particular.

'OK, so Jelena realises we have found the smashed-up car and knows we are going to accuse her of killing Dalibor Kubicek. Let us assume she killed him accidentally. It has been preying on her mind. The death of Evinka Whyte has also left her life in tatters. It all gets too much for her and she comes here to commit suicide and shoot herself in the head.' Drake wandered around looking at the floor, his natural stoop more pronounced than Grace had previously noticed.

'But if she really drove the car into Dalibor, why did she give us the car and garage keys. You'd think she would at least try to keep them secret. In truth, if she hadn't told us about it, we wouldn't have found it. That just doesn't make sense. Why would she have gone to Dalibor's house anyway? Did she think that he killed Evinka? But why ransack the place? What was she looking for?' Drake wandered some more, muttering to himself.

'OK,' said Professor Cooper arriving in the bed-sitting room. 'Sorry it took me a bit longer, the traffic is just dreadful today.' The pathologist went to stand over the outline marked on the floor where Jelena's body had lain.

'OK, now let's go over all this again,' he said. 'On the face of it, we have a suicide by shooting to the head. The first thing to say is that the wound and route of the bullet are both consistent with a self-administered shot. The gun we found has one bullet missing. The bullet I found in the brain of the deceased is of the type used by a Glock19 9mm handgun. It entered through the side of the head going in a slightly upward direction. It passed straight through the hypothalamus doing fatal damage on its way into the cortex. The hypothalamus has several duties and, with it so severely damaged, death would be inevitable and immediate. The bullet then ricochets around in the cortex causing considerable further damage. Jelena Novakova died from a bullet in the head fired from the gun we found next to the body.' Professor Cooper started walking around the room and pointing to the locations of the gun and cartridge case. 'The location of the body and the gun are consistent with a self-administered shot. The ejected cartridge case landed over here. That is consistent with the gun being fired just here and held up to the head like this. So far so good.' Prof Cooper stopped to make sure his students were following his account. Both nodded and he continued.

'I assume you have both heard of livor mortis?'

'Yes,' said Drake but I forget these days.'

'It's something to do with the blood after death,' said Grace.

'Excellent,' said Prof Cooper. 'It is exactly that. Once death has occurred and the heart is no longer pumping blood around the body, things start changing. The first thing is that blood is no longer being moved but remains under the influence of gravity. For this reason, it begins to sink and pool in the lower parts of the body as they are situated in the collapsed corpse. This in turn creates a colouring of the skin. We can use it as an approximate way of estimating the time of death. Once we have the body on the table at the mortuary we can thoroughly examine how far and where this has proceeded. What I can tell you, with considerable certainty is that the position in which we found the body is not the one it was in during the early phase of this process.' Professor Cooper stopped to see if his lecture had been received. It was Drake who broke the silence.

'Are you saying then that this body was moved some time after death?'

'Yes, I'm saying exactly that,' replied Professor Cooper. 'There must then be some doubt about our original assumption this was suicide. Of course, it still could have been but you would need to explain why someone else should move the body later.'

'A more rational explanation,' said Drake slowly, 'is that she was shot by someone else who later moved the body, gun and cartridge to make it look like suicide. If so, it was a fairly elaborate attempt at a hoax. So the other question is why? Was it her who ran over Dalibor in Evinka Whyte's car? If so, does someone else know and they have taken revenge on her? Or is all that a bit too far fetched? OK, everyone. Let's get back to the station. I need to look at my work boards.'

Drake was on the prowl. The others knew not to interrupt. He let out a couple of satisfied grunts that told them he was making some progress.

'OK everybody,' he said. 'It seems fairly clear where we should start but not how we start.' The others looked up from their various tasks and gathered round. Drake drew a deep breath and began.

'I'm afraid we may be back into an international situation,' he said gloomily. Evinka Whyte gave Jelena Novakova the key to the Kubicek house in the posh Mala Strana part of central Prague. She told us that she stayed there when visiting her sick mother. Separately, Evinka had also given the key to the same house to another of our characters, one Bohdan Pelech, the originator of the NmN injections. Remember that Bohdan, Jelena and Renata were in the second batch of children to be liberated from communist Czechoslovakia and had kept in touch ever since. I interviewed Bohdan Pelech while in Prague with Kapitan Havlik. I thought him to be an odd combination of a large and potentially threatening frame with a rather nervous disposition. He asked to be taken back to the house after the interview. He said he had lost the NmN company but was trying to develop new products in a lab he had set up on the top floor of the Kubicek family house. I went there and knocked on the door but got no response except for a brief glimpse of someone in the top floor window. I have since thought it must have been Bohdan Pelech. Jelena recalled seeing his lab and being a little frightened of him when he was angry at her apparently spying on him. There is little doubt that Bohdan Pelech is also Milan Schelling of Zurich who Grace had a somewhat nervous encounter with. I think the only sensible conclusion to all this is that Bohdan/Milan is still running the NmN company and became unhappy with Evinka when she told him she had discovered the opium in her injections. The money in her bank account as discovered at Dalibor's house suggests he started to pay her off to prevent her from going public. What if that was a temporary solution and he decided later to eliminate Evinka? If so, he thought the job was done but then Jelena appears and starts poking around. He resolves to eliminate her too in order to keep his secrets.'

Drake prowled off around his boards and began again. 'I think we need to see if Kapitan Havlik has any idea where Bohdan is now.' Drake looked at his watch. 'I'll call him now.' Drake sat in his chair with his notebook and phone. He dialled the Czech number of Havlik.'

'Hello, Kapitan. This is Drake here from Chester UK. How are you?...good, good. Have I what?.. Really?...How didn't I know this?...Oh sorry, I see. OK then, thank you. I'll let you know how we get on. Keep in touch.' Drake terminated his call and started poking around in his phone and cursing at what he considered to be its innate hostility. Grace smiled at Katie. Dave let out a hardly suppressed giggle. 'Ah here it is,' grunted Drake. 'Oh dear, my fault I suppose.' Then he realized the others were still waiting for him to tell them what on earth was going on.

'Apparently, my friend, Kapitan Havlik of Prague Police sent me a text a couple of days ago to say that Bohdan had left Prague on a flight to Manchester. I failed to see the text because this wretched phone must have decided to go silent on me. Grace, this is urgent. Get on to the airports. It seems to be Manchester again and check out flight lists for Bohdan Pelech going to Prague or, perhaps more likely, Milan Schelling going to Zurich. He needs to be arrested as a matter of urgency. If we've missed him and he's gone to Prague then we need to tell Kapitan Havlik. Then we get into tricky international collaboration territory.' The phone rang and Grace left the group to answer it.

'Good news everyone,' said Grace as she put the phone down. They've found Peter Sostre at his friend's house in Manchester.

I'm arranging for him to be brought over. Should be here in a couple of hours.'

35

'Dr Sostre,' began Drake. 'We would like to talk to you about the day of the opening gala concert at the new concert hall.' Grace held out a calendar and pointed to the appropriate day. Dr Sostre looked on impassively. 'Do you recall what you were doing and where you were on that day?'

'No. I don't remember,' answered Dr Sostre.

'Let me remind you then,' said Drake. 'Early in the morning, you organized a substantial group of demonstrators who broke into the building to make a protest. That is correct isn't it?'

'You can't prove that,' replied Dr Sostre, wearing a sullen expression and lounging back in his chair, which he had turned to forty-five degrees from the table. He had his right arm over the top of the back of the chair and he crossed his legs as he answered.

'We think we can prove it,' said Drake.

'You were wearing clothing which we have since photographed you in and you had a mask lent to you by Dr Laura Weeks.'

'So what if I was?' snapped Dr Sostre. 'There's no crime in holding a peaceful protest.'

'Maybe not,' said Drake 'But you forced your way into a building that was not at the time open to the public.'

'No comment.'

'Let us turn to later in the day,' said Drake. 'There was a gala opening concert. During the first half, did you enter the building again through the fire escape?'

'No.'

'We can show that you arranged to have the fire door wedged open.' Drake waited to get a response but none was forthcoming. He decided to play the trump card. 'You entered the building and walked down the main backstage corridor and entered the dressing room occupied by Evinka Whyte.'

'No. I wasn't near the building that evening.'

'That evening, Evinka Whyte died in unusual circumstances. We think you were almost certainly the last person to see her alive and that you may be responsible for her murder.'

'No, we never intended to murder her.'

'So you were there?'

'No. We didn't go there. You can't just pin a murder on me like that. I was nowhere near the place.'

'Do you have someone who can corroborate that?' demanded Drake.

'Yes, I was with my friend,' replied Dr Sostre.

'So why did you arrange for the door to be wedged open?'

'We changed our minds. We never intended to harm her.'

'What did you intend to do then, Dr Sostre?'

'No comment.'

'So you don't deny that you arranged to have the door wedged open and that you and possibly one or more accomplices intended to force your way into Evinka Whyte's dressing room?'

'We were going to talk to her. That is all.'

'What were you going to say to her then?'

'We were only going to persuade her not to perform.'

'What did you intend to do if she didn't agree?'

'No comment.'

'I put it to you, Dr Sostre,' that you had prepared a place to take her and that you intended to take her there against her will.'

'No comment.'

'So why had you prepared a place near Tarvin Village?' Dr Sostre suddenly took his arm off the back of his chair and leant forward.

'You can't prove anything,' he said.

'I think we can. We have a witness who has seen you there several times and we have seen the preparations you have made inside the house.'

'How do you know about that?' said Dr Sostre, suddenly looking disturbed. 'You can't prove we intended to hold her there. We were just using it as a place to go ourselves.' Drake waited for Sostre to think about the line of questioning.

'So why is the door across the landing upstairs fitted with a padlock on the outside?'

'No comment.'

'Abduction is a serious offence, Dr Sostre. This is not some trivial protest. It is a serious crime punishable by a substantial prison sentence.'

'We didn't do it. So you can't accuse us of it.' Dr Sostre's voice was raised and higher pitched than in his usual sullen responses.

'But you intended to?'

'Lots of people intend to do lots of things that they don't. That's not a crime.'

'So why did you change your minds?' demanded Drake.

'We never really intended to do it. It was just to keep Laura Weeks happy.'

'Can you elaborate on that?' asked Drake.

'Laura Weeks is Head of the School of Music. I have tried to help her with her research. She has a big thing about Evinka Whyte who was brought in by the VC and has treated Laura very badly.'

'So it was Laura's idea to abduct Evinka Whyte?' asked Drake.

'Yes. She had this idea that it would make a public demonstration of her unreliability and get her off Laura's back. Laura knows most of the major music critics. Apparently, it is common knowledge among them that Evinka Whyte took drugs but none of them thought it appropriate to write about it. One critic said he had evidence but wouldn't tell Laura what it was. We would have told her that we knew and would make it public. She would certainly have lost her job at the university and probably lost concert bookings once it was out.'

'That amounts to blackmail. You are collecting major crimes, Dr Sostre. That could attract a substantial prison sentence,' said Drake with a laugh.

'You would never be able to prove it though,' snapped Dr Sostre.

'Why didn't Laura threaten Evinka Whyte herself? Why did she need to get you to do it?' asked Drake.

'She had to stay clean in case it didn't work. The VC doesn't like her and is looking for any excuse to get rid of her.'

'We have evidence that you have searched the dark web looking for drugs, drugs that would perhaps immobilize Evinka Whyte. Is that correct?

'We thought about it but decided not to. The fact is we gave up on the whole project. I decided that there were too many people around and it was just too dangerous a project. Laura wasn't happy about that.'

'Did you tell her in advance that you had decided not to go ahead with the abduction?'

'No, it was only that day that we abandoned the project. After the demo in the morning, I realised that it was impractical. Laura was pretty angry about it. She can have a terrible temper at times, that woman. She made me go back and recover her blessed masks. We've sort of split up over it all.'

'What do we think?' Drake asked Grace. 'We now have two almost opposing accounts from Laura Weeks and Dr Sostre.'

'I have a feeling he is telling the truth. He's an odd character, full of rhetoric and bluster but surprisingly anxious about falling foul of the law.'

'Agreed,' said Drake. 'Either way round, we haven't got anything to charge Laura Weeks with. As for Dr Sostre, I think we should let him go but put Katie Lamb back on him for a couple of days just in case he makes a run for it.'

Drake went over to his boards and Grace made some coffee.

'I need some more time before we question Bohdan Pelech,' said Drake. 'If he just denies everything, we are going to struggle to pin it on him,' said Drake.

'I might be able to help you,' said Dave chirpily. 'I've been working on it and didn't want to speak about it until I had managed it. It's something I've never done before but I've managed to get fingerprints.'

'I thought we had given up trying to lift a fingerprint off the Glock19,' muttered Drake. 'Don't tell me you have had success. I've never worked on a case where we managed to lift a fingerprint off a handgun like that.'

'It's not the gun,' said Dave dramatically.

'What else could it be then?' demanded Drake.

'Well the gun has to be loaded,' said Dave with a calculated air of mystery.

'Oh so you found something on the magazine?' asked Drake.

'Nope,' said Dave. 'On the spent cartridge.'

'Surely that's not possible. The temperature of the explosion is far too high. The print will be boiled off.'

'It's not a new technique but I was told about it only recently.'

'Well if you do this, your forensics course has been worth the money several times over,' grunted Drake. 'Come on Dave, explain.'

'Well, the odd thing is that it is the temperature that makes it possible but you have to use a different technique. The good thing is that loading bullets into the magazine of a Glock requires quite a lot of pressure and accuracy. This is especially true for the last few. It's a fiddly job that requires a certain amount of force so the print is well and truly implanted as you press the bullet down against the spring into the magazine. You are of course right when you say the temperature eliminates a normal print, which is salty sweat. The firing raises the temperature of the casing of the bullet, vaporizing the water in the sweat. But non-volatile salts are left behind. At the high temperature involved, the salts are molten and they react with the metal. Effectively it causes a tiny etching in the brass of the bullet casing. It's then a bit like doing brass rubbings to show up the etched surface that results from the oxidising of the brass. You get lovely polished shiny brass where the fingerprint was and dull brass everywhere else. You need a nifty piece of kit to do it because you have to pass a high voltage through the bullet while sprinkling conducting powder onto it. My college has the kit required. The powder sticks to the corroded areas and hey presto!' With a great sweep of his arm, Dave placed the prints on the table in front of Drake. 'I'm afraid I'm still not all that good at comparing prints but I got a tutor to do it and there's a match with the right thumb of Bohdan Pelech.'

'Brilliant, Dave,' said Drake. Dave looked as pleased as punch. 'We've got him for the murder of Jelena at least.'

'What about Evinka Whyte?' asked Dave.

'Well he claims an alibi from a chap in Zurich,' said Grace. 'I think I know the fellow he's talking about. He's a waiter at the coffee shop in Zurich. It's probably a dodgy alibi but we haven't got anything else on him for the murder of Evinka Whyte.'

'OK,' said Drake. 'Let's celebrate our first victory. Grace, you'd better go and get him charged. That means we can keep him a short time to give us some chance of finding something else to pin down the Evinka Whyte murder.' Drake paused and looked at his notebook.

'Oh yes, then there's one more really important job for you. Will you catalogue all the pieces in that collection of Josef Kubicek manuscripts. We were looking at Overture IV. My daughter Lucy tells me that he wrote four overtures and that the fourth is the one used. If you can't find overtures one to three that might tell us they are missing. The interesting question then will be just where they are.'

36

'I've done that job on the manuscripts,' Grace told Drake. 'I couldn't find any more overtures. The next pieces in the collection are of the ballet itself. They are labelled as scenes of various kinds. It seems to follow a pattern that makes sense. I called Lucy and went through it with her. She thinks we have the complete ballet.'

'That is what I thought you would find,' said Drake. 'This gives us something to go on.'

'How so?' asked Grace.

'I've gone back to my work boards,' said Drake, walking over to them. 'Look here. The music director of the Smetana Hall in Prague said that Renata had told him that two manuscripts had recently appeared for sale. If true then where is the third?'

'It seems to have gone missing,' said Grace. 'Perhaps somebody has taken it.'

'As far as I can see,' said Drake. 'The only person apart from Evinka that we know had a key to the big safe was Dalibor. It was from his house that we got ours. I think we can assume that Renata hasn't got one or she would be able to take all the manuscripts to Prague for the museum, which seems to be her major project. I'll bet that she doesn't even know about the safe.'

'It's certainly well hidden,' said Grace.

'There are two people most likely to have taken the manuscripts from their folder. It could have been either Evinka or Dalibor,' said Drake. 'From what Renata told us, she was the odd one out of the three with the twins being very close and she obviously didn't know about the sales.'

'My money is on Dalibor,' said Grace. 'Remember he made those two payments into Evinka's accounts. I think the money came from those two sales. Perhaps we could validate that if we could find out who sold them.'

'I think there are only a few places with the resources to handle sales like that,' said Drake.

'I'll chase it up,' said Grace. Drake went back to walking around his work boards.

'I've tracked them down,' said Grace. 'It was surprisingly easy. The auction house recalled the sales. The music expert there remembers it because they were so rare. She wasn't prepared to tell me who put them up for sale or who bought them. She did give me the dates and amounts. It's exactly as we thought. That information matches Evinka's accounts quite closely. She also said that I wasn't the first person to ask her.'

'Right,' said Drake. 'So Dalibor Kubicek sold the first two overtures one at a time. Presumably, he would have sold the third when Evinka's accounts showed up another problem.'

'Do you think Evinka knew about this?' asked Grace.

'Difficult to say,' said Drake. 'But we need to know who took the third overture. Was it the person involved in the hit and run? Was that what they were after in the ransacking of Dalibor's study? The answer seems to be that this is pretty likely. So who was that?'

'I know we did at one time think it might have been Evinka's assistant, Jelena because she had the car keys,' said Grace. 'But now I'm inclined to think it might have been Renata. You have shown she was a vitally interested party. She might have discovered what we found. I think she was the person who enquired before us at the auction house.'

'OK,' said Drake. 'I agree with your analysis but, at the moment, I can't see a way of pinning that on Renata. She probably has as much legal right to Josef Kubicek's manuscripts as Evinka and Dalibor. How can we prove she was driving the car on that night?'

'I suppose we could challenge her,' said Grace. 'But there's no reason why she should own up especially since she could easily get a murder charge or at least seriously dangerous driving and possibly manslaughter.'

'Agreed again,' said Drake. 'Let's go back to the Evinka case for a moment. Do we think Renata killed Evinka?'

'I think she could have done if she had discovered that all the Josef Kubicek manuscripts had been hidden from her and, worse still, they were being sold off without her knowledge. She also complained about Evinka not helping her over her dismissal at the university.' Drake plodded around his beloved boards, not actually looking at them but in his usual stooped glare at the floor in front of him.

'We must be missing something,' he said. Grace sat thinking and wishing she could come up with a suggestion about the way forward. Suddenly Drake sat down in his chair. 'It's obvious what we should do,' he said. 'You know where Renata is staying don't you?'

'Yes, with a friend in Christleton.'

'OK, so the third overture was not found at Dalibor's house. It must have been taken by the person guilty of running over Dalibor. We assume that is Renata. Organise an arrest warrant for her and a search warrant for her host's house. The first thing we need to do is prove that she took the manuscript.' Drake went silent again and picked up his copy of The Times. Grace started her administrative task and all went quiet in the case room. The phone on Grace's desk interrupted the silence. She answered it while Drake plodded around.

'Greater Manchester Police,' she said putting the phone down and grinning from ear to ear. 'They have arrested someone calling himself Milan Schelling trying to fly out of the country to Zurich.'

'OK,' said Drake. 'Let's organize to have him sent over here. In the meantime, once you have those warrants, perhaps you could execute them. Take Katie Lamb.'

'Good afternoon,' said Drake, entering the interview room. 'This is Detective Sergeant Grace Hepple. I believe you two have met before. How shall we address you? Is it to be Bohdan Pelech or Milan Schelling?'

'My name is Bohdan Pelech.' He directed a weak smile in Grace's direction. Grace was hit again by the momentary wave of panic that afflicted her in Zurich. Bohdan or Milan, whichever he was, may be in captivity but he remained an intimidating figure. Grace was suddenly aware that Drake was talking to her.

'Put the name Bohdan Pelech on the charge sheet, Grace,' said Drake.

'What am I being charged with?' demanded Bohdan Pelech.

'We are charging you with the murder of Jelena Novakova. That will do, to begin with,' said Drake.

'You can't prove that,' snapped Bohdan Pelech.

'I'm afraid we can. Your fingerprints are on the bullet casing we found near to her body. The bullet had been fired from the gun we found next to her and you inserted the bullet.'

'I gave it to her loaded. She wanted to commit suicide,' said Bohdan Pelech.

'Mr Pelech,' said Drake. 'You made two mistakes. One was loading the bullets with your bare hands. The other mistake was in moving the body after death. I'm afraid that you didn't fool our pathologist. I'm confident that a jury will find you guilty.' Bohdan Pelech sat silently, shuffling his feet. Grace thought his penetrating stare had evaporated and there was a look of fear in his eyes.

'Why should I kill an old friend?' demanded Pelech stuttering slightly.

'Because she saw things you didn't want her to see in the Kubicek family house in Prague.'

'I don't know anything about that,' said Bohdan Pelech.

'You were making a product that her employer, Evinka Whyte had been taking in good faith,' said Drake. 'She had discovered what you were illegally putting into it. You have been trying to eliminate them both to keep your nasty little secret.'

'He's going to play a straight bat at all our questions,' said Drake to Grace back in the case room. If we want to pin the Evinka Whyte murder on him we will have to find some more evidence. I suppose we could organise a parade and ask people who were backstage at the concert to identify him.'

'I've met with a problem on our other line of attack,' said Grace. 'We have Renata Kubicek in custody but there was no sign of the third overture anywhere. She's waiting for us in interview room two.'

'OK,' said Drake. 'You have a go at her first. See if your gentle technique reaps any rewards.

'Miss Kubicek,' said Grace. 'Where did you get the key to Evinka's car?'

'It's always hanging on a nail in the cupboard off the hallway with the garage key,' said Renata Kubicek.

'The car was severely damaged in a collision with your brother, Dalibor.'

'Yes,' said Renata, showing no sign of emotion.

'You don't deny that you were driving at the time?' asked Grace.

'He ran out into the road in front of me waving his cricket bat like a mad thing. I couldn't stop. He's always been headstrong.'

'But you didn't stop after the collision,' said Grace. 'Failing to stop at the scene of an accident involving injury is an offence.'

'I didn't know that he was dead. I thought he just slipped off the nearside of the car.'

'You should still have stopped. He was bound to be injured, as it turns out, fatally.' Renata nodded her head.

'I know, I'm sorry and I'm really sorry that he's dead but it was his fault.' Renata sat staring defiantly straight at Grace.

'You had been in his house searching for something?'

'Yes. It was family property. I was only looking for what I was entitled to have. It was just a family argument.'

'You entered his house while he was away?'

'Yes, there is a key kept at my sister's house. We always have keys to each other's houses.'

'Did you find what you were looking for?'

'No.'

'What was it that you were looking for?'

'Just some family papers. I was as entitled to have them as he was.'

'You made an awful mess of his study.'

'I wanted to get out before he returned. I was right to. He came back in a furious temper. He chased me out of the house. He could have killed me with that cricket bat. I only just got in my car before he started bashing it. I drove off but it was a dead end. I turned and came back. That was when he ran out in front of me.'

Drake was collapsed in his chair and looking into the far distance. Grace was busy thumbing through her notebook.

'This bit about the cricket bat is new,' said Drake.

'Yes, I'm sorry about that,' replied Grace. 'I'm just trying to find if I made a note. One of the officers did see a cricket bat by the front wall of a house a bit further down the road. At the time, I didn't consider it as part of the crime scene.'

'If you can see it from the place of the body it is part of the crime scene until proved otherwise,' grunted Drake. 'If she is prosecuted it is likely to be brought up by the defence. However, it doesn't really change anything for us now.'

'She doesn't deny breaking in,' said Grace. 'She had a key and she was only taking what she was entitled to but she claims that she couldn't find it. I don't believe a word of it. She seems confident that we can't find it. She's hidden it somewhere.'

'I bet I can find it for you,' said Drake suddenly. 'I think I might know where she's hidden it. You'd better take our guests some coffees and leave me to find the third overture. I just need to make a phone call.'

37

'That's exactly as I expected,' said Drake, wearing a smug grin. 'I phoned the music director of the Smetana Hall in Prague, where they are planning, with Renata's help, to start a museum for Josef Kubicek. Renata sent the third overture to him. It's where she thinks it belongs. We can only assume that she doesn't know where all Josef Kubicek's original manuscripts are or she would have had them by now.'

'Renata is not as innocent as she tries to look in my view,' said Grace. 'I think she's jolly ambitious. She wants to become a big authority on her great grandfather. She will publish her book and become the curator of an important museum. With her sister and brother both dead, she has become the sole world authority on Josef Kubicek. She will be a minor celebrity. Her problem is in finding all the manuscripts. Perhaps she knows something we don't. I think it's just as well we have her in custody now.'

'So if Renata killed her brother, did she also kill her sister?' asked Drake from behind his copy of The Times. No one answered this question. Grace determined that Drake addressed the question to himself anyway. If so, he was not proposing to answer it now. He picked up his pencil to write in another clue in his crossword. Suddenly, there was a tremendous scream from the other side of the room where Dave was sitting at his beloved computer.

'Eureka!' he yelled.'

'What is the matter, Dave,' demanded Grace. Drake went back to his crossword.

'I've got the hang of these coded files now,' said Dave. 'This was on the USB memory stick that Grace brought back from the first safe in Evinka Whyte's house. I don't understand it all but I've got the gist of it and I'm sure it is important. I've sent a copy of it to your computers. Here it is, look. I'll get it up on the screen. Drake struggled out of his chair and limped across the room. The team gathered behind Drake who was stooping to examine Dave's exciting development. Drake started reading, grunting with satisfaction. He stopped and started again, this time reading aloud.

'This violin has wood and varnish that suggest it was made in Cremona in the eighteenth century. This alone makes it likely that this may attract a high price. It carries a label stating that it is a Guarneri del Gesu and there is no reason not to believe this. Guarneri instruments may be slightly less well known than those by Stradivarius. However, many rate his instruments as highly and even better. There is a body of opinion that a Guarneri produces a more mellow sound than a Stradivarius.

The label is in such good condition that it almost looks a fake but it is made of laid paper, which was generally found before 1750 as opposed to woven paper common post-1750. The label appears not to have been interfered with and has taken on the colour of the wood of the case, which is to be expected after that time. The label contains the letters IHS and there is a cross fleury. Both of these are to be found on all known Guarneri instruments post-1731.

The f-holes are characteristic of Guarneri as opposed to Stradivarius. This means they are more sharply angular with less pronounced ends to the holes. Moreover, the two f-holes are not identical which is also characteristic of Guarneri.

The bridge needs replacing and it needs a new D string. One of the tuning screws looks to be in poor condition. To avoid serious loss of value, a skilled luthier should carry this out. We can recommend one near Chester. If, when this work is completed, it plays in the manner expected of such an instrument then it could become recognized as a previously unknown Guarneri del Gesu violin.

If it is indeed the violin played by Josef Kubicek then its value could be further enhanced. Something in the range of twenty million pounds is not out of the question and should be used for any insurance.'

'Well I never,' said Drake. 'So the precious instrument really does exist and Evinka Whyte had it all the time. This looks like a report from a specialist in old instruments. Presumably, she kept the violin in that large empty space in the bigger safe, where Grace found the music manuscripts. Perhaps this was indeed Karel Whyte's beloved violin. Everybody thought it was just another ordinary instrument. When he moved into his care home, Evinka hid it away in her safe. However, she has had it evaluated and then realized that it could be extremely valuable. The next and obvious question is about where the violin is now. That may take a little longer to answer. Thanks, Dave. Well done.' Drake mumbled and grunted and then spoke again.

'We have to assume that Dalibor knew about it. Renata has told us that the twins Evinka and Dalibor were very close. Did Renata also know about it? If she believes that her siblings are hiding it from her and she is as ambitious as Grace thinks, she might also be ruthless enough to take the ultimate action. She can win both ways. Either she sells the violin for a fortune or she gets her new museum to buy it. I wonder where the violin is now? Certainly, my friend, the concert director at Smetana Hall didn't mention it. I'm certain he would have done so if he had it. In any case, you don't put something worth twenty million pounds in the post, do you? Let's ask Renata a few more questions. Have a go at her, Grace.'

'Miss Kubicek,' said Grace. 'Can you tell us more about your father's lost violin? Was it valuable?'

'I think it was a good fake,' said Renata. 'Actually, it played well enough. Though most of that might have been my father's skill and artistry. It might be worth a few thousand at best.'

'So you think your sister may have lost it?'

'Either that, or she sold it and didn't tell me.'

'Is that possible?'

'Oh yes. My sister was a wonderful artist but she also enjoyed money a great deal.'

'You don't think it possible that she had kept it?' asked Grace.

'I think it much more likely that she sold it. Dalibor would have known.' Renata grimaced. 'Things are a terrible mess aren't they?'

'My guess is she isn't sure about the whereabouts of the violin,' said Drake, when they gathered in the case room again. 'She may believe it was still somewhere in Evinka's house. If so, the problem is how to prove it. Did she murder her sister in order to be able to search the house?'

'I think she is capable of it,' said Grace.

'I wonder,' said Drake, slowly. 'I wonder if she collaborated with her lifelong friend, Bohdan, while she was in Prague and they were both in the family house. Bohdan would know how to get carfentanil.'

'And was seeing Evinka as a threat.' Grace chipped in.

'All this is pure speculation,' said Drake. 'Even if true, how would we prove it? OK, let's all be back here first thing in the morning and see where this gets us. At the very least we can charge Renata with dangerous driving and failing to stop at an accident.' Drake rose slowly from his chair.

'Right, I'm off. I'm rather keen to do some more flute practice. I'm gradually learning the fingerings and this evening I should have learned the whole of the lower register. That means I will be able to play some worthwhile pieces instead of the rather juvenile samples in my tutor book. The darned thing appears to think that

I'm about five years old in its choice of material.' Grace and Dave left as Drake wandered over to his work boards.

'I thought you were going, sir,' said Steve Redvers.

'I just need to make a couple of phone calls,' said Drake, wandering around behind the boards with his phone in hand. Steve Redvers heard him talking but could not make out what he was saying. Drake came round again and went over to his chair. Steve Redvers, keen to be at the centre of things, decided to stay. He watched and listened as Drake wandered around making notes and grunting. Eventually, he turned to Steve Redvers,

'I think my flute practice can wait a while. I might just do a little mental digging. You get off home.'

'I'm OK, sir,' replied Steve Redvers. 'I've nothing special on.' Drake was already lost in thought again. He slowly walked around the boards in his characteristic stooping gait. Steve had learned from the others not to interrupt. Then Drake stopped and went over to the coffee machine, which obligingly hissed and burbled. He took his coffee back to his favourite chair, put it down on the table beside him and started flipping through his notebook. Some while later, he struggled out of his chair and picked up his mug. Sipping gently from the lukewarm brew he wandered back to the boards. One more circuit and he appeared to reach some sort of conclusion. He grunted and turned to Steve Redvers.

'Since you are still here,' he said. 'I'd like you to drive me home and then do a small job for me.' PC Steve Redvers knew by now that the journey had to be in the Range Rover so he went and brought it round to the rear door. Drake flopped into the rear seat and sat looking out of the window. Steve Redvers drove back into the town centre, along Boughton and turned down Dee Lane along Grosvenor Park Terrace, round the Grosvenor Rowing Clubhouse, past The Moorings cafe and pulled up outside Drake's house overlooking the river. It was just going dark and the lights were coming on all along the riverside.

'Not here, Steve' said Drake. Please go four more houses nearer to the bridge.' 'Right,' said Drake, after the car stopped again. 'I need you as backup. We may have a little difficulty. I'm not sure of that but just in case, keep with me.' Drake looked down the front garden of the house and saw some lights on inside. He walked steady and more determinedly than Steve Redvers thought he was capable of and knocked on the door. There was no answer. Drake knocked again. Still no answer.

'It looks as if we have someone in because the lights are on,' said Drake. 'Do you have the big red key in the back of the Range Rover?' he asked.

'Yes, sir. I'm pretty sure there's one in there.'

'Fetch it then,' said Drake. Steve dashed down the front drive while Drake took a few paces back and peered at the upper floor window where there was a light. Steve Redvers arrived, rather breathless from carrying the door ram in both hands. Drake strode up to the door again. He knocked, turned the knob and pushed. The door creaked eerily as if to warn of danger. Drake pushed and the door opened.

'Keep with me Steve,' said Drake. Leave the big red key there.' Drake went in shouting 'police' repeatedly. He opened the downstairs doors. Those rooms were in relative darkness.

'Steve,' said Drake. 'You're young and fit. You go upstairs first and I'll follow.' They climbed the stairs and checked the bathroom and the two bedrooms. The one in the front had a light on. The wardrobe doors were wide open. A couple of pairs of trousers and a blue shirt with its buttons undone lay on the unmade bed.

'Drat,' said Drake. 'We're too late. Leave me here and take the Range Rover back to the station. Put out a call to all airports to intercept George Marshall. Unless I'm mistaken he'll be on a flight to New Zealand. He's probably going from Manchester.'

38

Drake arrived at the station a little later than usual. The others were gathered together wondering what was going on. Steve Revers had enthusiastically described the events of the previous evening. Drake came in with a satisfied grin across his face, made himself a cup of coffee and flopped into his chair. He took out his pencil and continued the work he had done on The Times crossword over breakfast. Grace was just about to ask him to explain when the phone rang. She dashed over to lift it off its cradle.

'Yes, DS Hepple...Oh I see...yes...thank you...goodbye.' The others were all looking at her except Drake who was struggling with 13 down. 'That was a call from Greater Manchester Police,' she said. 'They have intercepted George Marshall who was about to board the Singapore Airlines flight to Singapore with an ongoing connection to Auckland. Oddly, he had booked two seats.'

'That makes sense,' said Drake, looking up. 'He needed one for the violin. Well done everybody.'

'I think we need an explanation,' said Grace.

'It's simple,' said Drake. Steve came with me to George Marshall's house last evening. There was nobody in. There were clothes thrown around everywhere weren't there, Steve?'

'Yes, sir. It looked as if he had left in a hurry.'

'What are we charging him with?' asked Grace.

'The murder of Evinka Whyte and the theft of an extremely valuable violin,' said Drake nonchalantly. He looked at them with a stern expression, Grace started to laugh and one by one, the others joined in. Eventually, Drake started to laugh too and he clambered up out of his chair. 'I suppose you want to know how we did it?' he said.

'We, didn't know we had,' said Grace.

'Who had all the time and opportunity to go to Evinka Whyte's dressing room when everyone else was in the concert hall?' demanded Drake.

'OK, so we see that,' answered Grace. Drake walked over to the work boards and leant against them.

'Who has been anxiously asking all the way through this enquiry how we were getting on?'

'Of course but he had good reason to,' said Grace. 'There was nothing suspicious about that.'

'Who appointed Itzhak Stransky to conduct Evinka when the family feud was well known? Who appointed Anders Hagan and gave him a contract that would put him in direct and inevitably public conflict with Evinka Whyte.'

'These things don't seem suspicious in themselves,' said Grace, 'but now you mention them all together it does seem to add up.'

'True,' said Drake, 'very true. George Marshall hung on in there for a long time before he got spooked. Of course, once he made a run for it, things started to look rather different.' Drake paused and looked around at nodding heads.

'Professor Cooper eventually told us that Evinka was killed by a rare drug not in common use, carfentanil. One of several mistakes that, an otherwise extremely clever man made, was to tell me one evening when off guard that he had a brother who is a vet at a wildlife park in New Zealand. Prof Cooper told us that carfentanil is used by veterinary surgeons to anaesthetize huge animals like elephants and rhinos. His brother, who we must assume was in on the whole thing, sent him a supply. He was on his way to join his brother with the spoils and we must assume to sell the violin quietly for twenty million pounds. That sum would certainly have changed the lives of the Marshall brothers.'

'However, it was once we knew that the violin existed that everything started to come together. George Marshall had told me that he knew how to maintain and repair most instruments in the orchestra. Jelena Novakova told us that he had many long conversations with Evinka over two years while organizing the concert. When she and her brother moved their father into his care home, they would have gone through all his belongings. Amongst them was his violin, an instrument that had been handed down from father to son through the Kubicek family. Legend has it that this had been given to the great Josef Kubicek by Emperor Franz Josef in thanks for a private concert. This may or may not be true. I doubt we shall ever know. After escaping from communist Czechoslovakia, Karel Kubicek would never play it again in public, as he was terrified of being identified and found by the old Czech state. By the time it reached Evinka, the violin was in poor condition, she probably had no idea how valuable it was but had heard the stories. Her father by then had forgotten or at least couldn't correctly describe events. However, once we knew about the violin, what he said to us was actually completely correct. It just sounded confused.' Drake cleared his throat and started again.

'What could Evinka Whyte do? Perhaps she resolved not to bring the violin out in public until after her father's death. So she hid it securely. After she met George Marshall, she began to realize he might help her confidentially. He must have seen straight away that it might be a real Guarneri but I bet that he took the instrument and got the valuation done in London. Now, he is a hard worker but not appreciated, underpaid and given little support. His dream job was turning into a nightmare. I think it likely that he disapproved of Evinka's extravagant lifestyle. That probably resulted in him having no qualms about killing her. He worked out the whole thing carefully, even down to creating an obvious stooge in Itzhak Stransky. He knew they would argue and the building was organized so Stransky had a behind the scenes route into Evinka's room, so suspicion would fall on him.' Drake paused and looked around the room at the amazed faces of his colleagues.

'George Marshall may have organized it all carefully but he made another fatal mistake. I think he and Evinka had decided that the new bridge for the violin should be of a type of wood likely to have been used in making the violin, remember the little blocks with the label Acer Capestris, Lombardia. Maestro Stransky recognized them immediately as blanks for violin bridges. It's likely Evinka picked them up while doing her previous concert in Milan, which is the capital of Lombardy and only 40 miles from Cremona where Guarneri lived. Jelena told us that Milan had been Evinka's previous engagement. The irony is that Evinka was probably about to pass them on to George Marshall so he could get the new bridge made and fitted. I showed the blocks to him and he told us that he had never seen anything like them before. Of course, that is nonsense since he had learned how to repair violins. Why would he say that? Because he momentarily panicked at a clue pointing straight to him.' Drake paused.

'Of course, after administering the fatal potion to Evinka, Marshall didn't need to go to the house for the violin. He already had it and since it was a secret all he needed to do was bump off Evinka and twenty million pounds was his.' Drake went over to get his cold coffee and took a mouthful.

'Putting all this together, all I needed to do was just get some confirming evidence. I rang the auction house people who wrote the violin report and asked them to recommend a luthier near Chester. The name they gave me would have been the same as George had. A call to them to enquire if they would fettle a Guarneri violin and they rather proudly told me that they had another Guarneri violin on their current books. From what I know of the man, I guessed that George Marshall wouldn't have hidden the violin but would have it on display so he could look at it. If we could catch him with the instrument we could secure a conviction. A visit to his house was worth a shot. His departure makes it certain that he is guilty. I have thought long and hard overnight about what might have spooked George Marshall. The only thing I can think of is that I called the same luthier as he intended to use. Perhaps they had some immediate contact and the luthier mentioned my call to him. The evidence of the state of his house suggests that he left in a complete panic. I'm pretty sure we will find he went to a hotel near Manchester Airport last night having booked his tickets for the morning flight to Singapore and Auckland. Now that we have caught him, I doubt that he will try to deny it all.' Drake gathered up his bag. 'I'll leave you to do the honours, Grace. I'm off to get that flute practice I missed last night.'

A **DEGREE** OF **DEATH**
Bryan Lawson

A member of the Singapore Parliament is found murdered on a footbridge in Chester. A DEGREE OF DEATH is a crime novel about the past sneaking up on the present and making a real mess of things. It is September 2005. Murky oriental history is entangled with events at Deva University in Chester, a brand new institution doing its best to invent tradition. But do these new ivory towers hide more worldly pursuits, and what really goes on behind the genteel façades in the historic city of Chester?

DCI Carlton Drake is widely recognised for being as clever as he is tall and clumsy. He resumes duties after a sabbatical, taken for personal reasons, to investigate this diplomatically sensitive case. By contrast his high-flying young assistant Grace Hepple is stylish but inexperienced. Together they uncover an intriguing mystery.

The investigation takes Drake to Singapore where he discovers that the past is never far from the surface in this modern metropolis. Chinese societies, illegal ivory trading, academic jealousy and raw ambition jostle together to create a confusing and dangerous cocktail.

Readers say: -

"Highly recommended"

"The intricacies of the plot keep you absorbed and the conclusion certainly does not disappoint."

"From an ex-policeman…a good thought provoking thriller."

"I look forward to the next in the series of this detective duo."

WITHOUT TRACE
Bryan Lawson

Lord Richard MacCracken, a minister for the arts in the British Government, disappears during the interval of a performance at Covent Garden. He seems to have vanished without trace between the two acts of an opera. The nightmare gets darker when the postman delivers a copy of the Royal Opera House programme. It contains death threats and a set of the victim's bloody fingerprints.

DCI Drake and his assistant DS Grace Hepple are called in to recover Lord MacCracken safely and discover who is holding him. The kidnappers have covered their tracks with a web of deception that leads Drake around the world. The sinister and dramatic crimes he uncovers could have come straight from the operatic stage.

Readers say: -

"I really enjoyed it and found it extremely absorbing."

"Another great edition with exciting adventures and drama."

"The plot twisted and turned as a good detective novel should, leading to an unforeseen conclusion...

"...attention to detail in terms of background information from experts brought in to assist the case is incredible."

FATAL PRACTICE
Bryan Lawson

An internationally famous architect, Sir Julian Porter, fails to turn up to the public launch of a series of new landmark buildings for the UK Government. Detective Chief Inspector Drake and his assistant DS Grace Hepple are called in to investigate. They begin their work in the historic city of Chester where Porter's architectural practice is located. Drake soon discovers that Sir Julian seems to have made many enemies. Some strangely mutilated bodies become the focus of the investigation. One is in Chester and another on the Malaysian Island of Penang where the practice is designing a prestigious housing development.

These two murders appear linked but the question is how? The case leads Drake into dangerous water involving organised crime and a mysterious oriental cult.

Readers say: -

"Have just finished it. I enjoyed all the parts in Penang."

"As well as the intriguing mystery, it transports you to a fascinating part of the world."

"Just finished reading Fatal Practice – very entertaining. Makes me want to visit Penang one day."

"International intrigue and fascinating architectural insights enhance this clever and twisty mystery…"

Printed in Great Britain
by Amazon

25454752R00155